NOSFERATU

GHERBOD FLEMING

author	gherbod fleming
cover artist	john van fleet
series editors	john h. steele and stewart wieck
copyeditor	anna branscome
graphic designer	aaron voss
cover designer	aaron voss
art director	richard thomas

More information and previews available at
white–wolf.com/clannovels

White Wolf Publishing
735 Park North Boulevard, Suite 128
Clarkston, GA 30021
www.white–wolf.com

First Edition: September 2000

10 9 8 7 6 5 4 3 2 1

Printed in Canada.

...Like the vampire...dead many times, and learned the secrets of the grave.

- Walter Pater

NOSFERATU

part one:
shrouded beginnings

The tunnels, his home for years, loomed alien and threatening. As he ran, the mold-covered stones were slick and treacherous beneath his normally sure feet. Corridors he should have known seemed out of place, the landmarks all a jumble in his frantically racing mind. "Ulstead," he muttered unbelievingly, as if saying the name aloud might bring his clanmate back.

Pug whipped around a corner and flung his back against the wall. South—which damned way was south? He felt blood pulsing through his dead veins, the old involuntary responses kicking in. He realized that he was panting, wheezing as he drew air in through his deviated septum, and he made himself stop. Breathing would do him no good, and the sound would make him easier to find.

Gunfire. South be damned, he was running again, heedlessly through the darkness. *It's just Nigel*, he told himself after a few hundred yards, but he didn't stop. It wasn't Nigel that panicked Pug. Nigel wasn't firing his precious little sub-machine gun just to hear the pretty noise.

"Ulstead," Pug muttered again, shaking his head in disbelief. Ulstead was—*had been*— a rock of a Kindred, a walking, wart-covered, solid side of beef. He should have been able to snap the little man in two, or three.

But the Eye had opened, and the tunnel had been bathed in pale, blood-red light, and then…

Pug stumbled. He careened off a wall, almost righted himself, but then wiped out. He landed hard, a heap of short, flailing arms and legs.

The pale light had shone in the tunnel, and then Ulstead simply hadn't been there. A smoldering, writhing mass of what *had* been Ulstead had been there instead, the speckling of dark warts joining together as all the skin turned dark and then flowed away into a spreading, steaming puddle.

Pug lifted himself to his hands and knees and wiped his face with a sleeve, but the fabric was little improvement over the brackish water in which he'd landed. More gunshots, and not that far away despite Pug's headlong flight. *I shouldn't abandon him*, he thought for the first time. Nigel wasn't as familiar with the city; he was one of Colchester's people come up in the past few nights from Baltimore. *I shouldn't abandon him*, he thought again, then climbed to his feet and ran. Away. Let them call him a coward. If anybody called him anything, it would mean that he'd survived. Devil take Nigel, and Calebros, and the silent one, for that matter, and this Nickolai they were supposed to be finding.

Pug wanted to stop and get his bearings; he wanted—in a far more theoretical way—to go back and help Nigel, but his legs kept churning. *The fool should have had more sense, should have run instead of stopping to shoot.*

Pug turned another corner, and the world suddenly made even less sense. The bone-jarring collision snapped his head back. His feet flew out from under him. For the second time in the past few minutes, he lay in a painful heap. This time, however, his stunted limbs were intertwined with someone else's arms and legs.

"I almost shot you," Nigel said, shaking his head to clear the cobwebs.

The fog of fear and concussion was not so quick to lift for Pug. "Where did you…? How…?" He must have gotten turned around somewhere along the way, inadvertently made a loop. The shock wore away quickly now. The two disentangled themselves with all possible haste and scrambled to their feet. Nigel was shaken too, and not, Pug suspected, by the collision. The out-of-towner clutched his sleek, black Sterling to his side. Pug could feel the heat from the gun's barrel.

"I was coming back to help," Pug lied. "Did you…is it…?"

"Didn't even slow it down," Nigel said, shaking his head. His eyes were very small and dark and set close together. He had no chin to speak of. "Keep moving," he said urgently. "We need to keep moving."

"Moving," said the scrawny creature with the Eye, appearing from the darkness behind Nigel. "Yes, moving…"

Nigel whirled and fired. The shots that hit the creature's body drove it back a few steps, but the bullets striking the Eye seemed to sink into a bottomless swamp of fizzling plasma. The wan red light that covered them was not from the Sterling's muzzle flashes. Pug covered his ears and ran—*tried* to run. The stone beneath his feet was liquid sludge. He staggered and fell forward onto solid ground. Nigel sank. The sludge turned fiery hot and, in an instant, Nigel's legs below the knees ceased to exist.

More shots. Pug scrabbled to his feet and ran. Above the screams and the hiss of smoking brimstone, he imagined he heard the *click, click, click,* of the Sterling's empty chamber. There were no more shots, of that he was certain. But then there were only the sounds of a pounding pulse in his ears and his wheezing as he ran. And his own screams.

Tuesday, 1 June 1999, 2:37 AM
Mezzanine, the Fox Theatre
Atlanta, Georgia

The few, wispy clouds did not obscure the stars, but rather added an illusion of depth, of reality. Victoria leaned back in her seat, taking in and finding comfort in the expanse of crisp night sky. She did not care that the vista was "merely" a projection upon the grand auditorium ceiling. She did not care that the Moorish battlements were but a decorative framework for stage and balconies. In some cases—*very many*, it seemed—illusion was quite preferable to reality.

It was impossible to view the night sky in Atlanta. Oh, the sky was there, of course. But there were no stars, no sense of the infinite. Only a hazy pink glow, electric illumination bleeding from horizon to horizon, obscuring what, to a Kindred, was one of the few anchors in time. All too often, loved ones passed beyond; cities, nations rose and fell; forests burned; even mountains once impenetrable were scarred by modern man. Only the oceans and the stars, it seemed, remained constant, and this city offered observation of neither.

What it did offer, however, was opportunity.

"Good evening, Ms. Ash."

Victoria did not start, nor did she so much as look away from the soothing faux-heavens. She hadn't heard him approaching, but neither had she expected to—not if he didn't wish to be noticed. "Do you have what I asked for?" Victoria said, not rude but, at the same time, not encouraging familiarity.

"I do indeed," Rolph answered.

Not every member of his clan, contrary to popular belief, smelled as if he had rolled in week-old refuse. That was the first thing Victoria noticed after his unheralded arrival: the absence of stench. It made dealing with Rolph tolerable. Ugly, Victoria could abide for a short while, but those more aromatically challenged of Clan Nosferatu were never welcome in her presence. Not that she had anything against them *personally*. Victoria prided herself upon her magnanimity. She did not begrudge those more grotesque beings the hunting grounds that were beneath her station, or the filthy little burrows they carved out of the dirt; she merely saw no reason to allow those creatures to offend her sensibilities by coming near her.

She turned toward Rolph, reached out her hand. Thankfully, he wore a long robe with a hood that concealed most of his face. In the darkened theatre, she could barely make out the unnaturally pointed chin and the large nose, sharply bent. Rolph handed her a legal-sized manila envelope.

"Thank you," Victoria said. Rolph bowed slightly.

She opened the envelope and began to sift through the contents—casually, so as not to suggest that Rolph had done her *too* much of a favor. The Nosferatu were the elephants of the vampire world—they never forgot. The tiniest bit of aid rendered was filed away in their memories, a debt to be called due perhaps years later, quite often at the most inconvenient of times, and sometimes by a *different* member of the clan, in a different city or on a different continent, as if they shared some communal sense of recall.

"Is everything to your satisfaction?" Rolph asked.

Victoria continued to sift through the envelope's contents: photocopies of deeds, business records, cash withdrawals and deposits for various bank accounts. "It seems to be," she said nonchalantly.

In truth, the records were helpful, but hardly vital. They would help Victoria solidify her presence in Atlanta, her adopted home. The financial information pertained to the former interests of a former Kindred, Marlene, a Toreador of ill repute, who had met an unfortunate end. The establishments, each of which Marlene had controlled to varying degrees through intermediaries, reflected the banal vulgarity that had also been Marlene's dominant quality: strip clubs, adult bookstores, "lingerie" showrooms, and so on.

Victoria was not enthused by the prospect of peddling vice, but she did have her pragmatic bent. If a mortal proprietor was already accustomed to handing over profits to a mysterious silent partner, what could be the harm in assuming that role? It was also a very practical preventative measure to ensure that no one else moved in on what had been Marlene's territory. As the old saying went, "Nature abhors a vacuum," and Victoria thought of herself as nothing if not a force of Nature.

"Yes, I believe this will be adequate," Victoria said.

Rolph might have smiled within the shaded recess of his hood. "We are pleased that you have chosen Atlanta as your new residence."

Victoria smiled, recognizing, though still not averse to, flattery when she heard it.

"Despite Prince Benison's best intentions," Rolph continued almost conspiratorially, "there is a certain…cultural and artistic sensibility that is lacking among our Kindred. From what I have heard, I suspect you are more knowledgeable in those areas than was Marlene."

"Ha!" Victoria coyly raised two fingers to her scarlet-painted lips, as if to restrain further comment upon her predecessor.

"Forgive the unwarranted comparison," Rolph said quickly, lest he had offended. "Some of us remain hidden away from society, and polite conversation does not come easily to our lips…. That, and the Toreador we have grown accustomed to here have been of a certain…base element…."

"Well then," Victoria said at once, "we will have to show everyone different, won't we?"

"What do you mean?"

It seemed so obvious to Victoria. What could be more natural? She wasn't sure why she'd waited this long to embark on such a course of action. "A coming-out. A grand party." Instantly, her mind was racing; she formulated countless plans, motifs, decors, with each passing second. She could host the gala here at the Fox, or perhaps at the High Museum.

"Of course," said Rolph. "How fitting. Will there be art?"

"Ah, so you are the art lover, are you?"

"I appreciate beauty…from which I am so far removed."

Victoria felt a lump in her throat; she was nearly moved to reach out and actually touch Rolph's arm. How quaint—a beast pining for the beauty that was his antithesis. How her mere presence would enrich these creatures' lives, here in this southern, backwater city.

"Have you tried your own hand at the arts, Rolph?" Victoria asked, speaking as might a parent to a child.

The Nosferatu nodded. "But I have not had much success, I'm afraid."

Victoria nodded sympathetically. "What…sketching, painting?"

He nodded again. "And a bit of sculpting. Though my creations were as deformed as I am. Or more so…if that is possible," he added with a self-deprecating shrug.

How ghastly indeed, Victoria thought. But she was determined to show pity to this creature. "I will exhibit my private collection of sculpture," she said magnanimously.

"You have a private collection?"

"Most certainly. One of the finest in the world. And you will be invited." The words were out of her mouth before she could reconsider. Victoria's enthusiasm momentarily waned, but she maintained the veneer of her smile. She didn't relish the prospect of socializing with Nosferatu, but it was done. She couldn't uninvite Rolph, and the city as a whole would benefit from her largesse. So she would go about making her coming-out the event of the season, of the *year*, for this tired city, perhaps the decade. She began formulating the guest list at once. Dear, conniving Benito would have to attend, of course. And if all Victoria had heard about Prince Benison was true, then she would be able to instigate a delightful bit of mischief by inviting certain individuals: Benjamin, for one, leader of the city's Anarch resistance, who, nonetheless, would be granted safe passage to an Elysium; and the Brujah archon Julius came to mind as the perfect guest for her purposes. Perhaps he would be able to attend as well.

"I would be honored to attend."

"Hm?" Victoria had almost forgotten about Rolph. "Oh, yes. Of course." Yes, she would have to allow him to attend. Even in his inclusion, however, there was a sliver of redemption. Inviting a Nosferatu was the type of unexpected exploit that Victoria liked to undertake. Unpredictability, to her way of thinking, was synonymous with freedom. There were beings in the world—beings as arcane and mysterious to the Kindred as were the Kindred to mortals—that would usurp control of her destiny if she allowed them to do so. By doing what they could not have anticipated, Victoria asserted her independence. The more unpredictable the better. Even in such a small thing as this.

"Of course you will be welcome," she said to Rolph. "And your friends as well."

As Rolph bowed again and showed himself out, graciously not taking any more of her time, Victoria congratulated herself on her latest stroke of spontaneity, which no one—and no *thing*—could have predicted.

Calebros allowed Umberto to "lead" his elder along the unlit passage. Those younger occupants of the warren seemed to think that Calebros never left the grotto, his "office," that he never ceased poring over the countless reports and clattering away on his time-tested typewriter. Perhaps they were not grossly mistaken in those beliefs, he reflected. The particular curvature of his spine, along with the merciless arthritis that racked his every joint, did not make for ease of movement. Calebros preferred to stay put. The youngsters also would not be inaccurate to assert that, as for company, he preferred that of his Smith Corona to them. Still, they mistook his unwillingness to venture beyond his sanctum for an inability to do so. They assumed as much.

"Undisciplined," Calebros muttered.

"Pardon?" Umberto paused and turned back toward his elder.

"Keep moving or we'll never get there," Calebros scolded him. Umberto, crestfallen, continued onward.

Undisciplined intellect, Calebros thought. *Assumptions are but the signposts of an undisciplined intellect.* That's what his sire, Augustin, had always said, and truer words were never spoken.

For several minutes, the two hunched creatures continued onward, Umberto slowing his steps so as not to outpace his elder, Calebros slowing to avoid stepping on the shuffling fool before him. Eventually, they approached a ladder.

"There's a ladder here," Umberto said.

"Yes, I can see that," Calebros said, and, when Umberto continued to hesitate, added, "I do know how to use a ladder. Get out of my way." His talons clicked against the metal, but the slippery, fungus-covered rungs did not prove an impediment. There was pain as he climbed—his shoulder, elbows, knees, and neck—but the discomfort was no greater than that which challenged him when he rose from his resting place each evening.

The ladder led to another corridor, which ran past a small, cramped room where several more people were gathered and busy at a game of cards. Their familiar humor grew silent as Calebros passed. Either they feared attracting his displeasure at their idleness, or they were simply surprised to see him out and about, or perhaps a bit of both. Calebros ignored them and made his way to one of the next doorways, Umberto's computer room. Umberto slipped past and easily into the seat before the terminal. He began typing in commands.

"I thought you said he was ready," Calebros grumbled.

"He is. I'm just double-checking the link security." Umberto's nimble fingers tapping rhythmically across the keyboard sounded like the first spattering drops of a summer shower against a tin roof. His earlier hesitancy now vanished as he immersed himself in the embrace of technology.

"I could hook you up a terminal of your own," Umberto said without thinking, "if you got rid of that fossil of a typewriter and cleared off your desk—ow!" He jerked forward, away from Calebros, who had just boxed his ears. Umberto wiped a small trickle of blood from his right earlobe. Calebros took the seat that Umberto hastily vacated. An eardrum was a small price to pay to maintain the primacy of the pecking order, the elder thought.

"Is it ready?"

"Yes," Umberto said, rubbing his ear. "Just type in what you want, and then hit enter. Your text is displayed after the 'C'." Umberto busied himself with massaging his ear and stretching his jaw, mouth open, mouth closed, mouth open….

Calebros, seated at the terminal, stretched his legs to ease an aching knee, but met resistance under the desk. He pressed harder with his sizeable foot, eliciting a squeak of discomfort from below.

"Who's down there?" he asked gruffly, already knowing the answer.

"Me, Mr. C."

"Me? Mouse, get out from there, you half-animate furball. Some of us have work to do."

"Sorry, Mr. C."

As the mangy little creature squeezed from beneath the desk and scrabbled away, Umberto directed a half-hearted, perfunctory kick in his direction, but the elder Nosferatu had already turned his attention to the computer. Calebros's fingers, despite the long, gangly talons, moved with alacrity across the keyboard:

```
C: Hello? Are you there?
R: I am here. Are you well?
C: Well enough. What news?
R: I met with V. Ash three nights ago;
have since learned that she is planning
the party for the Solstice; probably
will take place at the High Museum, if
Prince Benison is amenable.
C: Do you expect him to be?
R: Hard to predict with him, but I don't
know any compelling reason that he should
object.
C: Is Ash suspicious?
R: Not at all. The party, of course,
was completely her own idea—as she sees
it. She has already made arrangements
for the particular statue to be trans-
ferred. I will see to it that H. Ruhadze
is on the guest list. Will June 21 al-
low you sufficient time to prepare?
C: It should. If Benito is on the guest
list. Do you know if he is?
R: He was one of the first she con-
tacted. He is planning to attend.
```

C: Splendid. I will inform Emmett. Any other news?
R: Hilda sends regards.
C: No time. Must go. Goodbye.

Calebros pushed back from the terminal, forgetting the chair he was in had wheels—unnatural, that—and nearly running over Umberto. "Can you print a copy of that and bring it to me?" Calebros asked.

"Certainly."

"Good." With much creaking of joints, Calebros lifted himself from the chair and made his way back down the hallway. He felt his mood noticeably improved. Rolph was a stand-up fellow, and arrangements in Atlanta were progressing nicely. Emmett would be pleased as well. The entire operation promised to be a quiet, tidy affair.

Calebros paused at the doorway to the room where the card game was taking place. He poked his head in. "Who's winning?"

A brief, dumbfounded silence followed before someone managed to reply: "Uh…Cass is."

"Good," said Calebros, as he continued on his way. "Very good, indeed."

"And then this dude says, 'If you on the schedule for that night, you better make sure you get off it.' Except he doesn't say, 'schedule,' right? He says, 'shedule,' like he got a damn speech impediment or something."

"He say what?" Odel asked, turning off the forklift so he could hear better.

"He says, 'shedule. Get off the shedule,'" Tyrel said more loudly, even though the forklift was off now.

"Why he say that?"

"I told you, I think he got a speech impediment. He always talk funny. I think he from Boston or New York. Maybe California."

"Naw, I mean why he tell you to get off the schedule?"

"*Shedule.*"

"What the hell ever. What difference it make to him?"

"He says he's doin' me a favor. Gonna be some action that night I don't want to be messed up in. He says stay away. Gonna be trouble. That's why I'm tellin' you too," Tyrel said.

"What kinda trouble?"

"Don't know. Just said trouble I don't want no part of. Now, listen. He's a strange one. He pay me sometime to tell him what I know about people. I don't know if it's drugs or what, but I figure if there's trouble, he mixed up in it, and he oughta know, see?"

"Huh," Odel scoffed. "He just tryin' get you fired."

"All I know, he ain't lied to me before. I gonna do what he says."

"Suit yourself."

As the forklift hummed to life again, a figure separated itself from the deepest shadows near the back corner of the loading bay and slipped out the open door. None of the dock workers noticed.

The knock on the door was faint over the clanking and hissing of the boiler, but Rolph knew who it was anyway. He didn't have many visitors, and only one ever knocked. He opened the door and was greeted by a lithesome young blonde in a short plaid skirt and white oxford shirt.

"Surprise!" she said, striking a pose.

"You do *not* look like a college student," Rolph assured her. "You look like a porn star pretending to be a Catholic schoolgirl. An *aging* porn star, at that."

"You say the sweetest things." Hilda stepped past him, giving him a peck on the cheek as she did so. "But don't think all your sweet talk is going to get you into my panties."

"Don't worry."

"You sly devil."

Rolph rolled his eyes. "Hilda. I'm a vampire. I'm functionally impotent. *Why* on earth would I want to get in your panties?" he asked, then added with more than a little cruelty, "Unless I had a very large truck I needed to park."

"Very large truck?" She seemed shocked, but then an evil grin spread across her face. "You sly, *euphemistic* devil!" She groped at his crotch, but he hopped out of the way. "How large is very large? Bring all that horsepower right over here."

"Dear God," Rolph groaned in exasperation.

"Funny. That's what they always say. Dear God. *Dear God. Dear God!*"

"Are you completely done? And stop humping the steam pipe."

"Spoilsport."

"What's news tonight?"

Hilda let her Catholic-schoolgirl facade fall away with a sigh. Her skirt was long and tattered, the crisp white shirt now dingy and bulging from the pressure of countless rolls of sagging flesh stuffed into too small a garment. Her haggard face was also a victim of gravity, with dark bags under her eyes and floppy jowls all dangling. Her grin was practically toothless, her teeth far outnumbered by the stiff stalks of hair that sprouted from her nostrils.

"More Sabbat action," she said. "London Tommy is warning some of his contacts away from the High the night of the Solstice party." With so few teeth, Hilda had a habit of smacking her gums together when she spoke. The effect was unappetizing, to say the least, yet still somehow managed to make Rolph thirsty.

"London Tommy," he repeated. "I suppose we'll need to pick him off once all this blows over. Can't have *too* many Sabbat hiding amongst our Anarchs, and he's one of the more active ones."

"What's wrong with now?" Hilda asked. "I say we do him now."

Rolph was taken aback for a moment. He was so often preoccupied with Hilda's other perversions that he tended to forget about her sadistic streak, which was, in keeping with anything relating to Hilda, fairly wide.

"No," Rolph said. "If we take care of him now, his Sabbat buddies might get antsy. This little raid or whatever they have planned for the High is perfect. There's some shooting, confusion. We grab Benito. Nobody is the wiser. They assume the Sabbat is responsible for him going missing. Emmett will love this."

"And there's the Hesha thing," Hilda pointed out.

"Right. I'll see to him myself. Was the statue there yet, with the others?"

"*The Dead Abel*," she nodded. "Unloaded tonight."

"I'll update Calebros."

"And when all this is over," Hilda said, rubbing her fat fingers together, "we'll run London Tommy through the meat grinder."

"Ah...yes." For a moment, Rolph pondered which would be worse: to be in Hilda's good graces, or her bad graces. In the end, he couldn't decide if there was much difference.

20 June 1999

FILE COPY

Re: Investigation

Spoke briefly with Rolph via SchreckNET
link———reports raid on Toreador party
in Atlanta will fall at midnight 6/22.
Some Sabbat activity in city, verified
by multiple sources, consistent with
report. — *some movement from Miami*

Raid should provide opportunity for
Rolph interaction w/Hesha's man — *Vegel*
(re: EoH); Emmett also planning
accordingly———reports arrangements
finalized; investigation matters to be
resolved, pursuance pending arrival at
Solstice engagement; hostess V. Ash.

Note: Julius to attend; likely result
Julius-JBH interaction obvious; cross-
reference also interaction matrix,
re: Julius-Victoria Ash;

   Julius-Eleanor Hodge;

   V. Ash-E. Hodge;

   V. Ash-Thelonious/Kantabi.

↳ file action update: Hazimel
file action update: Petrodon
↑ Note: query Rolph re: General (Mal.)

Monday, 21 June 1999, 4:12 AM
Service stairwell, High Museum of Art
Atlanta, Georgia

Rolph worked the corner of the putty knife expertly along the edge of the wooden door frame. The door's hinges and the padlock that ostensibly secured it were rusted but sound. No one on the museum staff used this particular door—a door that had not been marked on the building's original blueprints, yet which had served Rolph well on various occasions. The door itself, to be quite accurate, did not open. But, with appropriate pressure—a bit more than the typical kine might apply—frame and all would swing outward, allowing passage. It was a convenient route of access hidden practically in plain sight.

That was the problem. Rolph wasn't sure that Vegel would notice it. Vegel was Hesha's man, attending Victoria's Solstice party in Ruhadze's stead. Rolph and the Setite would transact their business just prior to midnight, and then the Setite needed to be spirited out of and away from the museum. The false door was to be part of Vegel's escape route.

"For Christ's sake," Emmett said from behind Rolph. "It seems obvious enough to me."

Rolph paused only briefly in his work, then continued with the putty knife, slightly enlarging the cracks that previously were almost invisible. "If he doesn't realize how it works," Rolph explained with forced patience, "he'll rip the entire door off, and I'll have to repair it all later—*if* someone else doesn't find it first."

"Hmph," Emmett snorted. He was pacing back and forth like a hideous, curmudgeonly metronome.

"I'm almost done."

"You might as well nail a giant stop sign to the door."

Rolph finished the bottom-most edge of the doorframe and slipped the putty knife into his pocket.

He reached into another pocket and, with a satisfied grin, produced a strip of yellow police-line tape.

Emmett stared in disbelief. "You're not really…"

"One thing I have learned about the other clans," Rolph said, "is not to overestimate them." He turned and tacked the tape across the door. "Just because a tunnel or an escape route or a hiding place is as plain as day—if you'll excuse the expression—to you or to me, does *not* mean that one of the others would recognize it even if he fell into it."

"Hmph."

"I've dealt with Vegel before. He's bright enough…for a Setite. But if there's a lot of confusion, which there should be…" Rolph waved his hands, rolling them at the wrists to represent distraction, and then ended the gesture with an almost apologetic shrug. "Well, he might need a little pointer."

"How about a neon sign?" Emmett suggested sardonically.

"I will deal with Herr Vegel in my way," Rolph said, deciding it was pointless to debate with Emmett. "You deal with Don Giovanni in yours. Would you like to look over the gallery again, or the main elevator, or the ramp to the lobby?"

"Thank you, but no. You've been quite the thorough host. I've got a map of the place right here." Emmett tapped his head with a gnarled finger. "I know what I want to do. I'll fill in the others."

"Then we should—" Rolph came up short and pulled the suddenly vibrating pager from his pocket.

"Who is it?" Emmett asked suspiciously.

"News from Boston." Rolph squinted at the peculiar message. "The graverobber has traded shovels."

"*Christ,*" Emmett hissed. "Benito has changed plans. No kidnapping in Atlanta, it looks like. Well, screw him. I'm not going to wait anymore. Let's get back. Now. I need to get on the horn to Calebros, and to Boston. Unless you have more decorating to do here…?"

Rolph ignored the jibe. His plan was still going smoothly, even if Emmett's was not. "No, I'm done."

"Gloat on your own time."

The two left the door and headed farther down the stairwell to one of several alternate exits. Rolph did not, of course, wish Emmett ill. After all, Emmett's task was far more vital to the clan than was Rolph's own. Rolph was settling an old debt, whereas Emmett needed Benito's information to settle a much more recent score. Still, Rolph did derive a certain perverse satisfaction from the turn of events and from the fact that his own operation was proceeding flawlessly.

Tuesday, 22 June 1999, 12:40 AM
The High Museum of Art
Atlanta, Georgia

Rolph was keeping his head down. Or up, rather. He was peering through the slats of the air-conditioning vent that was his current hiding place and gazing down at the Kindred below. They were resplendent in their evening finery: tuxedos and nineteenth-century suits; elegant gowns; even the occasional leather jacket and torn jeans carried a certain luster this evening. The Kindred of Atlanta and prominent out-of-town guests were here tonight to see and be seen. Rolph shared only the first of those two motives, and only he suspected that something was very wrong.

Not because of what was happening—the scheming, double-crossing, and backstabbing that was endemic to the goings-on of surface-dwelling Kindred—but because of what was *not* happening. Surely he should have heard something: a few gunshots, screams, perhaps a small explosion. Rolph had corroborated Hilda's reports through alternate sources both here and in Miami. The Sabbat was supposedly planning some excitement for tonight, undoubtedly a guerilla raid or the like to bloody Prince Benison's nose, wound his pride, and provide at least a propaganda victory to spur on Atlanta's Anarch element. The prince had been quite capable all on his own of grievously raising the ire of more than merely the fringe elements of Kindred society. The current rebellion among the younger generations (and of a select few, well-placed elders) was of his making, but the unrest was the type of situation that the Sabbat simply couldn't resist. Perhaps that was the method to Benison's madness—foment revolution against his own rule, and then flush out Sabbat moles in the city as they became more openly active.

Rolph, in his place of hiding, shrugged. Anything was possible with Benison. The Malkavian seemed to court disaster often, but his apparently rash and imprudent actions along with his inscrutable designs tended to keep his opponents guessing and off balance.

Regardless, there was no Sabbat raid. Not yet. Rolph's sources had seemed to think that midnight was the magic hour—but it had come and gone without event. What increased the oddity was the fact that Rolph felt certain that the Sabbat were out there. In the city. More so than usual. One of his sources in Miami had reported movements of certain individuals from that city, and Rolph himself had noticed an influx of Kindred—trying with limited success to keep out of sight—in Atlanta.

Rolph fished around in his pocket and pulled out a tarnished brass watch on an equally grimy chain. Quarter till one. No raid.

Despite his concern, Rolph found himself increasingly drawn into the drama unfolding beneath him. It wasn't in his nature to ignore the little games, the snubs, the plots. Victoria had really outdone herself. Not only had she invited into the sanctuary of Elysium Thelonious, one of the activists among the Anarchists opposing Prince Benison, but she had also included on the guest list the Brujah archon Julius. Julius had a history of animosity toward Benison—a sentiment the prince heartily reciprocated. Rolph was uncertain whether the archon was cooperating with Victoria, or if so how closely, but Julius had arrived almost an hour ago and had not yet presented himself to the prince. That was a lapse in decorum which was likely—and undoubtedly calculated—to rub Benison the wrong way, and possibly to lead to strife.

Rolph observed the unfolding events with interest. Would Victoria's scheming create a breach between herself and the prince? he wondered. Whatever damage occurred tonight would be linked only indirectly to her; she had merely mixed numerous, volatile personalities, and as a newcomer to the city would claim ignorance. But her choice of guests, at the very least, would attract Benison's suspicions, if not his outright enmity. It was a dangerous game she played. Benison was equally likely to laugh it off or to banish her from the city.

Yes, the morality play with Victoria, Benison, and Julius was the most significant focus of the evening, Rolph decided. The Sabbat must have bungled and aborted their raid. No surprise there. Furthermore, that increased the likelihood that Erich Vegel, entrusted with the prized Eye of Hazimel to deliver to Hesha Ruhadze, had left the area safely. Rolph had handed over the Eye just prior to midnight, anticipating that the raid would cover Vegel's hasty exit. With the raid failing to materialize, Vegel would have to make his own excuses should Victoria accost him in the future.

All thoughts of the Setite vanished from Rolph's mind when the shouting started.

"Do you see the bastard up there?" Prince Benison was yelling at a startled, cowering Toreador neonate.

Conflicting tides of Kindred swirled in and out of the main gallery, some rushing to see what was happening, others, deciding they didn't care to be so close to the enraged prince, hastily retreating. Benison's demands and curses rose above the commotion every few seconds. Then, as if by magic, the throng melted away and there, standing practically alone amidst the statuary and opaque glass dividers, were Benison and Julius.

"Behind you, Prince," Julius said perfectly calmly. He wore two sabers strapped to his back. Benison whirled to face the archon.

As the two traded threats, Rolph briefly wondered if perhaps Julius had cut some sort of deal with the Anarchs—get rid of Benison and everything goes back to law and order; no more threat to the Masquerade. Julius would certainly favor Thelonious, his clansman, over Benison as prince. But Thelonious was too active in the revolt. There would have to be a compromise candidate— perhaps Benjamin the Ventrue, or someone else of stature, someone like...*Victoria.*

Rolph craned his neck about in his perch behind

the vent covering. He tried to spy Victoria amongst the crowd, and Thelonious. Rolph wanted to see what their reactions were to the rapidly escalating conflict.

"Elysium be damned, I will punish your insufferable attitude!" Benison snarled with determination and twisted pleasure. Julius drew one of his twin blades—

And darkness covered the gallery.

Not a natural darkness. Not a darkness that penetrated the shadows of Rolph's hiding place. The inky blackness started a few feet below the ceiling and seemed to cover most of the gallery down to the floor.

"*Lasombra!*" someone below wailed in alarm.

That was no leap of intellect for anyone who had experienced the smothering shadow magic of that clan before, but even Rolph was amazed by the sheer scope of the blackness that descended upon the gallery. He could imagine the oppressive terror that must be crushing the Kindred unfortunate enough to be trapped within. Instinctively, he pressed himself farther back into the duct work.

Then a disturbing thought struck him: He should *help*.

But that would involve going *down there*, among the suffocating shadows. And now, he saw with growing alarm, there were Sabbat war ghouls wading into the fragmenting sea of darkness. As a result, not only were the shadows breaking apart, but *Kindred* as well, limb from limb, as if the war-ghoul monstrosities were ransacking a poultry plant and enjoying a giant game of "make a wish."

War ghouls? *What kind of raid is this?* Much more of one than he'd anticipated, apparently. And much more of one than he was going to be caught in the middle of. *Go down there?* He slapped himself on the face to banish the suicidal thought. *Not bloody likely!* Getting himself ripped apart, he reasoned, wasn't going to do anybody any good, least of all himself.

As if he needed more convincing, as the sea of darkness split into eddies that consumed individual Kindred, the gallery's windows shattered. Fist-sized orbs of flesh landed around the room, then exploded. Blood and pulpy body matter sprayed everywhere. The effect was very much like fishermen chumming the water. Several Kindred who had been holding their own lost it, went berserk, frenzied. Covered in blood and no longer able to control terror augmented by insatiable hunger, they pounced on whomever was closest, friend or foe.

The war ghouls took full advantage of the additional havoc to claim more victims. Many of Atlanta's Kindred were already down, although a few scattered melees lingered on. Benison and Julius, back to back instead of at each other's throats, seemed to be making a stand among the writhing and whip-like tentacles of shadow. Some other fool got himself launched through one of the few remaining intact windows—a four-story plunge to the street below; that was going to hurt.

Slowly, as if he could possibly draw someone's attention from the slaughter below, Rolph inched back down the ventilation duct. He'd seen enough. More than enough.

22 June 1999
re: (Anatole)

FILE COPY

Sighted so-called Prophet of Gehenna
outside J.F.K. Airport, 4:25 AM. No
luggage, companions, evident money or
other valuables. Followed him into NYC
to Cathedral of St. JtD. He went
straight to gardens, seemed to pray to
or with statue there.

At this point, I was forced away from
the site. I have no explanation for
this phenomena—some force made me move
away and out of sight. I summoned help,
but (the others) couldn't enter the
garden either, or close within sight of
it. We monitored the perimeter of the
cathedral all night, but Anatole did
not come out again.

→ Why now? Was he in the
air before or after Ralph extracted
the eye? Query Ralph on exact
timing.

→ Check assignment schedule.

Tuesday, 22 June 1999, 7:21 PM
A subterranean grotto
New York City, New York

Calebros sat quietly at his desk. With his tongue he prodded and probed a canker sore that had formed on the inside of his lip where his sharp, misaligned teeth rubbed. Not even the constant, jarring pain distracted him from the report he read over and over again.

The Prophet of Gehenna. In New York.

Calebros could not quite put his finger on what bothered him so much about Anatole's presence. Perhaps what pressed down upon the unraveler of secrets was merely the weight of history. And of the future.

Benito watched from the shadows as "art happened."
He didn't want to distract the artist, oh-so-talented
Pennington. But neither could the Giovanni intermedi-
ary stay away. Thought of the favors that the artist's
subject would owe made Benito practically giddy. What
was the worth of bilking some viscount, or expediting
the shipment of stolen art to aging Nazi refugees in Ar-
gentina, when compared to the indebtedness of a justicar?
Amidst the dust of dark clay and marble, something sweet
was in the air, like the smell of money, or of blood.

The apartment studio was sparsely furnished, completely utilitarian, every possible space given over to the
calling of the artist. *How very bohemian*, Benito thought.

The justicar, in all his splendorous bulk and foulness, sat perfectly content. The work was progressing more
smoothly now that Benito had given the photograph to
Pennington. The first few attempts had been maddening. Each time, the sculptor had worked for several
nights—until Petrodon had balked at some detail that
was not to his liking: the nose was too big, the eyes were
uneven…. Never mind that, if anything, Pennington was
doing the Nosferatu a kindness. But Petrodon would not
be placated, and they were forced to begin the work anew.
Time after time after time.

Then Benito's mysterious partner had quietly stepped
in. *Nickolai*. The name was all Benito knew for sure. He
suspected the man to be a warlock, but it made little difference; he'd suggested this scheme to Benito and charged
a steep finder's fee, but not beyond reason. Several nights
ago, Nickolai had provided the photograph—a picture
of Petrodon *before* his change. It depicted a handsome
and vainglorious man. One of those two qualities had
accompanied him into unlife.

And suddenly Justicar Petrodon had been completely satisfied, heaping effusive praise upon Pennington. Never mind that the evolving bust bore a more striking resemblance to the photograph propped by the sculptor's table than to the hulking monstrosity a dozen feet away. Petrodon could not have been more pleased. *And the customer is always right,* Benito thought. Let the justicar believe whatever he wanted to believe, as long as he paid up when the price came due.

"It seems to be going well," came the quiet voice behind Benito's shoulder. He started, and was relieved to see it was Nickolai, come unexpectedly. "I'm glad you are here tonight, Benito," Nickolai murmured. The words were innocent enough, but Benito did not care for the mocking, slightly ominous tone.

And then horror and chaos erupted. Within just a few minutes, the smell of blood truly was in the air.

Wednesday, 30 June 1999, 10:15 PM
The Sunken Cathedral
Cranberry Bogs, Massachusetts

Benito Giovanni lay still on the hard wooden pallet that was the only furnishing in his cell. His shirt was open at the collar, tie loosened, his shoes placed tidily together on the bare stone floor. His eyes were closed.

Emmett peered through the spy hole. He had learned much about his captive and his mannerisms over a week of observation. He wished he'd kept count of how many times Benito had tried to glance at the watch that had been removed from his wrist. That was exactly the obsessive sort of detail, Emmett thought, that Calebros would have noted. He would have charted the exact routes of Benito's pacing during his waking hours. Then Calebros would have discerned some pattern, real or imaginary, and spent weeks—or *months*—pouring through some musty tome, convinced that the prisoner's wanderings were part of an elaborate necromantic ritual, and searching for a way to counteract the infernal spell.

Not Emmett. For all of Calebros's strengths, the elder of the two broodmates lacked a sense of perspective, of *relevance*. Benito's reflexive habit of glancing at his wristwatch was merely a curiosity. Other facts were more telling. The Giovanni had been snatched from his Boston office nine nights ago and kept in isolation since. Even over that short period, Emmett had noticed Benito beginning to rise later in the evening. The difference was gradual, only a matter of minutes at this point. It was a physiological response, an attempt on the part of Benito's body, rather than a conscious decision on his part, to conserve energy—or blood. Benito had not been seriously injured during his capture, but he had not been allowed to feed since, and even the most minimal activity, over time, would exhaust whatever blood resided within his undead body.

The reduced activity might also be a psychological response, a coping mechanism. Captives, especially those kept in solitary confinement for extended periods, often developed sleeping disorders, losing the ability to rest altogether or, as in Benito's case, resting for increasingly prolonged amounts of time. The gradual nature of the increase in Benito's hour of rising, however, suggested that he had not yet suffered severe psychological trauma.

With time, of course, that would change.

Emmett had a certain amount of experience with observing prisoners, and with interrogation. He would know when the time was right for Benito to answer questions. With the proper amount of blood deprivation, it was generally not necessary to torture a Kindred extensively, and Benito did not strike Emmett as the type to possess any great loyalty to his conspirators. The Giovanni would talk.

Silently, Emmett slid the cover back over the spy hole.

"Are you ready?" Abbot Pierce asked in a near-whisper.

"*What?*" Emmett asked in return. He had heard perfectly well, but after a week, he'd grown irritated with the abbot's soft-spoken yet thinly veiled impatience.

"Are you ready to question him?"

Pierce wore a heavy robe, so heavy on his slight frame, in fact, that Emmett constantly expected him to collapse under the weight of the fabric. Judging by the abbot's few visible features—skeletal wrists and hands protruding from the loose sleeves, gaunt face set deep within the overhanging hood—Emmett imagined his clansmate to be little more than a walking coat-rack beneath the robe.

"Not yet," Emmett said, stepping past his host and beginning down the corridor.

Pierce fell in step behind him. "You must take him away from here. He endangers the cathedral."

Emmett gestured dismissively. "Moving him while things are so hot would endanger you more."

"Clan Giovanni is the power to be reckoned with this close to Boston—not your Camarilla."

"You mean…*our* Camarilla, of course," Emmett said meaningfully, then continued, "and the Giovanni would have found us out already if they were going to."

"Then you *weren't* certain that no one was following you when you brought him here." Pierce's insistent whisper struck a peevish tone with Emmett.

"Nobody was in a hotrod on our tails shooting at us, if that's what you mean, but the Giovanni have their ways—I don't know what they are, but they have them. Did I want to get old Benito a little farther from the city just to be on the safe side? Hell yes. I'm sorry if that inconveniences your little cult—"

"We are *not* a cult," Pierce snapped. "We are a spiritual collective, like-minded individuals gathered together to—"

"Yeah, yeah. Yadda, yadda, yadda. Save it for the promotional video." Emmett quickened his pace and drew ahead of the abbot. Pierce and the other "monks" grated on Emmett's nerves. Sure there was a chance that by bringing Benito here someone might find out about the collection of stone-lined tunnels and chambers they'd built beneath the bogs and then pumped out, and which they now somewhat grandiosely referred to as a "cathedral." But sometimes risks were unavoidable. Sometimes, especially in a matter as important as this, one had to be willing to take one for the clan. Besides that, Emmett was put off by the religious posturing that Pierce and his followers affected—like their spiritual whacking-off was all that mattered, and everybody else could—or would—go to hell.

"You know," Emmett said over his shoulder, "a *real* cathedral wouldn't have an abbot. A cathedral is the seat of a bishopric. You should be a bishop. There. I just gave you a promotion. That should make up for your trouble."

"Calebros will hear of your obstreperousness," Pierce said, actually raising his voice a decibel or two.

"I bet he will. He hears about everything sooner or later," Emmett said. "And, oh, he'll be real surprised too."

Sunday, 4 July 1999, 11:24 PM
Subway tunnel 147, Manhattan
New York City, New York

The repairs were still unfinished. They would remain so for the foreseeable future. The union refused to allow any of its laborers to continue the job, although the renovations were only a few weeks from completion.

Six workers. All that was found were their skeletons, relatively intact, the bones picked clean by rats.

Jeremiah made his way along the defunct metal umbilical of this aborted fetus. The third rail was dead. Purely from habit, he listened for trains that were not coming. Although he had fed earlier in the evening, Jeremiah was cold. The cement and unfinished tile seemed to draw the warmth from him. He imagined them leaching the very blood through his pores and drinking deeply of him. Had the tunnel workers felt that? he wondered. Had they felt the first nibbles of the rats? The first hundred bites, the first thousand?

Subway officials had speculated that the six workers had been overcome by some toxic gas mysteriously released into the tunnel. Jeremiah, noting the growing number of hungry eyes tracking his every move, questioned the accuracy of that hypothesis. But rats, even a large number, would never attack several strong, active, full-grown men. Would they? The victims were not sickly children. The workers must have been incapacitated in some manner. Jeremiah nudged an abandoned wrench with his foot. Had one of the workers tried to ward off the vermin before being overwhelmed? The Nosferatu spied an unused flare in the dust. He picked it up, inspected it, then tucked it into the canvas sack he was never without.

The six workers were merely a memory, but the rats were still very much in evidence. Municipal exterminators be damned. The rodents had returned like a conquering army after the fumigation. They had feasted on their poisoned brethren, whose tiny bones now littered the ground from which the mortal remains had been removed. Now the scavengers—hunters?—scuttled among the shadows. Watching through red eyes.

Jeremiah conducted his investigation, but he kept moving. He had the feeling that if he stopped for more than a few seconds at a time, he would be mistaken for carrion—or that he might become it, if he wasn't already. After all, what was he, if not a walking corpse? Only motion separated him from the more normal fare of the rats.

Jeremiah quickened his pace ever so slightly. He forced himself to continue looking for clues to what had happened. Was it his imagination, he wondered, or were the red eyes—growing ever more numerous—yielding less and less ground to him? The berth they granted him was not so wide as it had been. He could make out more of their forms—curved backs with bristling fur, distended bellies gorged on flesh. But there had only been six workers, and the attack had occurred almost two weeks ago. What else could these creatures be feasting upon?

Pausing in his trek, Jeremiah met the eyes of one of the encroaching horde rising like floodwaters. He was struck by the hostility in that gaze as he peered into the psyche of the creature. Their eyes locked, and an image formed behind the red eyes: a craggy expanse of concrete, its surface cracked and rough. More cracks formed—created by a rugged, splotchy vegetation growing at a speed reminiscent of time-lapse photography. The concrete bulged in areas, cracked, broke apart. Rats stormed in, thousands of them, and devoured the stalks. The strange plants…*not* plants, Jeremiah realized, but pustules of—

Flesh.

Jeremiah took a step back, jolted from the image and facing again the gathering swarm of rats. Flesh. Had the word formed in his mind or the rat's?

Flesh.

He heard it again. Or felt it. Like an echoing whisper spreading through the tunnel. Countless red eyes glared at him angrily, hungrily. He could feel the gazes boring into him, attempting to make contact as he just had with one of their number—attempting to gain control.

Jeremiah turned to continue down the tunnel, but found his way blocked. The circle had closed around him. A few of the snarling rats refused to yield to his advance. They crept closer. More were filling in beyond, filling the tunnel.

"Away!" Jeremiah barked with a threatening gesture. The throng wavered but did not break. He gestured again, "Away!" but to less effect. He felt a tremor of fear take hold of his hand. A different, quite distinct tremor rippled through the tunnel and the rats like a wave of chittering laughter.

Propelled by rising terror, Jeremiah snatched the flare from his canvas sack. In one motion, he ignited the device and flung it at the closest rats. They recoiled from the flash, but, in the next instant, their filth-encrusted fur was ablaze. They were packed so tightly that the panicked gyrations of the burning rodents carried the flames to those all around them. A piercing screech almost knocked Jeremiah to the ground. The sound was a single cry, a collective scream of rage and pain.

Jeremiah's first impulse was to cower from the flames as well, but he forced himself to take advantage of the few seconds he had. With all the strength and speed he could summon, he leapt directly over the sputtering flare and the burgeoning wildfire of rats.

He didn't turn back to see how long the fire burned or how many of the malevolent creatures pursued him. He ran for all he was worth, canvas sack flapping at his side and pounding against his thigh with each frantic stride. The screeching of burning rats filled the tunnel. He could not escape the sound, no matter how much distance he put between himself and the horde. Their screams lingered in his ears—their screams, and the single, drawn-out, eerily lustful word: *Flesshhh…*

part two:
beginning to unravel

Friday, 12 November 1999, 3:45 AM
West 132th Street, Harlem
New York City, New York

Pug scaled the ladder and slammed into the underside of the manhole cover so hard that it popped out onto the street. He clambered out in the cold night. The street was deserted. The area might be bustling with activity during the day, but people knew enough to stay away at night. Many parts of the city were considerably less hospitable after dark—especially these nights, with the Camarilla and the Sabbat taking their fight to the streets. Kine weren't stupid, just dense. They sensed that kind of thing even if they didn't realize it. All the violence and fires and accidents—the kine were staying home in droves. And that's where Pug wanted to be. Actually, anywhere but where he was would do. He was on his feet without hesitation and ready to resume his headlong flight when a deep, threatening voice checked him.

"Hold it right there, motherfucker."

Pug instinctively froze, but after the first instant realized that, no matter who this person was, he couldn't be worse than what Pug was already fleeing. He lifted a foot to run—

—And everything went black. His vision was swimming when he came to some time later, how long he wasn't sure. The sky was clear and starry. He was looking up at it. From his back. On the street. The pieces came together slowly. A shape was blocking part of the sky, and a face behind the shape. The shape was a gun, a big gun, pointed at his head. The face belonged to an angry-looking young woman. Her anger, and the fact that she was holding the gun, did not comfort Pug.

Then he remembered the Eye, and his vague discomfort spiked to sheer terror. He started to get up, to flee, but the woman jammed the barrel of the gun against his wide, flat nose. "Nuh-uh!" she grunted.

From somewhere behind her, came another sound—someone cocking a pump-action shotgun. Then another face was looking down at Pug, a man, a big man, a very big and very black man. Pug didn't get a good look; he was having trouble concentrating on anything except the gun pressed to his nose, and he kept going cross-eyed. He tried to look back in the direction of the manhole without moving his head.

"Gotta go," he managed to force out. "Gotta go. *Now.*"

"You'll be going," said the man, with a deep rumbling voice, "but it might not be *how* you wanna go, motherfucker."

"You don't understand. It's—"

"Shut the fuck up, asshole!" the woman yelled at him. She pushed him with the gun until his head was back down against the pavement. This woman seemed a bit too willing to splatter his brain all over the street. And she was strong. Kindred strong.

Fear and a fierce throbbing from the back of his head where he'd just been hit were mingling to make Pug feel sick. Beneath the veneer of terror that these people wouldn't give him a chance to explain, he was trying to guess whether they were Camarilla or Sabbat. At the same time, he kept trying to glance back at the manhole, but in a way that didn't induce anyone to blow his head off. He had to take a chance—it would mean his destruction if these two were Sabbat, but there was no time....

"I'm from Calebros's warren!" he stammered.

The woman pressed the gun harder against his nose. "I'm from Philly. Big fuckin' deal."

But the big man wasn't so hungry for blood. "Lydia, let him up."

"Huh?"

The man gently eased her gun aside. It was a pistol, a Desert Eagle, Pug could see now. It wasn't quite as big when it wasn't perched between his eyes, but it was still a handful for the small angry woman. She wasn't that much taller than Pug, and at least seventy-five pounds lighter.

"He's one of us," said the man, "if he's tellin' the truth." He extended a hand and pulled Pug roughly to his feet.

"I am!" Pug blurted. "One of you…I mean, telling the truth…both, *both*."

"Theo Bell," said the big man.

Pug was trying to shake his hand and leave all at the same time. "No time. It's after me…the Eye. Got the others already. Gotta go. We've gotta go…." He paused, cocked his head, and looked up at the man again. "Did you say Theo Bell?"

"Right as rain," said Lydia. "We're the fuckin' cavalry. Who is it that's after you?" she asked, more suspicious than helpful.

Two more shapes were materializing from the shadows. One held his head at a strange angle; the other had a long mane of red hair and was doing a poor job of hiding what appeared to be a broadsword beneath his long coat. Pug was still trying to pull away, to get away, but Theo Bell wasn't letting go of his hand, and Pug's considerable strength couldn't seem to break the grip.

"Did you say something about an eye?" Theo asked.

They were interrupted by a hollow voice, all too familiar to Pug, which emanated from the open manhole. "Yes," it said, "the Eye, it sees…. Mustn't find…mustn't harm her." The spiky hairs on the back of Pug's neck stood on end.

"Frankie, Christoph, spread out," Theo said, watching the hole warily. He let go of Pug's hand, and the Nosferatu, still pulling, stumbled to the pavement. He caught himself panting again, and wheezing, but he couldn't stop. And then the creature was pulling itself from the sewer. The Eye took them all in, and Pug felt himself rooted to the spot; he wanted more desperately than anything in the world to flee, but he could not find the strength to do so. The man who bore the Eye didn't seem so overwhelming out of the enclosed space of the tunnels; he seemed rigid and frail beneath the pulsating vibrancy of the orb.

Lydia turned to Theo. "You're not going to tell me that's one of us, are you?" Theo shook his head. "Good," she said, and turned and fired. She squeezed off seven quick shots.

Pug meekly raised a finger behind them. "That's not going to—" but the bullets were already slamming into the Eye. It sucked the slugs in like a putrid swamp embracing welcome raindrops. Lydia stared at the thing in disbelief. Theo leveled his shotgun at it—

The creature whipped its head to the side and spewed a spray of ichor over its assailants. The stink of burning flesh and the sound of screams filled the night. Lydia dropped to the ground, hands over her face, still screaming, and rolled. She clawed at her own face and chest, trying to rake away the burning, but the acidic ichor spread to her hands. Her fingertips instantly seared to bone. Theo also whipped around with a yell of pain. His face was steaming. The shotgun clattered to the street as he struggled to rip off his smoldering leather jacket.

From the other side of the Eye, Frankie was firing a pistol, and Christoph was charging from a different angle with his sword. Suddenly the pavement around the open manhole rippled—then stretched and *rose*, towering like a giant serpent. It snapped to the side and struck Christoph a bone-crushing blow, knocking him across the street, where he smashed into a parked car.

The huge black snake twisted and shot toward Frankie. The gaping maw—that seconds before had been the manhole—snapped closed on him. Frankie's head and right shoulder fell to one side, his legs to the other, but that was all. And just as quickly as it had struck, the black snake was gone, and only crumbled pavement remained.

Pug lay sprawled on the pavement. Mere seconds had passed since he'd fallen—seconds that seemed to drag on for years, for it seemed they would be his last. He tried to crawl, but all he could do was stare at the pulsating bloodshot Eye.

Theo, flesh dripping down his face like melted wax and his smoldering jacket at his feet, was all that stood against the creature. The Brujah archon reached down to retrieve his shotgun.

Pug saw the streetlight bend and swing at Theo. The Nosferatu managed to call out a warning, but the metal post was lightning quick. It flailed Theo from behind with a spray of glass and the sickening crunch of steel and bone. It knocked him to the ground, and then pounded him again and again. Finally Pug forced himself to his feet. He charged toward Theo, hoping at least to pull the archon beyond the reach of the metal post. But it abandoned Theo and struck at Pug. He saw it coming straight for his face, and then the impact, then…nothing.

He didn't think he'd lost consciousness, because the Eye was still there, the creature stalking toward Theo's prone body. But this blow to the head left Pug's vision blurry and clouded by…blood? He wiped a hand across his face, sniffed and licked at his own blood. He thought he saw the streetlight lying, broken, to his side.

Theo moaned. The Eye creature was on him now. Pug tried to get up again, but the world was spinning, the street shifting beneath him. He saw Theo roll over and weakly raise his shotgun. The creature reached out a hand. A flash and an explosion, a spray of white phosphorus and blood.

The creature stood above Theo, staring at its own stump of a hand. All the fingers and most of the palm were gone altogether. It rotated its wrist and stared curiously at the bloody mess. Theo and Pug and the others were completely forgotten as the thing turned and wandered away down the street, all the while staring at what had been its hand.

6 July 1999
Re: Benito Giovanni: Las Vegas

Montrose reports — two East Coast
Giovanni lightweights (Victor Sforza,
Chas Giovanni Tello) asking questions
about Benito; meet w/Milo Rothstein 6/
29; return 6/30 AM, unceremoniously
dispose of Rothstein. Tello flies out
next night; Sforza terminated by
unknown assailant(s).

Repercussions of M.R. death — few or
none; already cultivated connections
with other Giovanni-related elements in
L.V.

Commend Emett - False pointers
to L.V. successful

→ Now that the ruckus out west
has died down, Las Vegas might
be the safest place to move Benito.
They've already looked there.

15 July 1999
Re: Eye of Hazimel FILE COPY

Atlanta———Hesha's courier confirmed
among dead from (raid; Rolph reports———
no sign of Eye in city. Has it fallen
to Sabbat? Not according to info via
Vykos's pet assassin/ghoul.

Where IS the blasted Eye?

↳ HELL of a 'raid': Atlanta,
Savanah, Columbia, Charleston,
Raleigh, Wilmington, Norfolk,
Richmond, D.C. . . .

Note: file action update:
Pieterzoon, Jan, to arrive in
Baltimore tonight.

The light flickered incessantly. Finally, like a co-
bra striking, Calebros's gnarled hand shot out and cuffed
the lamp. The illumination shone bright and steady.
For several minutes, the tarnished bead chain became
a pendulum, swaying back and forth, tapping softly
against the curved metal shade of the banker's lamp.
All the while, Calebros unceasingly studied his reports.
The latest word from Las Vegas, from Atlanta, from
Boston, from London and Lisbon, from Calcutta…

Occasionally, he reached for his red pen and added
a note to one of the typed reports. He tirelessly examined and re-examined the countless details, the logic
behind the details. Endlessly questioning. Dissecting the
analyses, his own as well as that of others. Distinguish-
ing fact from assumption. The discrete bits of
information often fit together in unexpected ways but,
as with a jigsaw puzzle, forcing the pieces together,
though temporarily satisfying an impatient yearning for
order, served only to distort the overall picture in the
long run. But that was obviously what had happened.

Scrap paper. Calebros began sifting through the
piles of folders and loose papers piled and spread across
his desk, their placement seemingly the result of some
great explosion or catastrophic natural disaster. They
were stacked tall enough to give the impression that
his trusty Smith Corona was actually resting in a hole
instead of on the desktop. Eventually, he found what
he was looking for: a report that had outlived its usefulness. It was on the bottom of a stack, of course, but
Calebros skillfully extricated it without compromising
the structural integrity of his filing system.

He turned the piece of paper to its relatively un-
marked side, then paused and flipped it back over. This
particular report was a list, circa 1950, of suspected Com-

munist sympathizers in the New York metropolitan area. Page one of seven. He scanned the names, crossed off several, and circled several others, individuals it might be beneficial to check up on. Most if not all of them were certainly dead by now—such an unrewarding proposition, tracking a kine population over the long haul—but there was bound to be dirt on some. And a descendent or an estate executor was often willing, more willing than the potentially embarrassed individual would have been in life, to negotiate in order to keep damaging secrets just that—secret. Favors, knowledge, these were more useful to Calebros than, say, money, but one took what one could get. Cash had its uses as well; a good old-fashioned bribe was sometimes the very grease a wheel needed.

Not distracted overly long from his original task, Calebros turned the list back over and began jotting down assumptions to which Rolph, in the matter of the Sabbat "raid" in Atlanta, had obviously jumped. Several of those assumptions were, just as obviously, flawed. Calebros didn't spare himself in the critique. He should have recognized Rolph's less than rigorously analyzed conclusions for what they were at the outset. Calebros was just as guilty in the matter: By taking Rolph's word, by not demanding at least an accounting of more of the raw data, Calebros himself had fallen victim to slothful, undisciplined thought. He pressed down on the red pen, item after item, as his new list grew.

And then the light failed. His grotto office fell into total darkness.

Calebros sighed. A lamp, a lightbulb. Details. Mere details. But all the details were connected—in one way or another. One ignored even the slightest detail only at his own peril. Each puzzle piece was part of the larger picture. Still, Calebros was little more than irritated by this particular detail of existence. He preferred to concentrate on other, more relevant facts. But reading in the dark was tiresome, so he climbed painfully to his feet, tried to stretch out his back a bit, and then shuffled over to a free-standing rusted, metal cabinet. He slid aside three bulging boxes filled with newspaper clippings so he could open the cabinet, and took a package of small light bulbs from the second shelf from the bottom. Calebros took one of the last two bulbs, twisting it slowly in his talons, as if he were trying to screw it into thin air. For an instant, he was overcome by a sense of regret.

He felt for some reason that his time, like his supply of lightbulbs, was running out. He wondered which of his charges would some night take his place. Who would inherit the dilemmas that he left unsolved? Surely Emmett lacked the patience. Perhaps Umberto, with his interest in things electronic and modern, would be the torch-bearer. But Calebros had his doubts. He should put his mind to the matter, he decided. Soon. He should begin grooming a successor, just as Augustin had groomed him.

Then the feeling passed. Calebros continued twirling the bulb. He could just make out the edges as it turned in his grasp. "Hmph," he snorted. "Getting all philosophical about a damned lightbulb...and with so much else to do."

He changed the bulb. *A piece of junk*, Umberto had called the lamp. He'd been trying to get Calebros to replace both it and the Smith Corona, but Calebros scoffed at the suggestion. He was not of this new, disposable age. One did not simply cast away a useful tool.

With the new bulb in, the lamp again cast semi-adequate reading light over the mammoth desk. And almost instantly, the light started to blink and flicker.

"Damn you." Calebros smacked the lamp; the flickering stopped. Good as new. His own sire, were Augustin still around, would have disassembled the lamp years ago, rewired it, checked the switch, basically spared no trouble to make sure the device worked as it should have. Then again, Augustin had always been more the hands-on type—which was why he *wasn't* around any longer.

Before he sat back down, a distant sound caught Calebros's attention. Howling. Not wolves or lupines, but not wholly human either. The kennels. Emmett must be back. Good.

Calebros shuffled away from his desk, past bookcases and makeshift shelves in various states of disrepair, each crammed full of boxes and bundles of reports, newspaper clippings, letters, photographs secured with strings grown black and brittle with age. No crevice was wasted. Information of one sort or another was crammed into every available space. Calebros took hold of one metal shelf unit and wrenched it away from the wall. He hunched down and climbed head-first into the knee-high tunnel that had been hidden by the shelf and boxes.

His movements were a syncopation of popping joints and crackling vertebrae as he endeavored to force his corkscrew spine through the narrow passage. Not needing to look behind himself after years of practice—and unable to do so in the tight space, at any rate—he expertly hooked a foot through a metal bracket on the wall side of the shelves and pulled the weighty unit back to. He pulled himself along the tunnel by hooking his talons in ridges worn in the stone floor over many years of use. The orthopedic symphony lessened after his initial movements, but, of course, the discomfort remained just as acute. Jolts of pain shot periodically through his wrists and shoulders, neck, back, hips, knees, ankles. Despite the nagging physical pain, however, Calebros retained a fondness for the tunnel. Amidst the constantly changing world of his reports and messages from the outside world, this cramped stone crawlspace was a constant, a familiar place, a connection between present and past.

The tunnel sloped downward with mostly gentle curves. There was one sharp turn, precisely three fifths of the way down—Calebros had counted the talon indentations in the stone, estimated the distance, then checked his calculations with a series of tied-together tape measures. Minor curiosities sometimes took on seemingly obsessive interest among the monotony of the endless nights.

The chamber beyond the tunnel was dark, but Calebros felt the room open around him as he climbed free of the passage. The air against his face was cooler and distinctly sticky, salty. He could feel, too, his pupils stretched wide, as wide as a kine's entire eye. Before him lay water, his lake, the surface calm except for the few lazy ripples marking the air currents. It was, of course, more pond than lake, a glorified mudhole, some—notably Emmett—would say. Calebros realized this full well, but to Augustin it had been a lake, and Calebros had inherited that exaggerated fondness, along with much else.

Slowly, almost ritualistically, he removed his long jacket and laid it over a stone outcropping. He took off his shirt and trousers, laid them aside as well, and then waded naked into the pool. The water, never warmed by the sun, was cool against his ankles, shins, thighs. He came to the drop-off quickly. He paused, but there was no need. His hesitation was perhaps the last remnant of species consciousness, an evolutionary oversight. There was no great shock as he plunged into the icy water and pushed away from the shelf of stone that ringed the shoreline; there was no scrotum-tightening exhilaration from the blast of cold water. The water was not so much colder than his own body, than the tainted blood within it. He allowed his initial push to carry him out into the lake; he lay motionless below the surface. Gradually, he achieved equilibrium—of temperature, his body's dropping to match that of the surrounding water; of mass, his inert form maintaining a constant position a few feet beneath the surface of the water.

Gradually, he found peace. The briny water soothed and supported his deformed, aching body. The solid darkness crowded away the continual influx of information, the overwhelming stimuli of his nightly existence. The gentle swooshing of the lake filled his mind.

He opened his mouth, exhaled, allowed the water to enter him as the swarm of bubbles rapidly spent itself. By force of will, he averted his gag reflex. Slowly, he sank more deeply into the depths.

How tempting to keep going, to abandon his repose and kick, swim downward. And to find what? The center of the earth? The *Nictuku*, the great hunters? Is that what Augustin had done? Had he found what he was looking for?

Deeper still, Calebros sank. He opened his eyes, could not tell the difference except for the brief sensation of water against his corneas. He could have been floating in space, in a vacuum, beyond the reach of earthly promise or menace.

Silence...almost. Distant swooshing of water against shore, the sound of the heartbeat that was absent. Farther away, the howling, pain, exhilaration, rapture. There were deeper sounds, more difficult to make out. Rumblings of the kine, perhaps a subway train, or the rhythmic turnings of a monstrous printing press.

Calebros took these things into him like the briny water, accounted for them, factored them out.

Deeper...

He strained to hear that which he sought....

There. He heard it, felt it. Faintly. But then he was sure, like a searching finger at last finding the pulsing vein. A deeper sound, a hum, distant but strong. The sound of the bedrock, of the earth itself, of the world that was left to him, the world that was *forced* upon him. What a cruel gift, the steady hum of the earth, the subterranean world that was his legacy.

Augustin was foolish to seek out destruction, Calebros thought. They had eternity. Could the very earth whispering in his ear be wrong? Old wives' tales, the great hunters. Perhaps it was in the blood after all; perhaps Augustin had had no real choice in the matter, just as Calebros, night after night, had no real choice but to be true to his blood. To search for answers.

Calebros allowed his thoughts to float beside him, there far beneath the surface; he let them float away until thought, any thought, was his only in vague memory. There was the gentle hum of the earth. And nothing else.

Before he broke the surface, he heard the sand-like spray upon the water and knew who he would find beside the lake. Calebros made his way to the shore. He felt gravity take its hold upon him once again, felt it pull at his leathery flesh and his twisted body. He crawled. The stone of the beachhead was warm now against his callused knees. His talons clattered like the legs of a beetle. He retched, purging the eternal waters from this, his frail eternal prison. Water, bile, and blood mixed in shallow pools. Eventually, he rolled over and sat on his bony haunches. He neither clothed himself nor looked at his brother.

Emmett sat atop the canvas sacks of salt, sifting through the crystals, letting them run through his fingers like the grains of an hourglass. Every so often, he tossed a handful of the salt into the water.

"I guess you're a damn pillar of the community," Emmett said humorlessly. With his other hand, he played with the strand of knucklebones hanging from his neck, *his* inheritance. "You and your mudhole."

Calebros did not respond.

"Here," said Emmett. He took up from the shadows behind him a large goblet fashioned from bone and handed it to Calebros. The goblet was full of blood. "You gotta learn to take care of yourself. Scuba diving doesn't take the place of dinner, you moron."

Calebros took the offered vessel. The blood was tepid but not yet cold. The howling, the kennels. He drank.

"Geez, what am I, your mother?" Emmett asked.

"No," Calebros said. "You are my brother, my broodmate."

"Brood, litter, whatever. We were both chosen to suck the old blood tit, so who am I to ask questions?"

Calebros sighed. Blood tit, indeed. "That's not how you remember it."

Now it was Emmett's turn to sigh. "Don't do this. Don't get all… You always do this, get all touchy-feely we're-all-brothers-in-the-blood, when you soak your head, blah, blah, blah…"

"Make light of it if you will—"

"I will. Thank you very much. Got enough salt here?" Emmett flicked some at Calebros.

In the bags beneath Emmett, there was at least a ton remaining. Initially there'd been five times as much, or, if not in the truest sense of the word *initially*, there had been after Calebros had spent the better part of two years hauling sacks down here.

"You know," Emmett said, "if you get tired of bobbing in the Dead Sea, you could always just Embrace a masseuse. Now that I think about it, I bet Hilda would be willing to—"

"Have you moved him yet?" Calebros interrupted.

The effect of a smirk on Emmett's features was singularly unappealing. "Not yet. Soon as I get back. I wanted to check things out with you first, and not over the phone or SchreckNET, if you know what I mean."

"I do."

"So you don't want me to clue in Montrose. You're sure?" Emmett asked.

"I'm sure."

"Could cause problems later…if he finds out."

"Make sure he doesn't find out. Or can't you handle him?"

That elicited a wry laugh from Emmett. "I'll make sure he doesn't find out. I won't use our places in Vegas itself. Maybe Cactus Springs, or Shoshone."

"That's what I was going to suggest. How long do you think—?"

Emmett shrugged. "Not long. Maybe a few weeks." Calebros nodded. "You know," Emmett continued, "*Abbot* Pierce is a real pain in the ass."

Calebros nodded again. "That's one reason I thought it best to move Benito."

"From Pierce's to Montrose's." Emmett shook his head disdainfully. "I say when this whole mess is over, we sell both their asses down the river."

"You know we can't do that."

"*You* might know that," Emmett said. "What *I* know is that Pierce is a self-righteous, toothless excuse for a Kindred who'd rather piss his pants than cross the Giovanni, and Montrose…Montrose is a slimy son of a bitch who's so far in the Giovanni's pocket that he's sucking their collective dick."

"Eloquently put, as always."

"Pierce is a dick. Montrose sucks dick. That's how I see it."

"Didn't Pierce prove useful this time?" Calebros asked. "Would you rather have grabbed Benito on short notice and hung out in Boston, in the city, and waited for the Giovanni bloodhounds to track you down?"

"*If* they could."

"If," Calebros agreed. "But that's a fairly ominous *if* that we avoided. And we might not trust Montrose with everything, but he's another source of information about what's going on in Las Vegas, a source fairly close to the prince, I might add."

"Yeah, yeah. Whatever you say." Emmett's protests trailed off into incomprehensible muttering. Then he grew silent altogether. The two Kindred sat quietly, the only sound echoing above the underground lake the distant *plink, plink* of dripping water.

"You came all this way for that?" Calebros asked at last.

"'All this way.' Listen to you. Boston is not that

far. You really need to get out more. I didn't just walk from Las Vegas."

Calebros knew that, of course. Movement up and down a significant portion of the East Coast was not a great ordeal for the Nosferatu. Several generations of the clan had spent decades creating, through construction and appropriation, a network of underground tunnels stretching, more or less, from Boston to Washington, D.C. And with but a few above-ground lapses, a Nosferatu could travel as far as Richmond and even Atlanta in relative safety. Less safety, now that the Sabbat had swarmed through those cities, but it wasn't that difficult to stay out of sight. Of the Nosferatu that had thrown in their lot with the Sabbat, most knew of portions of the network, but even they weren't about to betray that information. The *antitribu* might have philosophical reasons for their sect alliance, but they had no great love for their "masters," the Lasombra or the Tzimisce.

Emmett had come only from Boston. Not that great an undertaking, true. But he was about to head west on an incredibly sensitive assignment. Calebros couldn't help but wonder if what had brought Emmett, aside from practical matters, was not something more…personal.

"What do you remember?" Calebros asked, finally. "It wasn't a litter. I don't remember you until after…after…"

"I don't remember nothing," Emmett said, "because I don't *need* to remember nothing. There was before, and now there's now. Right?"

Calebros knew he was right. There were some things that he and the clan would never forget: debts and debtors, favors and betrayals. Other things, there was no reason to remember. Nothing lay down that road except confusion and regret.

"Right?" Emmett asked, more insistently.

Calebros nodded. "Right." He stood up and gathered his clothes. The stiffness was returning to his body already. He picked up the bone goblet from where he'd placed it on the shore of the lake and handed the cup to Emmett. "Take this back. Please." To the kennels.

Emmett took the goblet. "Well then," he said. He nodded curtly and turned back toward the tunnel that had brought him here.

"Emmett," Calebros said. Emmett paused, turned back. "Good luck."

"Yeah," said Emmett. "You too." And then he was gone.

Thursday, 22 July 1999, 3:49 AM
A subterranean grotto
New York City, New York

Calebros hunched over his desk and typed madly,
compiling, composing. Emmett was on his way back to
Boston and then to Las Vegas. He would take care of
Benito; Emmett would do what needed to be done. That
was a relief. Maybe that was why Emmett had come in
person, Calebros pondered, pausing at the Smith Corona. Security was important, true, but there were
couriers that could be trusted.... Had Emmett come just
to set Calebros's mind at ease? Was Emmett capable of
such ulterior thoughtfulness?

Calebros laughed. If Emmett were, he certainly
would never admit to it. It was enough, Calebros decided, to have one less thing—one less *major* thing—to
worry about. There was still plenty else. Much of it dire,
and a significant portion ostensibly Calebros's fault.

The most potentially damning problem was that
of the Sabbat. At least the monsters had paused in their
rampage up the East Coast. In under two weeks, they
had stormed cities from Atlanta to Washington, D.C.,
in most cases annihilating the existent Camarilla power
structure and assuming, as far as Kindred were concerned, *de facto* control. It would take them quite some
time to root out the considerable Camarilla influence
in those cities. Perhaps the barbarian Sabbat would
never manage to scourge the halls of power. In this, the
computer age, physical proximity was not necessary to
exert leverage. Control on the ground, however, was
not a negligible advantage. Over time, Camarilla ghouls
would be found out, removed, destroyed.

The changes in territory were considerably less of
a burden to Calebros and his clan than to others. A
Nosferatu could pass unseen through a Sabbat city as
easily as a Camarilla one. With the shift in power, there
were still as many secrets, and, in a way, the services of

the Nosferatu became more valuable to his allies, for whom access to certain areas was barred, or, at the very least, far more dangerous. So the Sabbat advances could be seen, from that perspective, as a gain for the Nosferatu as well.

Not so for the Ventrue, who was accustomed to playing prince and having his subjects bow down before him. Nor for the Brujah, who liked to flaunt his defiance in the streets. Now those streets were filled with cavorting devils, devoid of reason or thought except to destroy their enemies and revel over the broken bodies. The warlocks were holed up in their citadels. The Toreador, normally parasites upon both kine and Kindred societies, would be lost. The Gangrel cared neither one way nor the other. No, the Nosferatu were likely to come out of this upheaval relatively strengthened. Therein lay the danger.

Perceived strength invited envy and fear. Envy and fear invited persecution. And what would be the justification? For surely the Kindred were too sophisticated a people to found genocide upon tenets so subjective as jealousy and hatred (for to fear is to hate)? The justification would be complicity, treachery. If the other clans, seeing the Nosferatu strengthened, ever had reason to suspect that the dwellers beneath had aided the Sabbat in their conquest, revenge would spring to the lips of every firebrand and echo throughout the halls of power.

And what reason might the others have to suspect the Nosferatu? Calebros, unwittingly, had given them ample grounds for suspicion.

His head was beginning to hurt. He leaned back from his typewriter, stretched his gnarled fingers, his arms and shoulders, his back. His vertebrae sounded like popcorn.

Even had his expectations of a minor Sabbat raid in Atlanta proved correct, Calebros knew, he and Rolph had still taken a chance. It was a calculated risk: withholding knowledge of the raid and risking Prince

Benison's profound displeasure. Rolph, being a subject of Benison and residing within the prince's territory, had borne the main burden of the chance. The two Nosferatu had agreed that the risk was worthwhile, the opportunities presented too great to overlook: resolution of the Benito matter, and repayment of an old debt to the Setite, Ruhadze.

But the raid had turned out to be a full-scale attack of a scope none had imagined the Sabbat capable of pulling off. Borges, archbishop of Miami and long covetous of Atlanta, could never have gathered, much less successfully commanded, such a force. Even Polonia, the capable archbishop of New York, could never have garnered enough support from the fractious warlords of the Sabbat. Sascha Vykos had been spotted, reportedly ensconced in Washington and installed as its archbishop. That, too, merely added more questions.

Jon Courier, as reliable and trustworthy a Kindred as Calebros had ever met, had established contact with an Assamite-playing-ghoul in Vykos's camp. A strange situation, that. The assassins had contracted with Courier independent of Calebros, which was how Calebros liked it. The fewer dealings with the Assamites and the less reason they had to know he existed at all, the better. Even so, the contact was a source of information, since Courier passed along what he learned. What Courier passed along these nights was that there was no sign the Sabbat was ready to continue its northward march. The initial blitzkrieg had left them as disorganized in victory, if not as desperate, as was the Camarilla in defeat.

So there it stood, the uneasy status quo, and any Kindred that found out about Calebros's part in the affair might be only too willing to point a finger and make accusations that could topple the fragile balance of power among the clans. Who else knew? There was Rolph, but he was in the same boat as Calebros. There were a few of his informants, and a few of Calebros's own in Miami. But how few? Calebros needed to know exactly; he needed to make sure that no one talked. No matter what. For the good of the clan. For several minutes, he struggled with thoughts that he didn't dare entrust to the permanency of writing. How far would he need to go, not merely to save himself embarrassment, but potentially to safeguard the very wellbeing of the clan? How far was he willing to go? Calebros knew what Emmett's answer would be to that question, but not his own.

He ripped out the sheet of paper that was in the typewriter. There was plenty else to worry about without getting mired in situational ethics—*hypothetical* situational ethics, at that. Time tended to answer many questions, and others it rendered moot, which, as far as Calebros was concerned, was just as good as an answer. Maybe better.

He turned readily enough to the next report, which dealt with another great concern: Hesha Ruhadze. The Setite shouldn't have been such a worry. He had a long history of dealing honorably with Clan Nosferatu. On occasion—the Bombay incident sprang to mind, but there were others—he had gone out of his way to aid Calebros's brethren. That was why it had seemed such a reasonable idea to hand over the Eye of Hazimel. Hesha had been searching for it for decades, and considering the curiosity's hiding place, Victoria Ash's coming-out party seemed the ideal place for the transaction.

How quickly things changed.

Now the Eye was missing, Hesha's man who had been sent to the doomed party was dead, and Calebros was left pondering a disturbing string of deaths and Assamite activity that conveniently coincided with Hesha's whereabouts on a disturbing number of occasions. Calebros shuddered. The thought of Hesha joining forces with the Assamites was almost too much to bear. His record of cooperation with the Nosferatu was no guarantee for the future. What if he blamed the

Nosferatu for the loss of the Eye? And what if he was prepared to address his displeasure by calling on allies who just happened to be lethal and fanatical assassins? Calebros tried to suppress another shudder but failed.

He took a very deep, unnecessary, yet highly therapeutic breath. Trying to convince himself that everything was the same as it had always been, he leaned back in his chair and propped his sizeable feet on the desk. Several of the piles of papers and folders stacked precariously on the desk quivered, but none toppled over.

Thoughts of assassination turned Calebros's mind naturally to Baltimore and all that was transpiring there. Just three nights ago, a band of Sabbat assassins had sneaked into the city and attempted to destroy Jan Pieterzoon, scion of a notable Ventrue line and the emerging leader of the Camarilla resistance—now that the sect was finally managing to regroup and mount a resistance. For a week or more, Calebros had almost expected the Sabbat war machine to keep rolling north, on through the Mid-Atlantic states, on through New England. But the blitzkrieg's momentum was spent by D.C, and there the Sabbat sat. For the time being.

The attack on Pieterzoon was not common knowledge among the Kindred. Ostensibly, morale might suffer knowing the enemy had struck so deeply into supposedly secure territory. More likely, Prince Garlotte of Baltimore was attempting to salvage his pride by keeping the attack quiet.

Marston Colchester, of course, had kept Calebros informed—of the attack, as well as of the change in Pieterzoon's mindset afterward. Until the attempt on his unlife, the Ventrue had been concentrating on shoring up the Camarilla defenses and consolidating his own power—there was Victoria Ash to contend with, now assuming the role of refugee ingenue; there was also Garlotte, his second-in-command Gainesmil, Marcus Vitel, and a smattering of others. After the assassination attempt, Pieterzoon turned his attention to the darker side of warfare. He had discussed with Colchester the possibility of hiring assassins of his own. At Calebros's suggestion, Colchester had made a recommendation—a killer who would strike fear throughout the ranks of the Sabbat because, by rights, she should have been one of their own. Only time would tell if Pieterzoon would follow Calebros's unseen lead.

Time. If only there were enough time. For the second instance that night, Calebros felt keenly the passage, the *scarcity*, of time. Relentless, irreversible. The sensation was strange. For countless years the clocks had seemed to tick so deliberately, so slowly. He had once spent eight months tracking the growth of iridescent algae on an underground pool—not by noting the new growth each week or even each night, but by watching intently, without interruption, hour after hour, night after night, for eight months.

The kine measured time by hours, by days and nights. What was a single night to the Kindred? A fraction of a second of eternity? Of what significance was the passing of a month, a year, a decade? A grain of sand, not within an hourglass, but upon an endless shore.

Somehow, that was changing. Calebros didn't know how, or why, but he could feel it. He could feel it in his blood. He could read it in the reports.

The desk lamp began flickering again and distracted him from his thoughts. His attention returned to the papers on his desk, to the problem of Hesha Ruhadze, to the lethal dance taking place within the Kindred halls of power in Baltimore. There was, as well, the wildcard that was the Prophet of Gehenna. As far as any of Calebros's people knew, Anatole was still somewhere within the Cathedral of St. John the Divine. To what dark purpose, only God knew.

Still, the routine of it all, of enumerating the various dots and then attempting to connect them, restored Calebros's sense of order amidst the swirling chaos. It restored his illusion of control.

22 July 1999

Re: Hesha Ruhadze

Report from Calcutta via Cairo———Hesha
arrived and presented himself to Prince
Abernethie; one of Prince's childer
subsequently terminated; coincidence?
Also: H. contacted local Tremere who was
then assassinated; Assamite suspected.

Rolph reports from Atlanta———probable
Assamite involvement in destruction of
Hannah, Tremere regent. Hesha's man
Vegel was there at the time.

Hesha allied w/ Assamites?
danger to us?
TRACK MOVEMENTS
as possible

22 July 1999

Re: Baltimore/Washington D.C.,

Courier reports—according to
Ravenna/Parmenides, no Sabbat plans for
imminent attack on Baltimore; slow
build-up/organization/consolidation
continues; no sign shift of forces
north, i.e., Buffalo.

Colchester to keep Garlotte,
Pieterzoon informed of info from
R/P re: D.C.

Pieterzoon not aware
of Colchester dealings
w/ Garlotte.

Keep it that way.

Thursday, 22 July 1999, 10:18 PM
Governor's Suite, Lord Baltimore Inn
Baltimore, Maryland

The suite was very much as Victoria had left it when she had stormed out three nights prior. She had packed away most of her belongings, the gowns and accessories, but not all. The Toreador had left in a huff, angry with her benefactor, Prince Garlotte, who had provided the lodgings as well as many of her other possessions. When she'd arrived in Baltimore with only the proverbial clothes on her back after the fall of Atlanta, Garlotte had taken her in, treated her well. She was his trophy Toreador. He would have given her anything she'd asked—anything except the favor she did ask, to banish Jan Pieterzoon from the city. Garlotte had refused to exile his fellow Ventrue. So she had left.

Now, Garlotte sat on a couch amidst the detritus of her pique, looking like little more than a cast-aside gift himself. Clothes that hadn't made it into a box or hanging bag were scattered about on tables, over chairs, hanging from the backs of doors. Marston Colchester, as he slipped quietly through the unlocked door, wondered if the prince had moved at all in the intervening nights or days since the Nosferatu had left him. Garlotte wore the same outdated suit and the same wistful expression; he sat in the same spot on the couch.

"My Prince," Colchester said. He curtsied awkwardly, knowing full well the mockery his lumbering, mangy-furred frame made of the gesture.

Garlotte acknowledged his spy's presence with a lackluster wave and sighed. Colchester was struck by the prince's uncharacteristic lethargy. The man was usually brimming, *overflowing* with energy. The prince, as often as not when he got an idea into his head, was instantly ready to ride off in five different directions all at once. He was a fair, if strict, prince, and one on whom subtlety was often lost.

No, Colchester reconsidered, that was not completely true. The prince was not blind to subtlety; he simply refused to abide it. As Colchester saw it, Garlotte was a five-color-crayon man, not the sixty-four-color-with-the-sharpener-in-the-back-of-the-box type. And that was by choice.

"What's she been up to?" Garlotte asked wearily, as if he didn't really want to know but felt he should ask.

"Ms. Ash?" Colchester asked knowingly. Garlotte glowered up at him from beneath his dark brow. "Ahem, yes...well, mostly she's been getting settled in at Gainesmil's."

From earlier conversations, Colchester knew he should leave it at that...but he just couldn't help himself in the face of the so obviously forlorn prince. "None of the old bump and grind as of yet," he said, adding a series of rather enthusiastic pelvic thrusts by way of illustration, "but it's early still. You know, I wouldn't have pegged Robert for a ladies' man, but I wouldn't be surprised to see him tickle her tonsils with the old one-eyed—"

"That is quite enough," Garlotte snarled. His face was noticeably reddened, dark with barely contained rage.

"Ahem. Yes, well, ah...she did meet with Vitel tonight."

Garlotte's eyes narrowed. "Yes?"

"Are you sure you want to know? I mean, I'm just the messenger—"

"What happened?" Garlotte drew in a deep breath and puffed up his chest.

"Well..." Colchester paused significantly and let the moment draw out, then, "Nothing much, really."

"Do not toy with me, Marston. I'll have your sorry head on a pike."

Colchester gulped. Threat of Final Death. Maybe it was time to play things straight. He knelt and bowed his head. "Forgive me, my Prince." He peeked up; Garlotte wasn't looking at him. "I'm perhaps not the most sensitive in dealing with matters of the heart."

"There *is no* 'matter of the heart' here!"

Colchester cocked his head to one side. "Uh-huh. I see."

"Stand up, you oaf. What transpired between Victoria and Marcus Vitel?"

Colchester climbed to his feet. "Oh, she made some innuendoes about how the two of them could rule the city. He politely ignored her." *And he didn't look at her the whole time*, Colchester thought. *How the hell did he manage that?*

"Ignored her, did he?" Garlotte asked, somewhat relieved.

"Oh yeah," Colchester reassured him, then added, "I was waiting for her to flash some titty. *That* would've got his attention. Yeah, baby!" He groped the air with his hairy fingers.

Garlotte was on his feet in a flash, his face awash with anger. Just as quickly, Colchester was three steps closer to the door.

"Do I offend? Forgive me my barbarous ways, my prince," Colchester said quickly and contritely. "These matters of the heart—I mean, of state…matters of state—"

"Not one more word. Not one!"

Colchester nodded emphatically. He waited, and as the silence lingered, Garlotte sat back down. He took a deep calming breath. "So, she did not attempt to…*entice* Vitel in the same manner as Pieterzoon?"

Colchester shook his head.

"And Vitel was not receptive to her entreaties?"

Colchester nodded affirmatively this time.

"Very well," Garlotte said. "Continue observing her."

Colchester nodded again. How convenient that his two clients, Garlotte and Pieterzoon, both seemed so interested in each other and in Victoria. It made Colchester's job easier. Even so, and despite his banter, he wasn't completely comfortable with keeping tabs on Ash. He could have one of his underlings take on the task, but, Colchester also knew, he would not. He would do it himself. Ah, the sacrifices he was willing to make for the clan.

Keeping an eye on Garlotte, the Nosferatu backed out of the suite. With the door safely closed, he sent a few more pelvic thrusts in the prince's general direction, then lumbered away down the hall.

"They would have *eaten* me, I tell you!"

"I believe you, Jeremiah," Calebros said in a forced, calm tone. He was tired of nodding politely, of reassuring his clanmate. Jeremiah could be a difficult person to like at times. This was rapidly becoming one of those times.

"Don't you humor me!" Jeremiah snapped. "I've been coming to you about this for *weeks* now."

Seems more like years, Calebros thought.

"And still you've done nothing. *Nothing!*" Jeremiah paced around, gesticulating wildly.

There was no second chair by Calebros's desk, and for this very reason. He mostly didn't like guests, didn't want guests, didn't want to encourage them to sit down, to take a load off and stay for a while. Most anyone who had reason or inclination to visit Calebros was irate, complaining, or tiresome. Jeremiah happened to be all three presently.

"That is not true," Calebros assured him.

Jeremiah snorted in disgusted. "What, then? Tell me. What have you done?"

"I have considered quite carefully your report."

"*Ha!* Like I said, *nothing*. Considered my report…" Jeremiah repeated contemptuously. "This is what I think of you and your reports—" he said, grabbing a handful of papers from the nearest stack on Calebros's desk. Jeremiah made to fling them into the air—

Instantly, Calebros's hand shot out and latched around his visitor's wrist. Talons pricked undead flesh ever so slightly.

"Believe me," said Calebros evenly. "You do not want to do that."

They faced each other for a moment, one monstrous creature restraining the hand of another.

Jeremiah's fingers, biting into the papers, were long and grotesquely thin, little more than needles of bone. His entire body was thin and hard and covered with knots, bulging masses of hardened tissue, like an old, gnarled swamp tree. Finally he stopped resisting Calebros and returned the reports to the desk.

"I'm sorry," Jeremiah said and resumed his pacing, just as intently if less frenetically.

"Think nothing of it," Calebros said. In truth, however, his attention was fully occupied by the sheets of paper Jeremiah had just set back down. Like all the reports, they were an odd lot, a jumbled collection of sizes, some handwritten, many typed, with addenda of scrawled red marginalia. Some of the reports were recorded on portions of grocery bags or thin cardboard, yet Calebros took each piece that had been disturbed and smoothed it down, gently, like a mother pressing the wrinkles from an unruly child's clothes.

Not until he'd attended to each report did he look back to his impulsive visitor. Jeremiah did not notice the cold glare leveled at him, nor did he seem to have been aware of Calebros's preoccupation.

"It shouldn't have happened," Jeremiah was saying, as much to himself as to Calebros. "Should never have happened. They were rats. Just rats. They should have responded to me. Just rats. But there was something else there too…something…emboldening them, joining them…"

"Joining them? Not physically."

"No, of course not. But their instincts, their anger… I reached out to the mind of a single rat, but I touched all of them." Jeremiah's pacing had fallen into the pattern of a triangle. Each time he reached the point nearest the desk, he changed direction, but he continued tracing the same lines over and over again. His eyes, almost hidden by a thick, drooping brow, seemed to glaze over as he gave himself to memory.

Calebros watched, waited. His accustomed role.

"It didn't feel like there was a conscious mind directing them," Jeremiah said. "Not giving orders, but there was something...anger...or maybe pure hatred."

He's been feeding from drug-addled kine again, Calebros thought.

"Let me take the Prophet," Jeremiah blurted out suddenly.

"What?"

"Anatole, the Prophet of Gehenna."

"I know damn well *who* you're speaking of, but why on earth—"

"I've done it before. I've led him around," Jeremiah said. He was pacing more quickly again, the words spilling from his mouth. "He hears so many voices, one more added to the mix is nothing unusual. He would know what I'm talking about. He'd be able to tell. I could take him down there. He'd know what it is." Jeremiah stopped at the edge of the desk and leaned forward on both of his bone-thin arms. His voice was no longer manic, but instead low and dire: "There is something dark down there, Calebros. We must find out what."

Calebros was taken aback by the sudden demand. He was accustomed to receiving reports from his people, mulling over the information, pondering implications, connections, ramifications of action. Every action, Calebros knew only too well, produced unforeseen consequences. Jeremiah did not seem to recognize that fact, else he would not be making such incredible pronouncements. *And that after disrupting my files!* Calebros thought.

"You saw nothing to justify such drastic measures," he said.

"*Nothing?*" Jeremiah's eyes bugged wide. "Haven't you been listening? Have you not heard a word I've said? I saw *nothing?*"

"I don't doubt what you saw," Calebros said calmly, "but neither have I reached the same conclusions that you seem to have reached. I do not say that you are wrong, no matter how fanciful your notions—"

"Fanciful!"

"But Anatole is not a toy or a pet, to lead around and play with as you please. You might well be able to guide him," Calebros said, hands raised to pre-empt his guest's protestations, "but the Prophet…" Calebros paused. He was not practiced in face-to-face debate, and words did not come quickly to his lips to describe his apprehension of Anatole. It was not the visceral fear that sapped his strength at the mention of the Assamites; it was more a deep, unsettled feeling. Was he more disturbed, Calebros wondered, by Anatole, or by what the Prophet might discover?

"The Prophet is here in the city," Jeremiah said. "We must use all the tools that are available to us."

"We *think* he is still in the city," Calebros tersely corrected him. "He entered the Cathedral of St. John the Divine a *month* ago. None of our people have been able to enter since, and our kine sources who've gone in have found no trace of him. So as to your one point, he's not exactly available to us, and secondly—"

"Calebros! Calebros!" The calls from outside the office cut through the quiet of the warren like a sudden clap of thunder. Cass Washington burst into the chamber, her skirt and loose sweatshirts billowing from her haste. "Calebros!" She didn't pause or apologize for the interruption. "Calebros, Donatello is in! He's gotten into the cathedral!"

Calebros, flabbergasted, looked back and forth between Cassandra and Jeremiah. She was excited and anxiously awaiting instruction. Jeremiah had crossed his bony arms and was looking quite pleased with himself.

"Well, calm down, girl," Calebros told Cass. "We've still to see what comes of it." Then he turned to Jeremiah. "And you, don't get smug with me. No matter what happens, you're to stay away from that cathedral. I'll not have you interfere just because of some…some old wives' tale."

Jeremiah protested, "I didn't say anything about—"

"You didn't have to," Calebros snapped. "You didn't have to." Calebros wasn't about to go chasing rumors and superstitions. *Nictuku.* Not even if those superstitions were the worst fear of his entire clan. Especially not in that case.

Friday, 26 July 1999, 12:47 AM
Amsterdam Avenue, Upper West Side, Manhattan
New York City, New York

Seemingly counting each step and placing each foot with care, the man walked nervously down the street. His lips quivered as they mimed his interior monologue. How far did he travel in a minute? How many steps did he take in a hour? It seemed he'd walked for miles in the passing of but a second.

He wondered, could it have been an hour already? The man did not wear a watch. In fact, he wore no jewelry or decoration at all—nothing but the angel that followed him more closely than a shadow—and somehow, suddenly, that disturbed him. He clutched at his neck, fingers seeking a chain or cord. The fingers prodded and stabbed at the top of his concave chest, where they slid back and forth in the cavity like a skateboarder out of control.

The man knew that his name was Donatello, but was somehow unable to make himself believe it. For all his careful and patient strides, he too was out of control. And despite his sagacious tread he was aimless.

No matter how he strove to make progress, he felt as though he traveled in nothing but circles. Every time he saw his reflection in the dirty windows of the brownstones that lined the street, Donatello felt it was the first time. He knew that hunchbacked, sinister, loose-fleshed outline was his own, but he knew it only in the vague way that allowed him to guess but not speak his name. It was like searching for the Holy Ghost in a coven of witches—surely present, but at bay.

So he kept walking, hopeful that as his feet made progress, his mind would as well. He grasped that he'd emerged from an experience of an extreme nature. It had been a gamble, that much he knew as well. But one that had paid off or not? Had he desired to forget himself? What manner of monstrous past might that horrid image in the mud-streaked window wish to hide from itself?

And with the inevitability of dawn, Donatello did begin to put his thoughts together. He wasn't sure if the walking helped, but he continued nonetheless. Regrettably, no other transformations accompanied the illumination of the past. His back, bowed like an angry cat; his jowls, sagging like a crone's breasts; his eyes, sunken with an addict's lack of will. These all remained. But the dim light of his mind began to glow.

With these remembrances came the revelation that the ills of his body were the curses he would bear to the end of his unlife. He was Nosferatu, and though he was one that excelled among his kind as his clan excelled among the other clans in the gathering of information, it gradually became clear to Donatello that the last three nights of his life were lost forever.

With a dread that he could scarcely comprehend, Donatello worried that the repercussions of a loss so miniscule in the context of an immortal life would reverberate in infinity. When would the butterfly of those few nights cause a hurricane in his life?

Donatello shook his head. "Soon," he muttered sourly. "All too soon."

He felt it would have been better to have lost three nights in the midst of a crazed Tzimisce ceremony.

Or three nights wandering lost and alone in a wilderness infested by lupines.

Even three nights of interrogation by the souls of the pious dead he'd instructed and directed centuries ago, when he'd been a priest of God among the mortals of this dark world.

But to pass three nights in the company of that most enigmatic of the Kindred, the Prophet of Gehenna, Anatole…

Three nights that he could not remember. Though fleeting images flickered in his mind's eye, Donatello felt certain the full experience of those days would never be recalled. He was uncertain why he was so sure this was the case. Perhaps he was giving more credence to Anatole's reputation than was warranted. Donatello sighed, kept walking, and strained hard to put concrete images to the few moments he could recall. As he had guessed and feared, by the time he was done, no new memories had surfaced.

Three nights with the vampire who knew the secrets of the end of the world, and Donatello could remember almost nothing. Frightening indeed.

He recalled his surprise when he'd entered the Cathedral of St. John the Divine. Some unknown force had for many nights kept any Nosferatu from entering the place. They could go so far, but no farther. They'd felt Anatole was within the cathedral, but they did not know for certain. He'd entered over a month before and had not been seen to exit, but in light of their inability to enter, it was equally likely that he was gone entirely as still within the walls. And what could he be doing for a month? How was he hiding from the mortals that swarmed the place every day, especially every Sunday?

The Nosferatu sent mortals to investigate. Even their ghouls—mortals with the Nosferatu blood within their surging arteries—were allowed entrance, and they detected nothing. One of these ghouls was even said to carry the blood of Calebros himself within her, and she still reported nothing. Another to enter was a wizard—not a Tremere, but a mortal wizard—who owed Calebros a favor of some variety, but he also could add nothing to the intelligence efforts of the clan.

Of course, now Donatello suspected the truth. They *had* encountered Anatole, but were denied the memory of meeting. But that raised the question of why they could not at least admit to the confrontation even if lacking memory of its content, as was Donatello's predicament. Perhaps they were physically unable to speak of it, just as Donatello could not bring his own name to his lips.

So Donatello's penetration of whatever force had kept him and his comrades at bay was a surprise. The Nosferatu recalled that as soon as he found himself able to enter the cathedral, he'd quickly retreated to the periphery to report this to one of the surveillance team members. A task force was quickly organized and a weeks-old plan for entry was dusted off and enacted. However, none of the others were able to take one step farther than any time prior. But Donatello still entered without resistance.

He laughed now at his foolish courage then. For he'd pressed on. He recalled telling his comrades that this was an opportunity that could not be forsaken. He would enter and report back as soon as he was able.

The chronology of Donatello's memory then frayed immediately, for the next event he could recall was praying with Anatole. The picture of the event in Donatello's mind arrived fully formed and realized from pitch darkness and deathly silence. Suddenly, there was an altar before Anatole and himself. Suddenly, Donatello heard his own voice, his memory making him feel as a passenger in his own body even though his memory of how he felt *then* was of himself completely at ease.

The Nosferatu also recalled Anatole beside him. The Malkavian prophet also knelt before the altar, and Donatello recalled thinking for an instant that this was odd. Little was known about Anatole, but the fact that he had forsaken God centuries before was largely accepted as truth—at least to the extent that any information about the mysterious madman could be accepted as truth.

But that quickly passed, and Donatello could also recall thinking that the Kindred's kneeling before the altar was proof. Proof that it had indeed been his faith that had somehow kept other Kindred from the Cathedral of St. John the Divine. This despite the fact that crosses and other religious relics held no power over the Kindred. Perhaps that, in turn, was proof that Anatole's visions and prophecies truly came from a source beyond anything other Kindred could imagine.

If all *that* was true, then Donatello accepted that he'd been able to enter because he'd been a priest of God in his mortal years. Not an especially caring—nor, to be certain, especially corrupt—one, but one who did what was expected by his elders even if that was not as much as he knew was expected by God. Evidently, it had been enough, and even now as he walked the streets of New York City, Donatello felt a flush of piety and faith wash through him. He clutched again at his chest for the missing cross. He still wore it during these eternal nights, though he'd thought the reason was pure derision of his mortal past and his own loss of faith. Now, he wondered if there was a deeper explanation.

And there had been Anatole himself, of course. It was Donatello's first memory of seeing him. His features were tranquil and smooth. A slight film of dirt and grime covered an otherwise Pentelic form. The Malkavian's blond hair had been pulled back in dreadlocks that in turn hung like ornate tassels around his downcast face.

Donatello had led the prophet in prayer.

The Nosferatu stopped walking and gathered himself. He had left belief in God behind long ago. Like others of his kind, he bore a beast within himself, but unlike any but others of the Nosferatu, he looked like a beast as well. He had been a man good enough in his mortal life to be allowed a mortal's death. When that was denied him, Donatello had gradually grown to accept that there was no God who made such decisions in the first place.

At a standstill now with the skyscrapers of Manhattan looming not far in the distance where their lights formed the new constellations by which—or to which—men guided themselves, Donatello's memory began to dry up. He felt his cursory communion with the almost entirely forgotten past drain from his motionless feet into the concrete below. And from there...deeper.

Through the bedrock and into areas of this mammoth city already forgotten in a span as short as a few hundred years.

And his thoughts dribbled deeper still. Not toward a fiery core of the planet, but toward something dark, something Donatello could not face and felt certain did not concern him in any event. He shuddered. Somehow, that thought sounded more hopeful than true.

What did concern Donatello were idle feet making for an idle mind.

The Nosferatu broke into a walk exaggerated so that he might psychically shake free of whatever he'd begun to glimpse. Had Anatole shared something of his apocalyptic visions with Donatello? The Nosferatu did not know, but this moment, when he was alone and fighting amnesia, was not the time to attend to such thoughts. As his stride slowed to the steady rate of before, images again began to tumble from an unknown compartment in his brain.

There were other memories of praying. Both of these other scenes were set in a garden of some kind, and they were bowed before an odd sculpture of a woman formed of welded metal.

And a brief glimpse of the past in his mind's eye revealed to Donatello a scene of Anatole sitting beneath that sculpture with his sandals on his hands, listening to Donatello's questions. The Malkavian would not say why he was in New York City. Instead, Anatole massaged the sandals together in a sort of act of supplication.

Or maybe, Donatello imagined, it was communication. Perhaps this was how—or at least one of the ways—he spoke to the heavenly powers. Or drew their attention. But Donatello could make no more of the scene, because his memory of it was so brief. Imagining it as a film, moving in frames through his memory,

Donatello guessed he had but three frames of Anatole; and to be honest, he could not tell if the sandals were being rubbed or clapped together.

Donatello knew that he should return to Calebros and report these little things he *could* recall. Or at least return to the cathedral. Perhaps even try to enter again, though he felt that would be folly. Besides, his shriveled stomach somehow managed to grumble in protest, and Donatello knew he was not yet made of the steely determination that bred courage and confidence. He would retreat to his subterranean home, draft a report, and be done with that matter.

Or so he hoped.

That hope was almost immediately dashed, for something still nagged at his mind. Something other than the darkness in the bowels of the earth that he thought he could still will himself to forget—a cruel turn of fate this evening when he otherwise struggled to recollect so much.

An image flashed in his mind, but it vanished before he could slow it down or even see it. It came again. A figure. Very close to him. Whispering. Surely it was Anatole.

Again. Yes, it was the Prophet. Whispering his parting words. Phrases uttered a mere hour ago, yet they were weighed down so deep in the sediment of Donatello's mind that he could barely uncover them.

Again, and the Nosferatu could hear some of the words. A riddle. Three nights spent with the Prophet of Gehenna looking at both Heaven and Hell and he walked away with a riddle? Donatello knew beyond doubt that the man was indeed mad.

And wise, so what was the answer to the riddle?

Donatello puzzled over it to distraction until dawn nearly overtook him. Then he hurried to a phone to call the warren at least before both he and Calebros slept the daylight away. Umberto answered and listened patiently as Donatello repeated the riddle a second time:

"One in a minute, and one in an hour. Walk a mile in but seconds to deliver my letter. Tell me, oh wise one, which way do I go?"

Donatello hurriedly pried open a nearby sewer grate. There would be safe sleeping somewhere near here. For a Nosferatu willing to scrounge, there was always safety close at hand.

Mouse had been just a few blocks from the subway
when he'd heard the world rumbling. He'd been rummaging through the sewers. Such treasures down here,
and he didn't have to worry about the upperworlders
seeing him. Nobody to hide from, nobody to mistake
him for a big dog if they did see him, and no Sabbat,
thank goodness. Both times the Cainite gangbangers
had seen him, he'd been able to ditch them pretty easily, but it made him nervous, and being nervous made
him shed, and shedding made him itch. Or maybe that
was just the multitude of critters that shared his shaggy
coat with him.

He'd been shuffling along in the shin-deep sew-
age to see what he could dredge up. And there! The
brief glint caught his eye but then submerged again.
So he reached down, cupped his hands beneath the
surface of the gray-brown muck, then raised them, letting the liquid run through his fingers. There. He
smiled. He was left holding a fairly intact pile of feces,
and sparkling up at him was a partially buried, perfectly good, wonderful, silver button. He plucked it
out and dropped everything else back into the flow.
The button he rubbed between his hands until it was
clean, then wiped his hands on his fur and clothes.
The button wasn't actually silver, of course. But he
could pretend. It was white plastic, but it was shiny,
and therefore a treasure. Mouse favored shiny treasures. He dropped it into his pocket, almost as pleased
as if he'd found a few tasty kernels of corn.

That was when he'd heard the rumbling. It wasn't
the familiar regular purr of the one train; that was a
sound and vibration that Mouse didn't notice anymore,
like the ticking of a clock that, after time, becomes more
conspicuous by its absence than its presence. This

sounded more like the buildings above ground, or maybe the streets, were tearing themselves apart. Not explosions really…maybe an earthquake? Except the disturbance seemed localized—not distant, but contained.

Mouse took a minute to set his bearings. He was nothing if not curious, so off he set. He moved purposefully through the sewers, up a rusted metal ladder, and then along a narrow access tunnel that brought him to the storm sewers, where there was easier and more frequent access to street level. By the time he reached a rain-gutter opening, the worst of the rumbling had ceased, but there was still *something* going on. He was less than a block from the big church that Mr. C. had said to stay away from. But the last Mouse had heard, that Anatole guy was gone, disappeared. So it shouldn't matter, Mouse figured, if he went a little closer, because that seemed to be where the noise was coming from now—window-rattling *thuds* and *whomps*, like somebody was dropping boulders off the scaffolding around the church.

Mouse didn't see anyone on the street, but he made sure to hide himself as he climbed out of the sewer and made his way down the block, just in case. He noticed at once the cracked and broken pavement—not potholes, which were nothing new, but stripe after stripe after stripe of crumbled asphalt, like ripples on a pond.

The noise grew louder the closer he got to the church. Mouse still couldn't place what he was hearing—it sounded like a pile-driver, distinct pounding blows but at irregular intervals. Each *whomp* clattered deep in his chest.

Mouse slowed as he drew closer to the church's gardens. He was feeling increasingly that this little expedition was not a good idea. Something about the violence of the sounds he was hearing put him off. There weren't any screams—screams were *always* a bad sign—but he thought he might have heard grunts and moans just below the pounding. As often was the case, his curiosity got the better of his prudence. Profoundly puzzled, he peered hesitantly around the stone wall and into the gardens.

He could do no more than stare dumbfounded at what he saw. Until he finally turned and ran.

"Come. Sit with me," Victoria Ash said.

A cheerful little ditty popped into Marston Colchester's mind: *Sit on my face, and tell me that you love me!* But he restrained himself.

"It's so good of you to come visit me," Victoria said.

"I guess you've been pretty busy since you got into town," said Fin, youngest childe of Prince Alexander Garlotte.

Colchester watched them from the far side of the room. Victoria had been a busy beaver since taking up residence with Robert Gainesmil, Baltimore's foremost native Toreador. She had put the bug in Gainesmil's ear that she would like to meet Fin. Gainesmil had obediently passed the word along, and now here was Fin. He was a beautiful boy, young and handsome. Somebody might as well have wrapped him up and put a bow on his head. Victoria was going to eat him alive. *And not in a way you're going to enjoy, buddy boy.*

"Alexander speaks fondly of you," Victoria said.

Funny, he speaks of fondling you.

There was a pause. "He did? Of me?" Fin asked incredulously.

"He most certainly does," Victoria assured him. "As for my being busy, there's actually very little for me to do here. You know how men are...all wanting to protect me from the grueling and dangerous work of defending a city."

I'll give you some gruel, baby.

"Well, the Sabbat's nothing to mess around with," Fin said. "Have you ever—"

"So it was very thoughtful of you to come see me," Victoria interrupted. "You know," placing a finger to her inviting lips, "Alexander hasn't said as much, but I do believe that you are the one he's grooming to succeed him as prince some night."

Colchester clapped a hand to his forehead, but no one took notice of him.

Fin laughed. "You must have me mixed up with Isaac."

"No. Isaac is an able sheriff, but I think Alexander has grander designs for you. I mean no slight to your blood kin." Victoria reached over and brushed aside a lock of Fin's hair. "But there are depths to you that I don't see in Isaac."

Fin's mouth dropped open. Colchester sighed, shook his head back and forth. Then he saluted, as if an unseen bugle were sounding Taps.

From there, it was just a matter of time. Not that Fin had had a chance from the start. As Colchester had been completely aware, the boy was *way* out of his league. *He's awfully cute, but not too bright.* A perfect vehicle for Victoria's spite. She fed him a steady diet of lies, everything that he wanted to hear and was only too willing to believe. She filled him with a grossly exaggerated sense of his own importance, and patently absurd ideas about what he should expect from his sire the prince.

"He prefers assertive childer," she assured Fin.

Ridiculous. Garlotte went out of his way to surround himself with yes-men. All he wanted from a childe was for him to bend over and take it like a man. *Thank you, sir. May I have another?* That made Colchester think of Garlotte's middle childe, Katrina. *There* was a hottie. *I wouldn't mind bending her over and—*

"So you think I should confront him?" Fin was saying. "In front of the entire council?"

"I think he would respect to no end such a public display of confidence."

Colchester sighed. This one was a lost cause. But then a smile came to the half of the Nosferatu's lip that wasn't pierced by his over-sized, upward-pointing tusk. There was no urgent reason, really, for him to tell

Garlotte about this little meeting. After all, there was no way the prince could expect him to keep up with every single conversation that Victoria had. And if Fin was so stupidly determined to go down in flames, there might as well be some entertainment value in it for the rest of them.

The truly difficult part came several hours after Fin's departure. Victoria spent the rest of night quietly in her rooms. She sat for much of the time with a coffee-table book about Baltimore architecture in her lap. She turned a page occasionally but did not seem to read the words or see the pictures; her gaze was distant, her mind on other things.

Colchester had little to occupy him—little except his own thoughts, and those he had trouble corralling. The perverse quips rang hollow when there was no one present for him to enrage or abuse. There was only the object of his desire. He could have left. It seemed increasingly unlikely as the night progressed that Victoria would go out or receive another visitor. She didn't seem to be expecting any news in the immediate future. She had wound up poor, dense Fin and sent him on his way, and now there was nothing to do but wait for him to collect his reward from the prince.

Victoria stared at the book in her lap—in the direction of the book in her lap. She said nothing. Colchester could not read her thoughts; he couldn't tell what memories or plans caused the hard, almost pained expression that crossed her beautiful features. There was nothing for him to learn, yet he was unable to tear himself away. He didn't want to tear himself away—he did, but he didn't. He could only watch and keep watching.

She wore a loose-fitting satin blouse, off-white, and pearls. Her knees were tucked beneath her in a long, clinging skirt. Sheer stockings covered her feet and ankles.

As the night wore on, Colchester began to creep

around the edge of the room. Inch by inch, he drew closer to Victoria, closer to her physical perfection. He positioned himself to her left. Her blouse pouched out slightly between buttons. Colchester stared at the downward curve of her white breast, he imagining his finger tracing that line, down to the edge of her bra. He struggled with his thoughts, making sure not to slip too far into fantasy. He was still concealed from Victoria's notice. He was skilled with the gifts of the blood, yet even with his expertise, the trick required a certain amount of concentration. A younger, less-practiced Nosferatu would never have pulled it off, but Colchester remained hidden.

He caressed her a thousand times as the hours passed, and all the while, a great ache was growing within him. Not hunger. Not even lust exactly—Colchester was well acquainted with that, his most frequent of emotions—though lust was certainly the seed of this deeper, more profound distress. He wanted almost desperately to reach out and touch Victoria, to stroke the satin of her blouse, the silk of her skin. He wanted to undo one of the smooth buttons, and then another, and another....

"Is there anything I may do for you, Ms. Ash?"

Colchester's every muscle tensed. Blast his infatuation! He had not heard the butler's approach, the door to the suite opening—the door directly behind him. The Nosferatu's black eyes grew wide with alarm, but he held his position. He was crouched exactly between the door, to his rear, and Victoria, to his front. The butler obviously did not perceive him—his voice and question were too casual, too routine—but now Victoria was turning to respond to the butler.

She looked directly at Colchester—looked *through* him.

"Nothing, Langford," she said.

Colchester held his tense pose. He heard Langford withdrawing from the room, gently closing the door behind him. For the longest of moments, Victoria stared after Langford and through Colchester. For those drawn-out seconds, the Nosferatu allowed himself to believe that her green eyes—they were flecked with gold, he could see now—saw him and loved him. She did not flee in revulsion or attack him. She looked upon him, saw him for what he was, loved him.

It couldn't happen. Colchester couldn't allow it. He couldn't allow her to see him. If she had, she would have responded with shock, anger, fear, some combination thereof. She could never see him for anything other than a deformed freak. She or anyone else. But for those seconds, he could imagine—

And then she looked away. The illusion faded, and Colchester, hidden as ever, felt more keenly the ache.

He wasn't prepared when Victoria shifted in the chair, set down the book, and got up. Had she turned toward him, she would have tripped over Colchester. He was lucky she went the other way, and he knew it. He cursed himself, not for the first time, for nearly making a complete muddle of this job.

That's what it is, a job, he reminded himself. There was too much going on in and around the city for him to turn the job into a voyeur's wet dream. There'd be plenty of time for that later. *All the time in the world*, he thought, and the notion made his chest seize up, the ache growing unbearable for an instant. He tried to climb to his feet but staggered; he caught himself just before he crashed into an end table and lamp. He feared for a moment that his distraction had unmasked him, wasn't completely sure that it had not, but Victoria was walking the other way, into the bathroom. She clicked on the light.

Colchester stared after her, the open door calling him, inviting him.

There's nothing else to learn here, he told himself. His legs felt weak. He knew he should go. He had more than pressed his luck already. Both Garlotte and

Pieterzoon had asked him to watch Victoria, to report back to them. A twisted smile came to Colchester's lips. Both of the Ventrue envied him. He knew, he could tell. Each of them wished, in this one instance, that he could switch places with Colchester and *watch*. Only watch. Not have to put up with or avoid Victoria's schemes. Only watch.

If they only knew! Colchester thought. He was doomed for eternity *only* to watch. Garlotte showered gifts upon her, and Pieterzoon—Pieterzoon! She had thrown herself at him! He could have had her, and for such a small price.

Idiot! Colchester wasn't sure whether he meant Pieterzoon or himself, as he took awkward steps toward the bathroom door. *There's nothing else to learn here.* But he kept moving forward. He paused at the threshold, took another step, and another.

Victoria's clothes were draped over the edge of a counter. She sat before a vanity mirror, a plush, white, terry-cloth robe belted tightly at her waist, and with a wash cloth and cold cream was removing her makeup. She rubbed small circles on her face, gradually exposing more and more of her skin. The skin of one of the kine doing the same thing would have turned rosy from the rubbing, but Victoria's face, a portion at a time, changed from the pale tone of her makeup to the blue-white complexion of a corpse. Colchester thought the change made her only more beautiful. Her emerald eyes shone more brightly in the mirror, and her fine auburn hair was more strikingly rich in contrast to the pallor of her skin. She took on the beauty and perfection of death, leaving behind the pretensions of the living.

Colchester felt that he was seeing her for the first time, that he was seeing her as perhaps few others ever had. She cleaned her nose, cheeks, and upper lip, then her chin, the rest of the right side of her face, and then up and around her forehead, the left side of her face. Colchester watched the transformation as it unfolded;

he watched this woman who would retain her place among the kine as she shed the mortal coil and became a queen of ice and pure snow, a goddess of elemental beauty.

But then a scowl chased away the serenity of her features. She was still rubbing the wash cloth in small circles, but now with more pressure and speed. Her motions grew more fierce, as did her expression. She scoured the left side of her jaw, hard enough that it seemed, if she continued with such ferocity, her skin would begin to peel away. She stabbed the wash cloth violently into the cold cream and attacked her jaw again. Colchester watched with growing curiosity.

Only when she finally threw down the rag in frustration could he see the tiny blemish that so enraged her. It was a strange shape…was it a curled snake? He leaned closer…no…not a snake, but…a dragon, twisted round in a circle, swallowing its own tail.

Victoria was leaning close to the mirror looking at the mark herself. Colchester drew back as an animalistic growl sounded from deep within her throat. As the growl grew louder, Victoria reached out. The mirror had perhaps three dozen light bulbs set into its frame. She grasped a bulb in each hand and squeezed. The bulbs exploded with a loud *pop!*

She did it again and again. Shards of thin glass showered down on the makeup table, and all the while her throaty growl rose, grew louder, more intense, until it was a deafening, bestial screech. With the crescendo of the primal scream, she smashed a fist into the mirror.

All was silent.

Victoria stared into the ruin of the mirror, triangular shards of glass in a web pattern emanating outward from the point of impact. Colchester, never taking his eyes from his winter goddess, stepped carefully toward the door. He had seen enough and the night was growing late. As he did so, Victoria abruptly stood and whipped around from the mirror. The Nosferatu's blood froze, but she did not see him. Her scowl was hardened like a ceramic mask, but not directed at him. She crossed the small room, hands clenched into fists, and ignored the fragments of light bulbs on the floor that sliced into her feet and peeled the skin from her soles.

Colchester, ready to take his exit, found himself suddenly unable to move as Victoria turned on the hot water to draw a bath. The ache, subsumed momentarily by his curiosity about the mark on Victoria's jaw, claimed him again. He could not overcome his urgent desire. There were plenty of *mortal* women he could watch, he tried to tell himself. He could watch them as long as he wanted, and then have them—in a way; he could claim their blood. But that, he knew, would not satisfy his longing.

As he debated, Victoria untied the terry-cloth belt around her waist. Colchester clapped a hand over his open mouth lest he moan aloud. She pulled the robe off her shoulders and let it fall to the floor. Colchester blinked. And blinked twice more.

She stood before him for merely seconds, but for Colchester, it was as if eternity were revealed to him—an eternity of that which he would be denied. He might *see* Victoria, he might watch her, naked, climbing into her bath, but he would never have her. Her, or any other woman. Even were he to force blood to the dead, dangling flesh between his legs, even were he to force himself upon Victoria, he would never know intimacy, only violence. Touching her would be no more than feeding from a kine, than taking that which was not given freely. His lust was a cruel mockery of love, but it was all he had. All he would ever have. And thus the desperate ache took hold and ruled him.

Colchester, as desperately as he wanted to touch Victoria, wanted just as desperately to flee into the night. She was reclining in the tub now as it filled with steaming water. The mirror, a mosaic of jagged shapes, was covered with a thin film of fog. More steam billowed out the open door.

He stepped closer to her. Another step. And another, until he stood over her mostly submerged naked body. Her eyes were closed. The scalding water returned a semblance of rosy color to her, drawing blood closer to the surface of the dead flesh.

With trembling hand, Colchester reached for her. He stopped as she moved, turning off the water and then stretching luxuriously. She lay back again in the water, closing her eyes.

The ache was too much to bear. He knew it would do no good, he courted disaster, but he could not help himself as he reached for her. His fingertips, quivering, were inches from her perfectly rounded breast.

And he saw the mirror. And himself in the mirror. Fragmented and disjointed to be sure, but the dark, looming figure reflected beneath the layer of steam was him, a grotesque, colossal monster. And as he looked on his own horrified image, a single, triangular shard of glass teetered and fell.

Victoria's eyes sprang open at the sound of the glass striking the table. She sat up with a start, setting off waves that lapped over the edge of the bathtub. It was only a piece falling from the wall-mounted mirror that she had smashed. All was as it should be.

She started to sink back into the steaming water, but heard a sound from the outer room. The door closing, it sounded like.

"Langford?" she called, then, "Robert?" But again there was no response. She waited for several seconds, listening, but heard nothing else. Perhaps she was mistaken. She reclined again in the bath and took solace in her isolation.

"Tell me again," Calebros said, "how it was that you came to be at the cathedral four nights ago."

Mouse's hair was falling out in clumps. His coat didn't have a beautiful sheen at the best of times; as it was, he could very well be totally bald by morning. And he couldn't stand still. He itched all over. He kept fidgeting and scratching. It was all he could do not to fall to the floor and writhe on his back to get some relief. Meanwhile, Mr. C. was sitting behind his big wooden desk and asking the same questions again and again. Mouse could barely see his elder over all the clutter, stacks of papers and boxes. Mouse was sweating all over too. A thin bloody film that made him itch all the more, and so he scratched, and more of his hair fell out, and that made him itch more....

"It's all right, Mouse. I'm not angry with you. I just need to know."

Mouse wiped more bloodsweat from his face. Was it a hundred degrees in here or what? He felt as if he were ringed by bright hot spotlights, although in truth there was only the erratic lamp on Mr. C.'s desk.

"Come over here," Calebros said. He motioned with his curved talons that Mouse should come closer.

Mouse did as he was told—always the best course of action with Mr. C. Old Crookback did not care to be defied, and, as often as not, disobedience brought with it a cuff to the head. Not that Mr. C. was cruel, he just expected to be listened to and obeyed. Period. Mouse edged around the old desk and, as Calebros indicated, settled down on the floor at the elder's feet.

"There. That's better" Calebros said. "Now we can speak properly."

Mouse smiled weakly. He sat slightly hunched in a

perpetual half-cringe, awaiting a blow to the head should he misspeak.

"So, you were near the cathedral. You were hunting…"

"Yes," Mouse nodded. "For treasure." He reached into his pocket, pulled out the shiny button he had found that night, and showed it to Calebros.

"Yes." Calebros nodded and kindly patted Mouse on the head. "Very nice. So, you heard something—something loud, and not that far away. You went to investigate. What did you find?"

Mouse hesitated. He stared down at the button-treasure in his hand—the treasure that some of his brethren had told him was no treasure at all. *Nothing more than a plastic button. Don't be foolish!* That's what Mr. C. had said, and then he'd smacked Mouse on the back of the head. That was right at first, when Mr. C. had been pretty excited, and Mouse hadn't said what his elder had wanted to hear.

"What did you find at the cathedral, Mouse?"

"The hand man, and the melted man." Mouse had already said this before. Mr. C. had *seen* the melted man, because Mouse had dragged him away from the church, down the storm drain, and back to the warren. The melted man, beneath all the burned clothes and dripping skin and muscles and fat, was a vampire. Mouse had been able to smell that, and the sun had been about to come up, so he'd pulled the thing to cover. It was in the sick room now. Mouse watched over it.

"The hand man," Calebros prodded gently, "the one with the funny eyes, he was leaving when you arrived?"

Mouse nodded. It was true in a way. The hand man was leaving when Mouse arrived the second time, after he'd run away and come back. "He was carrying a statue hand, and it was moving. All the fingers were wiggling," he said in a hushed voice. Statues weren't supposed to move. Not like that. No one had believed him about that part of the story at first. That was why he hadn't mentioned what else he'd seen. He was certain that no one would believe him, and Mr. C. might hit him.

"And that's all you saw?" Calebros asked.

Mouse didn't hesitate; he nodded again. If he changed his story now, Mr. C. would know that he hadn't told everything before, and then Mr. C. *would* hit him…and maybe take him back to the kennels. Mouse *couldn't* tell him about what he'd seen the first time he'd peeked into the garden at the church—the big metal statue *moving* and *beating* the melted man, only the melted man hadn't been melted yet. Mouse hadn't said anything about that before, so he couldn't say anything about it now.

"I see," Calebros said. He sat quietly for a few minutes. Absentmindedly, he gently scratched Mouse's head with his talons. It felt good. But Mouse itched all over. He wished that Mr. C. would scratch his back, and his shoulder, and his leg…but Mouse was afraid to ask.

"Thank you, Mouse," Mr. C. said at last. "You can go back to your patient."

Relieved, Mouse crawled around the desk and then scurried out of Mr. C.'s office. Mouse felt important now that they were letting him take care of the melted man, although there wasn't really much to do, except wipe up the bits that dripped off. Still, Mouse felt that he'd found two treasures, even if only one of them was bright and shiny.

Calebros watched the youngster scuttle away. That interview had not proven overly productive. He really shouldn't have spent the time on it, he decided. The "melted man," as Mouse called him, though enigmatic, was of little real concern, other than the fact that the mystery of what had happened to him had the entire warren abuzz with rumors and speculation. That was the main reason that Calebros was interested. If he could figure out what had happened, he could dampen the agitated atmosphere. Otherwise, the severely burned stranger was of little import.

I shouldn't have wasted the time, Calebros thought.

Time. There it was again—the sense that time was running out. But why, and for whom?

It's just that there's so much going on at present, he told himself. *Gather the pieces. I will reconstruct the puzzle.* That was what he'd told his young Nosferatu charges, much as Augustin had often told him. Yet, truth be told, Calebros felt profoundly unsure of whether or not he was up to the task. The puzzle pieces were still all a jumble.

There's not so very much going on, he tried to convince himself. *It merely feels that way.* Expectation could be worse than crisis. So many loose ends dangling; so many axes waiting to fall. But still, he was making progress.

There was no substantive news from Emmett yet, but that would change. Calebros had every confidence in his clanmate. And as for the Sabbat, they seemed still to be stalled in Washington. The storm was gathering, certainly. Calebros had no doubt of that. But from Jon Courier's reports, there seemed to be dissension brewing among Vykos, Polonia, and Borges, and perhaps others. That was to be expected. They were a fractious, bloodthirsty lot, and the longer they were holed up in one place, the better for the Camarilla.

For their part, the defenders of the seven clans were not sitting idly in Baltimore. Jan Pieterzoon had acceded to Calebros's suggestion, which Marston Colchester had discreetly passed along—despite his air of perverse buffoonery, Colchester was, in fact, capable of acting discreetly. At any rate, along the lines of psychological warfare, Pieterzoon had hired an assassin. And not just any assassin. Lucita, wayward childe of Cardinal Monçada of Madrid. Lucita would certainly remove the targets whom Pieterzoon had chosen for her, and her activities would force members of the

Sabbat, from the high command on down, to think twice about their every move. Beyond those benefits, however, there was another potential payoff, though it was far from certain. There was the chance that Lucita's involvement in the war might possibly prompt the attention of another infamous assassin, a certain Assamite who seemed to have maintained a heated rivalry with Lucita over the years. But only time would tell if that came to pass.

Time.

Calebros sifted through the papers on his desk. Despite the press of weightier matters, he couldn't manage to dismiss the melted man that Mouse had found. Something about the grotesquely disfigured victim struck a resonant chord. Perhaps that was it, Calebros mused: He identified on some level with this Kindred, ostensibly *not* a Nosferatu, who had been so hideously deformed. Seemed a reasonable enough explanation.

No time for sentimentality, you old fool, he chided himself. There was Benito Giovanni to consider, the Sabbat, not to mention the still-missing Eye of Hazimel. And Anatole! The Prophet, presumably after keeping all the Nosferatu out of the Cathedral of St. John Divine for weeks, had allowed Donatello in, but now, Donatello could remember nothing of what had happened—nothing except a single, childish riddle. As if they had time for *that*. And to top it all off, when more of Calebros's people had entered, Anatole was gone. Without a trace. And then these new unexplained happenings at the cathedral with the melted man...

Blast it all to hell. Calebros tried his best to put Mouse and his enigmatic melted man out of mind and get back to work.

4 August 1999
Re: disturbance at Cathedral of
St. John the Divine

7/31---none of our people witnessed;
statues deformed; damage to connecting
streets for several blocks---path?

Found one body; badly damaged and
burned---<u>Kindred</u>, but unrecognizable.

8/1---Cassandra sighted two Kindred
prowling around the same area; didn't
recognize either.

→ Not responding favorably
to treatment.

"When do I get a chance to practice on him?" Kragen asked.

Emmett swiveled on his stool beside Benito's cot. "You don't. Interrogation is my job." Emmett stared coldly at the two Nosferatu outside the jail cell. Kragen was a brute, no two ways about it. He'd already cracked three wooden door jambs here in the "off-limits" basement level of the lockup by forgetting to duck. Rhodes scholar he wasn't, but he possessed a low cunning and a sadistic streak that made Emmett feel like a humanitarian. Behind Kraken stood Buttface. He'd come by his name honestly. Emmett was sincerely grateful that he didn't have to go through eternity with such an affliction.

"How do I get good at interrogatin' if'n I don't get to do it?" Kraken grumbled.

"You don't have to get good at it. That's why I'm here," Emmett said.

Kraken snorted but didn't complain further. Buttface didn't say anything. He wasn't a big talker. These two were the local talent. Purely small-time. *And I thought Montrose was an ass*, Emmett thought, then caught himself in the awful, unintended pun. And, of course, Montrose *was* an ass, but that was beside the point.

Emmett's own men, whom he'd brought with him from the East Coast, were in the other room. They were merely insurance. There wasn't much chance that Clan Giovanni would find out about this operation. The biggest worry was keeping Kragen and Buttface away from Benito. Emmett felt pretty confident that, given half a chance, they'd be a little overzealous with the prisoner, and before long there would be no prisoner left. Benito was the one locked up here, but it wasn't to protect the Nosferatu from him.

"Look," Emmett said finally to Kragen, "you bother me. Why don't you take Hemorrhoid Boy there and scram."

Kragen didn't take insults kindly, but he obeyed, and that was all that Emmett was worried about. *Those two aren't going to keep quiet after this is over*, he thought as he watched them shamble out the door, Kragen remembering to duck this time. *They're going to grumble and spill their guts to anybody that'll listen. Then again, that might not be all bad.* If everything went well, secrecy wouldn't be so important after the fact. It might be *better* if word got out that it was the Nosferatu that had abducted Benito. It would send the message that the clan wasn't going to sit back meekly and take insult and injury. The Giovanni might get a bit nasty, but it wouldn't be anything that Emmett and his brethren couldn't handle—he hoped. Conveying a position of strength to the other clans would more than make up for any complications from the necromancers. Again, he hoped.

Emmett took a miniaturized tape recorder from his pocket, turned the device on, and set it on the floor beside Benito's cot. The Giovanni had definitely seen better nights. He was blindfolded, and Kragen and Buttface had unceremoniously stripped him and stuffed him into an orange Inyo County jumpsuit the first night Emmett had arrived with his captive. That was the night that Emmett had decided the two southwestern sociopaths would not touch the prisoner again. Emmett was fairly certain they had broken Benito's arm, as well as opening a deep gash in his head, in the process of changing his clothes. Benito had been torpid at the time, so he hadn't made much of a fuss. Still, Emmett was determined that if any carnage occurred, it would be at his direction.

The gash in Benito's head remained open, attracting flies. His arm was still broken as well, but it looked straight enough. Probably it would heal—if and when

Emmett allowed him a sufficient amount of blood.

The jail cell, without the lurking presence of Kragen and Buttface, was calming in the same way as a cheap funeral parlor, minus the flowers. The stark cinderblock walls were painted that washed-out, institutional pink. The toilet, in this case, was superfluous.

Emmett carried the keys to the barred door in his pocket. He leaned over and slid a briefcase from beneath Benito's cot, dialed the combination and opened the case, from which he removed one of several glass test tubes. All were full of blood. Emmett also took an eye-dropper, which he filled from the test tube. He leaned close to Benito.

The Giovanni had always been fairly fleshy for a Kindred. Fat city living—or unliving, or whatever; Emmett wasn't one for semantics. Currently, however, Benito's pasty white skin was drawn tight over his bones, like a shriveled plum. Emmett snickered at that thought. *Yeah, I've got a giant, vampire prune here.* "It's good for you," he said. "Keep you regular." Then he remembered the tape recorder, picked it up, rewound, and started recording over again.

Before feeding drops of blood to his captive, Emmett brushed the flies from Benito's lips. Where Emmett's fingers brushed, the skin flaked away like scorched paper. Very gently, Emmett pulled Benito's mouth open slightly and began squeezing in droplets of blood.

Almost instantly, the Giovanni drew an involuntary breath between his parched lips. He was trying to drink, his body attempting to draw the sustenance it so badly needed. Another drop. Benito's gray, withered tongue stabbed weakly at the air, like some meek but desperate subterranean creature testing the light of day.

Emmett fed him two more drops of blood, then leaned very close to Benito's ear. "Gary Pennington," the Nosferatu whispered. He dripped two more crimson droplets. "Gary Pennington," he whispered again.

The small amount of blood, even had Emmett fed him the entire dropper's worth, was not nearly enough to restore Benito's strength or to allow him to begin to heal his injuries, but it did serve to draw him slowly toward consciousness. Beneath the blindfold, there was the movement of spastically blinking eyes. Benito's tongue continued stabbing at the air, searching desperately for more blood.

"How the mighty have fallen, you pompous fuck," Emmett hissed. "I'm going to know everything you know. It's just a matter of time. We've waited two years, we can wait two more if we have to."

Emmett placed a droplet of blood on Benito's cheek, just beyond the reach of his striving tongue. Benito tried to buck but hardly shook the bed. He didn't have the strength. He didn't have the strength to lift his hands, even had they not been tied beneath him.

"Gary Pennington," Emmett said, a bit more loudly this time. "He helped you, didn't he, Benito? He was in on it. And then you killed him, didn't you? I want to know it all. I want all the details. You're going to tell me everything, Benito. Did you contact him, Benito? Was it your idea? Benito…"

Emmett squeezed the rubber bulb on the end of the dropper, holding his fingers together so that all the blood ran from the dropper into Benito's slack mouth. The Giovanni's tongue sprang to life again at once, darting from side to side, soaking up every speck of blood it could find. For the first time in many nights, sound escaped from Benito's throat—a faint gurgling moan.

"Gary Pennington. Tell me, Benito…."

Emmett reached for another test tube and refilled the eyedropper. He would bring Benito along slowly. The art connoisseur was little more than a torpid mass of primal instincts, a hungering pile of undead flesh, but Emmett would bring him back. Ever so slowly. All Benito would know was that he hungered, that he desired blood. And with each drop he would hear the name.

"Gary Pennington. Tell me, Benito…."

First to return would be a few of the most basic of motor skills, and then, slowly, the blurriness would begin to recede. And Emmett would be there leading him all the while.

"Gary Pennington. Tell me, Benito…."

After three hours and three more test tubes of blood, Benito began to speak. At first he merely responded to the names that Emmett whispered, but soon he spoke names himself, different names. *"Nickolai…"* Benito rasped. By the beginning of the third cassette tape, he had progressed to sentence fragments. He wasn't quite ready for dates or addresses, but Emmett was confident those too would come, as would all the plans, all the vile schemes.

Oh, yes. They'll come, Emmett thought. It was just a matter of time.

"Lie still, my friend." Nickolai lifted the *I* ♥ *NY* sweatshirt that he had bought for his troublesome patient. The deep gut wounds had been the ugliest—shredded organs and muscle and sinew—but they were significantly healed. The internal tissues had knitted back together, and even the surface-entry wound, which had been wide and gaping, was largely repaired. The quintuple lacerations on both chest and left shoulder were completely mended, use of the left arm returned. All that rejuvenation merely from the blood of two prostitutes.

No, more troublesome than the patient's physical well-being was his mental condition....

"She is here? That's what you said—that she would be here," he said.

...His mental condition, and the fact that his stinking, sputtering Eye kept seeping acidic pus onto the sheets.

"Yes, Leopold. She'll be here. I promise. You can trust me," Nickolai reassured him.

Leopold was, in layman's terms, fried. Intelligible sentences from his lips were the exception rather than the norm, and on the rare occasion that he did manage to utter a comprehensible thought, invariably he was asking after *her*. His right eye, the normal one of the pair, stared crazed and fanatical. The other, the Eye, bulged out dramatically, as if it might pop from the too-small socket at any moment. The fleshy membrane that served as a lid was obviously darker than Leopold's own skin—as if there might have been any doubt that he was not the original owner of the Eye. Adding to the overall foulness was the intermittent fizzling and dribbling of a pungent, gelatinous ichor from the orb.

Nickolai was envious. *Fascinating*, he thought, at least once every few minutes. How, he wondered, could such a rank neonate stumble across such a wonderful...*thing*? The secret, for now, was safely tucked away in Leopold's addled mind. Along with other secrets. Nickolai had surmised something of Leopold's mental state over a week ago, but when the warlock had actually, physically, found the boy five nights ago, wandering north of Central Park and caressing a stone hand—*and being caressed by it!*—Nickolai's suspicions had been confirmed. Leopold remembered nothing of their previous time together.

Leopold did remember. He gazed up at the teacher through the fantastic prism of Sight. *Nickolai* was the teacher's name; it was a name Leopold knew. He knew many names. And he remembered a great deal.

Truth, to Leopold, was a great, dark, underground river. He walked along its chalky banks. In places, the river ran straight and sure, flowing inexorably toward its destination. In other places, the river grew wide, and the current was not so strong. The water meandered, split into separate channels, wandered between rocks and beneath the knobby roots of blighted swamp trees, their branches pulled low by crimson Spanish moss—all beneath the vaulted darkness of living rock.

Leopold stepped closer to the river. Who was this person he was watching? The name escaped him now, when a moment before it had been as familiar as family. No matter. The paunch-bellied man was not *her*, not Leopold's Muse. Leopold had thought he'd found her again, thought that she'd taken him by the hand, but he was no longer sure. He could feel her presence, her nearness, in the dragon's graveyard, but would she reveal herself to him again? She had already given him so much. He must not be greedy. She had led him to the cave and presented him with the tools he'd needed.

My masterpiece...

Leopold stared down at the water. Blood dripped from the hanging moss and painted circles on the river, ripples carried lazily downstream, spreading as they moved, leaving the point of their impact smooth and clear until the next drop fell. Leopold dipped his foot into the water.

He stood in the cave again, his masterpiece towering over him. Never had he known such contentment, such peaceful exhaustion, awash in the afterglow of the most skillful and elusive of lovers. His Muse had brought him here with whispered promises, and she had proven as good as her word.

The wolves stared at him. Surely they understood the honor accorded them, their droll existence graced by the opportunity to partake of perfection, to *become* a fragment of perfection. Rivulets of blood clung to the mammoth column of sculpted stone, sweat upon his lover's brow.

Another face watched Leopold. *Teacher?* No, nor the Muse. Another woman, a seer, whom Leopold had touched and studied. She had placed her seed in him—Leopold laughed at the irony—and he had birthed her anew.

There were others—so many visitors. A troublesome man who'd left very quickly. And also Leopold's teacher.

"I've been searching for you, Leopold," he had said. But Leopold had been so busy. For three days and three nights he had labored. The Muse had directed him, and the teacher had watched over his shoulder—though, in truth, Leopold had been too enthralled to be constantly mindful of the other's presence. And when Leopold was done, the weight of all the stone had seemed to press down upon him, to force him to his knees, to his belly.

He'd awoken to find the Sight gone. Taken from him. *Stolen.*

"Do you want it back, Leopold? I can help you." The teacher again. But so *stupid* for a teacher. *Did he want it back?* Did blood call to blood? Did greatness call out to the worthies?

"I shall have it!" Leopold had screamed. "I-shall-have-it!"

The mere memory was too painful. Leopold withdrew his foot from the water. He waited until the ripple of his passing was swept downstream, then tested the waters again.

He was in the dragon's graveyard, Sight restored, brought to the city by his teacher. *I can help you.* Stepped through the portal. Leopold had found the thief, the *snake*, and shown him the error of his ways. That was before. The righteous indignation was ebbing already. No lasting harm was done, after all. The Sight was restored, and Leopold was holding the hand of his Muse—but not his Muse.

"Just a piece of a statue," his teacher was saying, "but I can help you find your Muse again. Come with me, Leopold. Didn't I help you find the Eye?"

Leopold pulled his toes from the river. His foot was covered with blood. He watched the red water flow past. He was unsure what to do next; his Sight was restored, but his Muse was gone. He tried to listen to the teacher, Nickolai—that was his name. But the teacher seemed so far away.

"Leopold?" Nickolai couldn't trace the blank stare of the neonate's right eye—it gazed at some nonexistent sight in the far distance. Nickolai was more interested in the left Eye, distended and constantly in motion, like some ever-curious creature. *Or ever-hungry*, he thought. Continuously shifting position, gangrenous pus ever percolating and seeping.

Fascinating.

Even when Nickolai had reached Leopold's troubled mind, when the artist had collapsed from his supernal exertions in the cave and had been robbed of his "Sight," Leopold had seemed to know where the

Eye was. Nickolai had merely transported the enraged victim of treachery to the city, and Leopold had done the rest. And now he had the Eye once again. Nickolai had nursed him back to health—physical health, at least. He feared that Leopold's mind, however, had been stretched beyond its limits.

The Eye, blinking, oozing, watching, did little to dispel that impression. Yet there was much to learn; there was much power here. And the gods knew that Nickolai would be in need of it. Leopold might, perchance, prove a fine tool indeed, a fine weapon. For Nickolai's enemies were searching for him. His secret was revealed—or would be in time.

Nickolai turned away from Leopold. The Eye watched, as always, but the right eye still saw some specter projected by a broken mind. The warlock stepped into the next room. He took up a vial filled with blood. He'd collected just a drop of blood—not the blood of his enemy, but of his ally—on the night of that fateful attack, but the sorcerous arts were nothing if not practical. One drop had become two, and two four, and so on until the vial was full.

Standing before an ornate quicksilver mirror, Nickolai unstopped the vial and poured a small amount of the blood onto a cloth of pure silk, the death shroud of a long-dead king. The warlock wiped the cloth across the face of the mirror, and where the fabric passed, the reflection of the hotel room was replaced by another scene—cinderblock and bars; a hideous beast leaned over poor Benito and whispered lies in his ear.

Nickolai did not need to watch for long. The truth was clear enough to see. Benito had betrayed him, and soon the hoarders of secrets would possess his own secret. *Damn them!*

He went back to the other room and stood over Leopold. *An unexpected boon, this Eye,* Nickolai thought. There was much to prepare, and who was to say how soon his enemies would fall upon him.

NOSFERATU

Curiouser and curiouser. Calebros pondered the strange new twists that the perversity of the gods had seen fit to toss his way. Not only was there no single member of Clan Nosferatu who was able to tell him the whereabouts of one Hesha Ruhadze, Setite, Esquire— and the snake was last reported seen here in the city, in New York! Infuriating!—but now there was some strange little Ravnos, with a Gangrel girlfriend of all things, who was also trying to find Hesha and who was making demands of the sewer rats.

This Ravnos, by the name of Khalil, was not a savory sort of fellow. His demands, some of them at least, were a bit on the extreme side, and he was apparently subject to some type of seizures. Odd. All very odd.

It was possible, of course, that this Khalil might be able to deliver on his promises of payment. The fact remained, however, that, even were Calebros resigned to bargaining with the youth, the Nosferatu didn't know the answer to what Khalil was asking. Galling, that. Had Calebros known Hesha's whereabouts, he still might have turned away the Ravnos on principle, but the inability to fulfill a potential bargain struck a nerve.

That was the course of Calebros's thoughts when Umberto scurried into the room, his mouth all screwed up in apparent distaste at the message he brought— although Calebros had learned long not to rush to judgment based on the facial expressions of a man with no lips.

"Um…news in," Umberto said, brandishing a printout unenthusiastically.

Calebros feared his first impression was correct. "News" would be bad news. "Yes?" He steeled himself to receive it.

"Report in that…um, Anatole has been spotted."

"Oh?" That was not so bad. After his tête-à-tête with Donatello, the Prophet of Gehenna had disappeared. Without a trace. The Nosferatu, masters of hiding and of uncovering the hidden, didn't seem to be able to find *anyone* these nights. This sighting, however, was doubly fortuitous, for Calebros had decided to accept Jeremiah's urging that the clan make use of Anatole's presence. But not in the way Jeremiah had so vehemently suggested. *Teach him to hold my reports hostage*, Calebros thought. No, he wouldn't waste Anatole's talents on Jeremiah's superstitions, hungry rats or no. The news that Emmett had forwarded, however, *that* was worthy of Anatole's insight. If Jeremiah was right, and he was indeed able to lend guidance to the Prophet's peculiar skills, then a great service to Clan Nosferatu might soon be fulfilled. The first step would simply be having Jeremiah catch up with Anatole.

"Where was he spotted?"

Umberto hesitated. "Um…on a…uh, that is…getting on a…a bus."

"A bus," Calebros said coldly. "For where, pray tell?" *Say, 'Crosstown,'* Calebros pleaded silently.

"Chicago. Red eye."

Calebros blinked. "Red eye. Then that would have been—"

"Several hours ago. Yes, sir."

Unbelievable. "And why that long? Who—?"

"Uncle Smelly."

"Oh. I see." Uncle Smelly was well respected among the Nosferatu, but he did tend to operate on his own schedule, and nothing Calebros or anyone else said was going to change that in the slightest.

But all was not lost. Not yet. Calebros raked his talons along his lumpy scalp as he thought. Considering the information that Emmett had uncovered from Benito, Chicago, of all places, was one of the prime locations that Calebros had intended for Jeremiah to *take* Anatole. Coincidence? In dealing with the Prophet,

Calebros did not believe there was such a thing as co-incidence. Still, he was undecided as to whether this revelation bode well or ill. One thing, however, was certain.

"Track down Jeremiah at once," Calebros ordered. "Give him the information about the bus number, destination, etc., then get him to Jaffer at LaGuardia on the double. I want him waiting at the station when that bus rolls in. I'll have a packet ready in fifteen minutes for someone to take to him at the airport. See to it."

"Gotcha." Umberto scurried out of the room, undoubtedly pleased that the situation required immediate action and there wasn't time for Calebros to be angry.

Calebros himself wasn't completely sure whether he should be angry, mystified, or frightened.

A few hours later, a courier sent by Colchester arrived from Baltimore. The news he bore was grave indeed, whatever level it was taken on—collapse of the Camarilla, or onset of the Final Nights?

Jeremiah had wanted his time with Anatole to revolve around superstition. Well, here was something else to keep him busy during his vigil with the Prophet of Gehenna.

8 August 1999
Re: Gangrel

FILE COPY

Baltimore, Colchester reports———
Xaviar claims Gangrel to quit
Camarilla; the justicar is not given to
idle threats! Claims Antediluvian
destroyed all Gangrel, upstate NY;
referred to prophecies of Endtime,
"Final Nights at hand."

Xaviar repeatedly mentioned
Antediluvian's eye———connection to
Eye of Hazimel?

file action update: EoH

Have Jeremiah begin
observation of Anatole.
Just in case.

Friday, 12 November 1999, 11:47 PM
The International, Ltd., Water Street
New York City, New York

Although he was standing in the command center of the Camarilla reconquest of New York, few noticed Federico diPadua. The Nosferatu archon was simply one ruggedly handsome, well-dressed Kindred among many. As was his wont, he watched and waited as others received and made calls, directed couriers, and scoured countless maps of the city. He had bloodied his hands last night while Justicar Pascek had held himself in reserve should significant trouble arise. Tonight Pascek was venting his bloodlust while Federico played the role of backup. Lucinde, the second justicar in the city, was elsewhere and not so keenly interested in taking a direct part in the battle. The presence of the third justicar was unknown to any Kindred outside of Clan Nosferatu.

Here, in the American offices of the Dutch-based Jan Pieterzoon, that Kindred was directing the Camarilla efforts. "Are these the latest lists?" he asked his ghoul assistant, van Pel, who handed him a sheaf of papers, names and last reported locations of squads that were overdue.

"Current as of 11:30."

Pieterzoon began poring through the pages. "Still no word from Archon Bell?" he asked after a moment.

"None, sir."

The command center had been moved to the heart of the Financial District in Manhattan after two nights of operating in Queens, among the offices at the Aqueduct Racetrack. Despite significant losses, those first two nights had gone well and had seen the destruction of Armando Mendes, Cardinal Polonia's chief lieutenant. Much of the Sabbat presence, which would normally have made the city virtually impregnable, was away to the south, sacking Baltimore—just as Pieterzoon and Archon Bell had hoped they would. That was not to say that the City That Never Sleeps had been empty of Cainites. The invaders had met fairly organized resistance in Queens, but that had crumbled beneath the two-pronged onslaught from the staging areas at La Guardia and JFK. Brooklyn, where Federico himself had spent much of last night, had been more chaotic, and there were still isolated skirmishes breaking out at intervals. Otherwise, however, the Camarilla had succeeded in breaking the Sabbat power in those two boroughs, driving the enemy survivors north and west as far as the East River.

Much of the southern half of Manhattan was already a Camarilla stronghold. That line had been pressed north beyond Central Park. That left Staten Island, where Pascek was attempting to establish a beachhead, and the Bronx, with Harlem and Washington Heights as something of a no-man's land to the west. That was the area that Theo Bell had been prowling with great success, and also where he was last heard from early last night.

Pieterzoon seemed more at ease tonight than he had the past nights, though the absence of word regarding Bell obviously concerned him. Perhaps Jan's confidence was restored because the attack was well underway, and to all accounts largely successful thus far, or perhaps because Pascek was in the field tonight and not watching the Ventrue's every move like a hopeful vulture.

"Edwin," Pieterzoon said, handing the pages to a Kindred who appeared right at home in the fast-paced world of corporate America.

Edwin Mitchell straightened his tie and adjusted the headset he wore, then began to examine the MIA reports himself. He was the youngest of Prince Michaela's three remaining childer—the three that remained prior to the attack, at any rate. The eldest was a confirmed casualty, and the second was listed among the missing from last night. Michaela herself was leading the squadrons in the Bronx, the territory most firmly held by the Sabbat. That her assignment to the most treacherous portion of the city by Pascek was a clear rebuke, possibly handed down from as high as the Inner Circle, was lost on none.

"You can mark me off that list," said Theo Bell from the doorway, but his reappearance was a relief for only a brief moment—until those in the offices took a good look at him. His face was badly scarred and streaked with what appeared to be patches of melted skin. A wet cloth he dabbed against his jaw came away bloody. His bulky leather jacket, which looked lived-in at the best of times, was torn and speckled with burn marks. The buzz of conversations and phone calls that pervaded the command post fell away to nothing.

"What happened?" Pieterzoon asked quietly, but his words carried in the silence.

"Fuckin' Eye thing," Theo said. "I never seen anything like it."

"Did you…?"

Theo shook his head. "It got away. Or hell, maybe I was the one that got away. I don't know. But it cost me a good man, and two other laid up for I don't know how long."

"In Harlem?" Jan asked.

"Yeah. It was last night, but I couldn't get back before now. I was too wiped out."

Jan took that in and began to synthesize the information into the mosaic of reports and updates coming in from all over the city. While the uncomfortable silence lingered, Mitchell pressed a finger to the earpiece of his headset. His brow furrowed deeply.

"Heavy fighting from the Bronx," he relayed to Jan. "The prince's forces are engaged…being pressed. Identified among the Sabbat are…Lambach Ruthven…." He pressed the headset more firmly against his ear. "Repeat, please." He nodded gravely, then looked up at Pieterzoon. "And Polonia."

Federico stepped forward without hesitation. "I am ready," he said to Pieterzoon.

The Ventrue nodded acknowledgement, then asked Mitchell, "What is her position?"

"Current position?" Mitchell asked. He paused. "Just north of Whitestone Bridge."

"Federico," Pieterzoon said, "the reserves are yours. Use Throgs Neck. We'll send the Manhattan units from the west and encircle them."

"That would be my territory," Theo Bell said.

Pieterzoon gave him a long look, sized up the archon's injuries and fatigue as much as possible. "I don't think so. I need you here…in case anything else comes up."

"I can do it," Mitchell said. He might not have experienced field command before, but his prince, his sire, was out there, and all present could see the intensity burning in his eyes.

"Very well," Pieterzoon said. "Get to it."

Federico was already slipping out the door.

Calebros and Hesha sat silently. Waiting.

The Nosferatu was still chagrined, a month after the fact, that he'd had the infamous Setite, *the melted man*, under his nose, at times quite literally, at the same time the intense worldwide search had been going on. How much time and energy had been wasted, Calebros could only imagine. He'd been wracking his brain trying to find Hesha and the Eye as well, while both were in his backyard, practically over his head, and one the victim of the other. It would have been impossible, Calebros kept telling himself, to have recognized Ruhadze when Mouse had found him in the gardens at St. John's. It was still difficult. The Setite was a collection of raw scabs and weeping sores. He looked more the part of ragged beggar than influential Cainite. He was far from recovered, but compared to his earlier state, he was wondrously spry. Whether the oversight was avoidable or no, Calebros still had not forgiven himself, and recent events had done little to improve his mood.

Other than the seats he and Hesha occupied, one other empty chair, a few exposed pipes close overhead, and an electric lantern that blazed in the corner, the dank stone-walled chamber they were in was bare. Occasionally Calebros drummed his talons on the yellow legal pad in his lap. He stopped when he realized that, in his agitation, he had punctured the top sheet. He tucked the page under and began scribbling notes on the next.

"No harm was done," Hesha said softly, his voice still the slightest bit scratchy from the ordeal he'd undergone.

"As you say," said Calebros, not looking up and continuing to write furiously.

"You concede without agreeing." Hesha laughed quietly. Calebros's head whipped up. Angry words were ready on his lips, but the Egyptian's smile was not mocking. The Setite obviously realized the weakness of his position, physically and strategically, as well as the fragility of their alliance. "Candor is important between friends," Hesha said. "Otherwise, perceived insults take hold and fester."

"I am quite accustomed to festering," Calebros said curtly.

"I fear that I'm growing so as well," Hesha said, squeezing one of the boils that stood raised about one of his many open wounds until the canker popped, and frothy pus ran down his arm. He laughed quietly again.

Calebros punctuated a written sentence with a particularly violent period. "Your woman willfully disobeyed her instructions."

"She exercised discretion," Hesha countered.

"She blatantly disregarded the safety of my people."

"If anything had gone wrong," Hesha said, "it would be Pauline lying torn on the ground. Your people would have faded into the night, none the worse for wear."

Calebros fumed. Probably Hesha was correct—but the Nosferatu was not about to admit as much.

"I will speak with her," Hesha said reasonably. "She has not encountered those of your clan before. She's not aware of how strongly your predilection for…"

"Cowardice?" Calebros suggested accusingly.

"*Prudence*, I was going to say. She's not aware of how strongly your predilection for prudence runs."

Good choice of words, Calebros thought. But, then, Hesha always chose his words carefully, always seemed to know just the right thing to say. It was discomforting in a way, how easily the Setite could alleviate tension with just a few words. *Go ahead, Eve. Take a bite of the apple. Adam might like some too.* But it seemed that they needed one another—and that outweighed their natural and mutual tendencies to distrust one another. Just barely.

It seems we each have our story, Calebros had said a few nights ago. *We each also have no way to prove our own or to disprove the other's.* Hesha had agreed. Calebros knew for a fact that he had not acted in bad faith toward the Setite; Hesha claimed that he had not betrayed the confidence of Clan Nosferatu. *It would also seem,* Calebros had said, *that it is in my clan's best interest for the Eye to pass to less…shall we say, conspicuous ownership than that of the present time. Fewer questions about how it got out and about. You remain interested in possessing it?* Hesha was. And thus they had entered into a marriage of convenience, of common cause. It was true that Ruhadze had treated honorably with the Nosferatu in the past, but the past was no guarantee of the future. Especially with a Setite.

Calebros had been left to act on instinct. No amount of scribbling or note-taking or arranging of facts could give him a definitive answer. And so he had acted. To cement the deal, he had gone so far as to entrust to Hesha the secret that Calebros wished he could reclaim from his own clansmen: that he had known an attack of some sort was to fall on Atlanta. Hesha would have pieced as much together on his own, given what he already knew. So there was little real damage, and hopefully the Setite would take the admission as a sign of good faith on the part of the Nosferatu. Although still the disclosure grated.

Just as the indiscreet use of discretion on the part of Hesha's underling grated. The bargain with Ruhadze had seemed safer somehow when the Setite had had barely enough strength to sit up in his sickbed, when Calebros and Cass had just figured out that the blistered corpse they had in their possession was actually Hesha Ruhadze. Each night, as the patient's strength had slowly returned, Calebros's control of the situation ebbed that much more, as did his comfort with his decision. Hesha was still covered with bleeding wounds, injuries caused by the Eye, that would not heal. *Can I be certain,* Calebros wondered, *that, when he is again whole of body, his loyalty will continue?*

"I would think your underlings would be more obedient," Calebros, attempting to maintain his ire, chided Hesha.

"She is new to the family," Hesha admitted. "Given time, she will grow to learn exactly how I would have her respond in any situation."

"Given time..." Calebros muttered to himself.

They did not have much longer to wait. Calebros heard the footsteps first. Four sets. Umberto, obviously disgruntled, entered the chamber first. He was followed by Hesha's underling, the Gangrel, and Cassandra. Both Umberto and Cass wore their best faces, so to speak—normal human visages, neither noticeably handsome nor beautiful, but not hideous either; nothing to attract attention. Neither Pauline nor the other girl, Ramona, had been subjected to the full brunt of facing a Nosferatu. Not until now, that is, when they were brought into Calebros's presence. He did not hide his true appearance from them. And he could read the dismay, the fear and disgust, on their faces. Of the two, Pauline made the worthier attempt, *attempt*, to maintain her demeanor of professional detachment—perhaps Ruhadze *had* taught her well. The Gangrel, unsurprisingly, was not so couth. She gawked, both at Calebros and at Hesha in his current condition, and she hid her revulsion quite poorly, if she tried at all.

"Welcome, Ramona Tanner-childe," Calebros said.

She stared hard at him, eyes narrowed. "Hesha?"

"No," Hesha said, repressing a chuckle. "I am Hesha Ruhadze." Ramona looked back and forth between the Nosferatu and the Setite with his ragged, festering wounds. Hesha added to his underling, in a harsher tone, "That is all for now, Ms. Miles."

The woman's earphone was dangling at her shoulder, a token of her disobedience at having revealed the identity of her Nosferatu guardians to Ramona. She nodded to her employer and retraced her steps from the chamber.

"Likewise." Calebros gestured for Umberto to go as well.

"Are you sure?" Umberto asked, but then he, along with Cass, retreated beneath Calebros's cold stare.

"I would think your underlings would be more obedient," Hesha said—with a straight face, no less—once the two younger Nosferatu had left. Calebros ignored him.

Ramona, apparently having grown somewhat accustomed to the hideousness of her companions, was glancing uncomfortably at the low ceiling, the pipes, the cold walls all around. She was a pretty girl, Calebros could see. Not beautiful, but pretty beneath the grime. Her hair was wild, like a panicked flock of swallows. She was slightly built, but wiry with muscles, strong, *tough*, like shoe leather. She scratched at the packed-earth floor with bestial clawed feet.

"We must get you some boots," Calebros said. "Large, but…you'll grow accustomed to them. There is the Masquerade to be maintained."

Ramona glared at him as if he weren't speaking English, then looked back at Hesha. "Pauline said you wanted to talk to me. I'm here. Talk."

Hesha bowed slightly. "Allow me to introduce our host, my friend, Calebros. *Your* friend…if you are wise." Ramona looked at Calebros again, a more measured look this time, trying to see through the deformities.

Good girl, Calebros thought. *Young and brash, but not stupid.*

Eventually, she turned back to Hesha. She looked at the third, empty chair, did not sit. "What do you want to talk about." Still guarded, but less hostile this time.

"As I understand it," Hesha said, "it is you that has been asking after me."

"Not me," she said.

"Your companion," Calebros said.

She was instantly on edge again, but trying not to appear so. "He ain't my *companion*." She spat the last word distastefully.

"He," said Hesha. "Khalil Ravana."

She hesitated for a long moment, staring, one after the other, at the two beasts before her. "He said you could find the Eye," she said at last to Hesha.

"Did he, now?"

"Yeah." She waited. "So can you?" Her every word was hard, an accusation.

What have you seen that makes you so angry, so bitter, little one? Calebros wondered. *Family killed? Have you been betrayed? How many times, I wonder. You'd best get over it, if you hope to survive.*

"I do possess the means to find the Eye," Hesha said.

The gem, Calebros thought. *The black and red stone.* If Hesha had told him the truth about it.

"Why is it," Hesha asked Ramona, "that you want to find the Eye so badly?"

Ramona hesitated again. She obviously had many questions of her own, but she was being very guarded about what she said. *Quid pro quo, my dear,* Calebros thought. *Quid pro quo.*

"I have my reasons," she said, kicking at the dirt some more.

Hesha shook his head, disappointed. "That's not good enough if we're going to work together, Ramona."

"I didn't say nothing 'bout working together," she said.

"Do you really think Khalil can get you what you want?" the Setite asked. She didn't have an answer for that, so Hesha continued. "You were with Xaviar...in the mountains. You saw what it could do."

Calebros and Hesha had speculated as much over the past nights, but if the Setite's assertion was a gamble, then Ramona's wide-eyed expression was the payoff—and confirmation of the truth of his words.

"I want to kill it," she said, finding her tongue after a few seconds. "Leopold, the Eye." Her words dripped with hatred. She was not one to hide her feelings, this Gangrel whelp.

"I will make sure that it harms no one else," Hesha said, the casual tone of his conversation gone, his words even and cold. "I will find it with or without your help. But you have seen it; you, like I, have survived it."

"I'd say she did a *better* job of surviving it than you did," Calebros suggested.

"I would like to think," Hesha went on, ignoring the interruption, "that we could help one another. Are you better off with me, or with Khalil?"

"I'm not *with* Khalil," she snapped at him.

"Of course you're not," Hesha backtracked, somehow without seeming to, "but he's the best you've done, and I suspect he has told you more lies than truths." Ramona was obviously not convinced; she regarded the two elders warily.

"We are trying to bring about the same end," Calebros insisted. "For you to trust Khalil over us is insanity."

"I didn't say nothing 'bout trust neither."

"Perhaps a token of good faith," Calebros suggested. "We've already brought you here safely, and I have guaranteed your safe passage—whether you help us or not. What if Hesha provides you with something that is a marker of his trustworthiness? And you…? Khalil mentioned a way to cure wounds inflicted by the Eye…."

Ramona's hand moved absently to her cheek—the cheek that Calebros knew had been scarred but now was healed. Cassandra, who had seen the wound, seemed to think that the injury was the same type as those Hesha bore, though less severe.

"I'll tell you that," Ramona agreed. The thought of counteracting the harm done by the Eye seemed to sit well with her—either that, or she was excited by the prospect of undercutting Khalil's bargaining power.

"And in return?" Hesha asked.

This time the Gangrel whelp did not hesitate at all. "I want Liz freed."

Calebros cocked his head, not fully understanding. For an instant he thought he saw surprise register on the Setite's scarred and bandaged face—but only for an instant.

"What are you saying?" Hesha asked, sounding slightly suspicious.

"Khalil has been keeping her chained up," Ramona said. "I want her free of him. I want her free of you, too." Her hard, accusing stare didn't waver from Hesha.

She can see his injuries, Calebros thought. *She knows she has him. He has no choice.*

"You have my word," Hesha said solemnly.

Ramona crossed her arms. Her scowl, which seemed to be her only expression, deepened. "Your word, huh? Once I tell you how to cure yourself, why should you still help me?"

Calebros sighed. "I am more than willing to vouch for—"

"Do I *know* you?" Ramona asked pointedly. "I mean…your name, and this is your place, yeah, but…as far as I'm concerned, you're on his side." She nodded toward Hesha.

Calebros took no offense, though he was caught off guard by the whelp's audacity. *I shouldn't be*, he reminded himself. Maybe what Emmett said was true, and he didn't get out enough. When, Calebros tried to remember, was the last time he'd spoken, face to face, with an outlander? Or, before Hesha, with a Kindred of any clan other than his own?

"I give you my word," Hesha said, "and if that is not enough…" His hand was in one of the pockets of the wrap the Nosferatu had given him to wear. He took something from the robe and tossed the small object to

Ramona. She started to flinch, as if the Setite might be attacking her, but then snatched a small key from its lazy arc in the air. She studied the key intently.

"I promise that Elizabeth will be free," Hesha said. "At the very least, you can free her yourself."

Calebros, uncharacteristically, found himself a few details short. Elizabeth? Khalil was keeping someone Hesha knew prisoner? The Nosferatu assumed that Ruhadze would fill him in after this meeting. Hesha had proven remarkably forthcoming throughout their discussions. Still, Calebros wondered about the possibilities, about exactly *how* forthcoming the Setite was being with him, and with Ramona. Hesha promised this Elizabeth person would be free. Immediately? Did that include being alive? He'd tossed Ramona a key—but not specified whether or not the key actually matched Elizabeth's bonds. Was Hesha making a symbolic gesture that he knew the Gangrel would misinterpret? A great deal of truth could be skirted without lying.

"Turmeric root," Ramona said. "Light it, press it down in the wounds good."

"Light it," Hesha repeated. "On fire?"

"Yeah, but let it burn out. You know, so it's just smoldering. Hurts like a motherfuck, but it works."

Hesha thought about that for a long moment. He did not appear to relish the idea, and Calebros couldn't blame him, not considering the amount of the Setite's body that was covered by the Eye wounds. The very thought of pressing burning *anything*… No, Calebros would not think about it.

"You should know this, Ramona Tanner-childe," Hesha said. "We have arranged a meeting with Khalil tomorrow night. He has agreed to tell us the secret of healing these wounds—agreed to *sell* us the secret. All he wanted was cash. It seems he's no longer interested in finding me…or the Eye."

Ramona glared. She seemed skeptical but not surprised.

"Know this also," Hesha said. "I believe what you have told me—and, regardless, I will know the truth of it soon enough. I believe just as strongly—no, more strongly—that Khalil will lie tomorrow, that he cares not one whit about this bargain, or about you, or Elizabeth. I ask you to come tomorrow night, to listen secretly, and to make up your own mind. I do not expect you to trust me unquestioningly...but I do *know*, for a certainty, that you will better achieve your aims with me than with Khalil."

Ramona considered that. "I'll be back tomorrow night," was all she said.

"Be here by nine," Calebros said.

Ramona nodded and left them.

"Cut away as much of it as you can," Hesha instructed.

"Yes, sir." Pauline stood behind her seated employer. Even so, he had to lean his head back for her to reach the wide, seeping rend in his forehead. She was not a tall woman, but she wielded her butterfly knife with a degree of expertise. She was not *comfortable* with being ordered to cut her master, but neither were her hands trembling. She proceeded with grim determination.

Calebros watched, fascinated. Other than a telltale clenched jaw, Ruhadze did not seem to feel the blade slicing away his flesh. Granted, much of that flesh was blackened and rotting, and the nerves undoubtedly destroyed, but still...

The three were in the small room that Calebros had moved Hesha to once the Setite was well enough. It was damp, and the rough brick walls were bare except for a few fungus-covered 1950s pin-ups. Even so, it was more private than the communal shelter that Hesha had initially shared with any number of hard-luck cases and restrained lunatics.

Hesha raised a mirror to inspect Pauline's work. "More," he said.

"More, sir?"

"As much as possible," Hesha explained with forced patience. "I would rather feel the knife than the fire…. And yes, Calebros, I would think my underlings would be more obedient."

Pauline took that as a rebuke, but Calebros grinned. The woman cut more deeply, and though this was largely healthy meat that she carved away, still Hesha betrayed no signs of the pain he must certainly have felt. He raised the mirror again. "That should do, I think."

Pauline set down the knife and took up the turmeric root that Calebros had sent Umberto for, and a lighter.

"Wouldn't that be the height of irony," Calebros said, "if a Gangrel whelp tricked a Setite elder into taking a torch to himself?"

"*Irony* is not the first word that comes to mind," Hesha said dryly. Pauline looked nervously back and forth between the two Kindred. "Proceed." Hesha closed his eyes.

Reluctantly, Pauline lit the lighter and raised the flame to the turmeric. The root sputtered, and what the flame did catch quickly gave way to glowing embers.

"Do it," Hesha said, sensing Pauline's reluctance. "Make sure to get it all."

With a steady hand, she lowered the smoldering root to his forehead. Undead flesh crackled and burned away. Hesha's fists tightened on the arms of his chair. As she moved the turmeric to cleanse all of the wound, Pauline peered through the acrid smoke that billowed forth from her point of contact on Hesha's brow. His skin crisped and curled before the embers. Finally, she pulled the root away.

Hesha neither opened his eyes nor relaxed his grip on the chair. Pauline, horrified, stared at him as if she'd sent him to his Final Death. Then, one at a time, Hesha did begin to unclench his fingers. He drew in a deep breath—full of the smell and taste of his own burning flesh—and opened his eyes. He raised the mirror and nodded, satisfied. Before their eyes, the gap in his forehead began to heal over. The skin was pink and tender against his dark complexion, but there was no sign of rot and corruption. The fiery root seemed to have done its job.

"One down," said Calebros. "What…a few hundred to go?"

"I will require blood," Hesha said. "Much blood."

"I'll see to it," Calebros said. "I think I've seen enough here." He left them and headed for the kennels. He was glad to leave the scent of burning flesh, as it gave way to the familiar, comforting smells of the sewers.

Tuesday, 31 August 1999, 2:57 AM
Piedmont Avenue
Atlanta, Georgia

Jeremiah huddled in the corner. The friendly shadows would help him remain hidden—from Anatole, and from the "Queen of Apples," who was descending the basement steps even now.

Near the bottom, she paused for a moment to survey the cellar cum *atelier*. It was a cluttered and dirty affair, full of work tables and partially destroyed statues. Anatole, his blond hair shorn close tonight, did not look at the woman, did not acknowledge her presence now that she was with him.

There was only one undamaged piece of sculpture in the studio, and from Jeremiah's vantage point, the bust was aligned almost perfectly with the new arrival. The two faces were all but mirror images, but Victoria Ash—she whom Anatole called the Queen of Apples—had only seen the back of her stone twin.

The Prophet met Victoria's gaze at last, and Jeremiah was rewarded by the sight of the Toreador staggering in the presence of one more compelling than herself. Jeremiah smiled as he took his notes. Victoria descended the final stairs in a daze.

Anatole was smiling also. "Welcome to your parlor," he said.

Jeremiah shared the little joke and dutifully jotted down every word, but Victoria was puzzled. She moved around the bust to see the face, and laughed, impressed with the likeness, and with her own beauty, no doubt.

"You knew this was me?" she asked.

As she and Anatole engaged in a guarded bout of wordplay, Jeremiah grew too preoccupied with recording what was said—each exact word—to worry out the meaning of the Prophet's seeming nonsense. "My riddles do not hide a lie but attempt to reveal the truth," he said at one point. As Victoria rummaged half-heartedly through a cardboard box of *bozzettos*, scaled models, the sculptor's thumbnail sketches, Anatole told her, "Keep looking to find what we need."

Victoria pressed him for his meaning, but her attempts were not fruitful. She continued sifting through the box as she and the Prophet feinted and parried. Jeremiah had long since given himself over to observing Anatole rather than understanding him. The Nosferatu, unlike Victoria, recognized greatness. Calebros might not have seen fit to allow Jeremiah to seek Anatole's insights regarding the malevolence beneath the earth, but Jeremiah could not ignore the great honor accorded him by way of this assignment. He had taken Anatole to Chicago, to the studio of Gary Pennington, and now here to Atlanta and Leopold's studio. Soon they would travel far to the north, to the mountains and a scene of a great atrocity. But for now, there was this room, and Victoria. Even the Prophet's seemingly inconsequential mutterings with this woman, Jeremiah thought, must have some greater significance.

Jeremiah looked up from his notes to see Victoria reaching for one of the *bozzettos* on the table next to the box. The model was darker than the rest, so dark it was almost black compared to the smooth gray surfaces of the others, like midnight against the pale white of Victoria's skin. It was more the color of the clay models he'd seen in the Chicago studio. It was also, Jeremiah suddenly realized, a likeness he recognized.

He was on Victoria in a instant—not touching her, not giving away his presence. Jeremiah was far too skilled for that. But he slapped at the *bozzetto*, striking the hardened clay model a glancing blow precisely as her hand came to it. It was enough. The model toppled and fell, smashing to pieces on the floor.

Jeremiah recoiled from Victoria and retreated to his position in the corner. She gave no indication of seeing him, or of attributing the accident to anything but her own carelessness. Jeremiah watched Anatole as well. The Prophet was pacing, wandering aimlessly about the room. He seemed to take no notice of Jeremiah. The Nosferatu was still nothing more than one voice among many, both a guide and a follower.

Victoria continued her rummaging, though her mind was not focused upon the clay at her fingertips—nor the shattered *bozzetto* at her feet. She was perturbed, obviously unused to the wisdom of the Prophet, he who spoke in his own time and his own way. The Toreador was accustomed to having her suitors cater to her every whim, yet this time she was the suitor, who would have truth as her bride. The prospective bride, however, was shy and elusive.

After sixteen and one-half minutes of this forced silence—Jeremiah, when not recording dialogue, which itself was rare when Anatole was alone, had taken to timing such apparent minutiae as the Prophet's sandal rubbings and periods of silence—Victoria resumed her hectoring of Anatole. "You are not making anything clearer," she grumbled at one point.

Anatole merely shook his head, almost mockingly, and then he confounded her. "You have already found what you need. At least we did."

Jeremiah cocked his head. The words had meaning for him, if not for Victoria. The smashed *bozzetto*, the grotesque figure… *You have already found what you need*.

The Prophet was not done. "And as for the sculpture, it is indeed important, for the young wizard's sire is within the clay." If first eye-contact with Anatole had staggered Victoria, then these words struck her like a stake to the heart.

Glancing up at her horror, Jeremiah scribbled furiously. If the "young wizard" Anatole often referred to was indeed meant to be Leopold… Victoria was moving away from the Prophet. She reached out to the air to steady herself, then sat heavily on one of the lower steps. She was shocked that her secret was revealed.

If only she knew how *revealed*, Jeremiah mused, *and to whom*. But of course she did not.

Thursday, 2 September 1999, 2:37 AM
Interstate 85 Northbound
Greensboro, North Carolina

The young wizard's sire is in the stone. The words had been haunting Victoria for hours, for two nights. Anatole must be mad…well, of course he was. But he must be *wrong*, as well as mad.

The young wizard's sire is in the stone.

She could not be his sire. It was not possible. She would *know*, she would feel the bond. *I would remember, damn it!* she thought. Embracing a childe was not the sort of thing a Kindred ever forgot. It was not the sort of memory that could be obscured…was it? Some Kindred could reach into the minds of others—Victoria could do it herself in certain situations. It was simple with the kine. But she was no kine, nor a neonate, to be toyed with so. To have wiped such a consequential fact from her mind— that she had sired a childe—would have taken…would have taken…

Victoria squeezed the steering wheel more tightly. She would not go down that road. She could not allow herself to do so. She would drive. She would not think. Not about that.

She had fled Atlanta again. The journey south had not been a complete loss: She had seen her Tzimisce former gaoler destroyed, as well as the Lasombra usurper of the city—*the city that was so damn nearly mine*. But she had gone back to Atlanta to find out what she could about Leopold, and the one thing she'd found out, she could not share with anyone else. She would not. At least she had been alone when the Prophet had cast his aspersions like stones.

The young wizard's sire is in the stone.

She was on her third vehicle now since the police cruiser which she had appropriated after her very literal run-in with the Sabbat. Finding a kind person to lend her a car was no trouble. Any rest area or truck stop would do. There was no need for struggle. The kine in question invariably, of his or her own free will, handed over the keys, was *pleased* to do so, in fact. It was enough to renew Victoria's belief in the generosity of the human spirit. The only problem was that she could not always travel in a style that suited her. The shiny Saturn she was in now, for instance, was a tad below her standards. *But beggars and choosers, and all that…*

She had been speeding north for several hours now, concentrating more fiercely on the route her thoughts followed than the road beneath her. She was not enthused about returning to Baltimore, to the suspicious stares of those who thought she might have turned to the Sabbat. How patently absurd! The Sabbat had ruined her chance for power in Atlanta. They had ransacked the museum, destroyed her art collection…and a few Kindred as well, she supposed. The Sabbat had tortured her, done horrible things…. For her own Camarilla allies to believe that she would serve the fiends—*ridiculous*.

But her memories of Baltimore, if less perverse, were no more comforting than those of her time among the wolves. Instead of the Sabbat, Jan Pieterzoon and Alexander Garlotte had stepped in to persecute her. Theo Bell probably had something to do with it as well, she'd decided. The Brujah archon was too closed-mouthed, too seemingly indifferent to her. He must have been up to something untoward.

Why should I return? Victoria wondered. As so many people had pointed out, the Camarilla was not a governing body *per se*. She was not under orders—as if there was someone in Baltimore with that authority. She had come south out of the goodness of her heart. For the cause. There was that little Leopold matter also…but regardless, she had suffered for the Camarilla. She had done her part. Let those arrogant bastards who had persecuted her do the rest. They could survive, or not, on their own. Victoria would go wherever she wanted.

Which left the question of where she wanted to go.

Ahead was a sign for I-40 West. Her first impulse was to take that exit...but instead her foot was easing off the accelerator, she was slowing and pulling to the side of the interstate. The shoulder was narrow. Her car stopped mere inches from the guardrail. Victoria was frozen by indecision. She felt the hand of Fate upon her shoulder—not in the form of an impersonal deity, but an old and powerful creature, one of her own kind that would have her do its bidding. She absently raised a hand to her jaw, to the tiny blemish. *Damn you!* she wanted to scream. *Damn all my elders!*

Like Jan and the others, she wasn't able to trust her own thoughts and decisions. She blamed them, all the same. Demons without, demons within. The scent of corruption and manipulation was almost palpable. Something was trying to use her. How else could she not remember that Leopold was her childe?

"No!" she screamed. She dug her fingers into the dashboard. "He is *not!*"

Regardless, she would not follow a predetermined course. She required the reassurance of randomness lest she go mad. *Mad like Anatole. That is what comes of toadying to the gods!*

Her car was on the side of the road. Two lanes curved past on her left. The next car that passed—if it was in the near lane, she would follow her present course and return to Baltimore. If it was in the far lane...

At that instant, a huge semi, all lights and rushing wind, rounded the curve and rumbled past—in the near lane. The Saturn lurched and swayed at the passing of the giant only feet away. Victoria had her answer. She was anxious to be away—not to be somewhere in particular, but simply away, anxious for everything to be different. She peeled from the shoulder and gunned the protesting engine to eighty.

She gripped the steering wheel tightly with both

hands, imagining for an instant that the black road was a snake—a serpent, a dragon—stretched out behind her, chasing her. But it lay before her also.

Suddenly Victoria wrenched the wheel to the side. The Saturn shot across the road and barely made the rapidly approaching exit ramp. Interstate 40 West. "Ha!" Victoria cried. Let the gods attempt to fix her path. Let them! She would outwit them. She'd not return to Baltimore. She'd drive west, perhaps Chicago, but regardless, she was done with this damnable war

Damn Fate, damn the gods, damn the hidden ones! They will not have me. I will not let them.

Monday, 6 September 1999, 9:50 PM
Piedmont Avenue
Atlanta, Georgia

Rolph carefully made his way down the steps. The rest of the house was empty, and he did not expect to find anyone in the basement. There were no signs of forced entry, nothing to lead him to believe that anyone had set foot inside since Jeremiah left. Even were there someone waiting in the basement, Rolph had taken precautions so he would not be seen.

His concerns proved unfounded, but caution was never wasted.

All was as the reports suggested it would be: work tables, broken statuary, fine dust, one intact bust, boxes of clutter...and one mostly shattered, hardened clay model on the floor exactly where Jeremiah said it would be. Rolph stood over the *bozzetto* and studied it. Even with part of the face broken away, the likeness was clear enough: the large curved proboscis; one of the two eyes, practically vertical in its orientation; the gaping maw with walrus-like fangs. Leopold did possess a certain amount of talent, Rolph had to admit. But the young Toreador should never have laid eyes on that particular subject.

Rolph took a Ziploc bag from the folds of his cloak and began gently placing the clay fragments inside. When he was done, he poked a bit at the other models on the table and in the box. Doing so, he noticed something beneath the inward-tucked flaps of cardboard. He shoved the models to one side and pulled the flaps open. A photograph was wedged against the side of the box. Rolph opened the Ziploc and placed the picture with the broken *bozzetto*.

That done, he took another look around the room. The surviving bust attracted his attention. Another fine likeness. Rolph wondered how many artists had made how many representations of Victoria Ash over the centuries. She was not one to discourage imitation and, by extension, flattery. Surely one could fill a huge museum with renderings of her visage in stone, on canvas. *And let's not forget the sonnets,* he thought. There must be thousands.

His hand was drawn to the sculpture; he ran his fingers across the cool marble, so similar in hue to the subject's actual skin. His fingertips lingered at the lips, where the piece was slightly marred. Rolph leaned over and examined the disfigurement. The flaw, to his thinking, brought Victoria closer to perfection. But what had happened—another pair of lips, perhaps? Had someone felt compelled to kiss her unchanging face?

Rolph chuckled. *Good thing Colchester wasn't here,* he thought, *or the indentation in her mouth would be shaped differently.*

Friday, 24 September 1999, 10:00 PM
The underground lake
New York City, New York

The taste of salt. Water puffing up his atrophied lungs. The quiet whispering of the earth.

Calebros floated several feet below the surface. He let words float in and out of his mind like gentle swells in a tidal pool: *One in a minute, and one in an hour. Walk a mile in but seconds to deliver my letter. Tell me, oh wise one, which way do I go?*

He hoped the earth would whisper an answer to him, but it was not to be. Calebros allowed the words to wash from him again. Surely the Prophet of Gehenna could have been more dignified than to have left them a silly children's riddle. Or perhaps the Nosferatu was merely irritated because he had not solved a silly children's riddle.

The taste of salt. Water puffing up his atrophied lungs. The quiet whispering of the earth.

He must relax. The riddle, if it was part of the puzzle, would fall into place. Eventually. Or it would not. Even if it did not, as those surrounding it did so, the truth of what the missing piece contained would become evident. So many of the pieces had already come together, yet still there were many holes.

Emmett had provided many of the pieces and helped Calebros to place them. The younger broodmate would be back soon. He was nearly done with his work in the West, nearly finished with Benito. Although Emmett was not the most patient of Kindred, his presence would ease Calebros's mind.

Other matters, more concrete and immediate than a riddle, remained up in the air. The Sabbat were growing restive to the south. They grew increasingly aggressive toward Baltimore each and every night. Soon they would pounce, which was why Pieterzoon and Bell had set in motion a desperate plan. They had reached

an uneasy alliance with Prince Michaela of New York—
prince of Wall Street, perhaps, Calebros had scoffed, *but
not of the rest of the city, God knows*—and would attempt
to shift the Camarilla forces north when opportunity
presented itself. Calebros estimated their chances for
success at fifty percent, and that because he was feeling
charitable.

On other fronts, there was no word from Jeremiah
since Syracuse. Had he come to harm? After confronting
Victoria in Atlanta, Anatole had fallen upon his clansman, Prince Benison, and slain him. Had he done the
same to Jeremiah once the Nosferatu had led the Prophet
to the cave that both Ramona and Hesha had described?
There was no way to know. At what point, Calebros debated, should he send someone to find out? The uncertainty
gnawed at him like rats after the last sliver of flesh upon a
bone.

The taste of salt. Water puffing up his atrophied
lungs. The quiet whispering of the earth.

At least Hesha was doing well. The turmeric root
was working its magic, though the going was slow and
painful. Each night, Pauline burned Hesha, cleansed
with fire and root the corruption of the Eye, allowing
the blood to do its work. And Ruhadze needed much
blood. He was growing stronger, and that, too, was a
cause of concern for Calebros. Would the Setite, once
he was no longer dependent, remain loyal?

Ramona was proving a pleasant surprise. She
seemed to sense, finally, that Hesha and the Nosferatu
meant her no harm. She was not such an unpleasantly
feral creature as she had first appeared. Once it had
become undeniably clear that Khalil was a rake and a
cad, she had seemed almost relieved to have the company of the Setite and his underling, and even several
of the brethren.

Khalil was another loose end to be knotted some
night. He'd proven as good as his word—which was not at
all. *Poor Mouse*, Calebros thought. For a childe of the ken-

nels, existence could be short and cruel. The Ravnos had fled, but it would do him no good. He had stopped in Chicago for the time being, and Calebros had his sources there. There would be a reckoning. The Nosferatu did not forget.

But those were harsh thoughts, and Calebros wished to relax his mind. The taste of salt. Water puffing up his atrophied lungs. The quiet whispering of the earth.

One in a minute, and one in an hour....

25 September 1999
Re: Fatima

Courier reports——helped Fatima contact
Ravenna/Parmenides; unable to learn what
passed between them.

Our people aided Fatima in Hartford as
well——quite a list of favors
accumulating; remind her of that if
necessary. (Our ploy) to lure her out seems
to have worked.

More help for her than I would
have liked, but how do you turn
down an Assamite — esp. Fatima?

file action update: Fatima al-Faqadi

→ Not necessarily. Other possible factors—
increased Assamite activity worldwide
What is their agenda?

Saturday, 2 October 1999, 2:20 AM
Crown Plaza Hotel, Midtown Manhattan
New York City, New York

"Try again, Leopold. And *concentrate* this time."

"She was here? Before?" Leopold was so crestfallen that Nickolai thought the boy might break into tears. That in itself, of course, was potentially quite interesting.

"Yes, she was here," Nickolai lied. "We tried to rouse you, but you would not wake."

Leopold dug his fingernails into his scalp and muttered to the floor. His right eye was squeezed tightly shut in consternation, yet his other Eye stared ahead. It was almost always open these nights. Watching. Secreting its pungent discharge.

Surely it knows I'm lying, Nickolai thought. It must know that the Muse had not been present, that, in the weeks they'd been secluded in the hotel, no one other than Nickolai had set foot in the suite of rooms. Nickolai had seen to their isolation. No employees of the hotel were allowed on this floor, and the warlock had set powerful wards to keep him and his charge hidden from sorcerous eyes. *It must know.* Nickolai could sense a brooding sentience about the Eye. He had no way to be sure, no empirical evidence, yet somehow he knew.

Whatever the Eye might or might not be able to discern, none of the information in question had dawned on Leopold. The neonate did as he was told, if grudgingly, as if his will had been eroded away. At times, gazing at the unblinking Eye, Nickolai fancied that he and it were, in a sense, co-conspirators, the truth known to them but unseen by Leopold. Nickolai believed that the Eye must have come to the same conclusion that he had: namely, that Leopold's time was running out.

The boy was a candle that had burned too bright and too hot. The Eye had pushed him far beyond what he was capable of, and now he was little more than a clump of wax awaiting the last dying flicker of its wick. Many nights he did not achieve consciousness, or he did so for merely a handful of hours. Perchance he would soon slip completely into torpor, never to return. Nickolai detected no sense of loss or regret from the Eye. At times he decided that he was only imagining signs of higher sentience from the orb, but other times…

For Nickolai, Leopold's demise would prove troublesome. It was a cruel Fate that had brought Leopold back to him for the end, so that the circle might be complete.

"Try again," Nickolai said. Leopold, beyond solace, reluctantly turned to the blocks of stone that Nickolai had provided. "*She* said that if you do well with these, she will return. Soon."

"What shall I do with them?" Leopold asked, his hesitancy and despair draining away, down the deep well that had already claimed his resolve. He held the blocks, one of granite and one of marble, in his hands.

"Perhaps a nice flower."

Leopold nodded glumly. He lifted the two blocks, neither larger than half a loaf of bread. Almost instantly, his fingers began to dig into both marble and granite as if they were no harder than wet clay. The rectangular blocks elongated in his grasp, and, when he pressed them together, the light and dark stones flowed one into the other.

But Leopold paused. He sighed and set the now single, irregular block of fused marble and granite on the table before him.

"It is done," he said weakly.

Nickolai touched the stone. It was cold and solid. He rotated it on the table, noting the interwoven channels of stone toward the center. Top and bottom were still separate, unmarred marble and granite, so that the entirety formed a sort of "x."

"This is not a flower," Nickolai pointed out.

"It is done," said Leopold, not looking at the stone.

"You must concentrate, Leopold. *She* will be very displeased with this."

"It is done," Leopold repeated. "Will she come?"

"Not if this is the best you can do. Finish the flower."

"Will she come?" Leopold asked again, as if Nickolai had not answered him. There was, perhaps, a trace of desperation in Leopold's right eye. The Eye looked on dispassionately.

"Are you tired?" Nickolai asked, but Leopold did not respond. He was watching, with his right eye, some faraway scene. "Yes, she will come, Leopold. Soon."

The boy's attention slowly returned to the here and now, his pupil contracting and struggling to focus. "Good," he said. "I am tired, I think?"

Are you? Nickolai wondered. *Or did my suggestion make it so?*

"Rest, then," Nickolai said. "I have other matters to attend to."

Almost before the words were completely spoken, Leopold had retreated to that faraway place. His eye and the Eye both remained open. A dollop of ichor dripped onto the stone and sizzled away to nothing, but Leopold took no notice.

Nickolai returned the stare of the Eye. *And what will I do with you once our Leopold is gone? I wonder,* he thought. There was the rub. Leopold had outlasted his usefulness—the moment the foul Nosferatu had seized Benito, Leopold could no longer serve any purpose for Nickolai. But now, with the Eye that Leopold had somehow come upon, the boy was handy, if only as a glorified pot holder. What *would* Nickolai do with the Eye if Leopold continued to deteriorate? *I certainly won't use it myself.*

He thought for a moment that he saw a gleam in the Eye, almost like laughter, or a dare. His imagination, surely.

Nickolai lifted from the table the x-stone. It was

dense and heavy. Leopold offered no response, gave no indication that he was any longer cognizant of Nickolai's presence or anything else. Nickolai lugged the stone into the next room and placed it on a table beside four other sculptures.

The first sculpture, the oldest, was a perfect orchid. The stem was flawlessly woven strands of white and mottled gray-black, and each petal alternately one of those colors, marble and granite. The leaves curved gracefully, each so thin that it seemed it should fall of its own weight. But the orchid stood, the composition balanced precisely.

The second sculpture was an orchid as well. Although where the first was a perfect flower that happenstance had seen rendered in stone, the second was a crude facsimile. The stem was a bit thick and too rigidly straight. Seams were readily visible where marble and granite met. One of the leaves was proportioned poorly and cracked. The petals, rather than distinctly separated, were a single structure with little detail.

The third sculpture lay on its side, too top-heavy to stand. It might have been a daffodil, or a rose, with thick awkward leaves. The fourth was a vaguely pyramid-shaped clump. The half-fused x-stone was the fifth.

Nickolai stared at the strange collection, each piece commissioned, as it were, within the past two months. Had Leopold merely lost interest? Did an orchid no longer hold the slightest wonder for him? Nickolai thought that was not the case. The deterioration of Leopold's skills mirrored quite closely the deterioration of his grip on reality. Not that he had ever, since the night Nickolai had found him wandering north of Central Park, been the model of lucidity, but Leopold was spending increasing time in that faraway place of his mind.

More disturbing to Nickolai, however, was Leopold's decreasing potency in utilizing the powers the Eye seemed to confer upon him. Nickolai remembered the great sculpture in the cave. The warlock, upon learning that Benito had gone missing, had immediately begun to seek out Leopold. The bond between them assured him that he would find the boy, and Nickolai, reaching out with his mind and spirit, had indeed found Leopold. He'd found him at the cave, waist deep in living rock and mangled Gangrel. Nickolai was not the one to critique the boy's artistic vision, but the warlock had marveled at his *power*—at how the very earth had responded to Leopold's merest whim. And when Nickolai had brought him to the city, Leopold had, *without possessing the Eye*, laid waste to several blocks' worth of city streets and much of the gardens at the Cathedral of St. John the Divine.

Since then, however, he'd been fading fast. Nickolai feared that the row of orchid sculptures illustrated, not a wandering of interest, but a dwindling of vigor. It confirmed his thoughts about the candle: too bright and too hot. And now time was running out.

Damn him! How dare he? Especially when he was to be Nickolai's defense against the foul sewer dwellers! They would be coming for him. The only question was when.

Strangely enough, despite Leopold's slide, the Eye itself appeared completely undiminished. It seemed vigorous, almost—and Nickolai suspected this was but his imagination—*cheerful*. It was quite possible, the warlock surmised, that Leopold had passed some threshold, that the Eye had taken him to a certain point and the boy was capable of going no further. But neither could he maintain that existence, and so he'd begun this long descent into madness—or not that long, perhaps.

Yes, that was possible. But remembering Leopold's great masterwork at the cave, Nickolai considered other possibilities as well. He did not sense within the Eye power of the magnitude that had created that living statue and tomb of the Gangrel, nor in the scope of destruction surrounding the cathedral gardens. Perhaps it was merely the wiles of the orb—it wished to be underestimated, so that a potential user might believe himself capable of controlling it.

Or there was something else. Something greater than the Eye, something augmenting it, or something that had seized upon it as a focus for its own power—something that had seized Leopold. The boy had exhibited considerable acumen for the mystical arts, even when he was without the Eye. He had performed at a level that should never have been possible for him, even were he some night to discover his true heritage.

Nickolai studied the five sculptures before him, from the sublime to the mundane, and shook his head. He could not be sure of the forces at work…not without the proper experimentation. Almost immediately, new plans began to take shape in his mind. *It might work…it could work.* He might yet bend Leopold to his designs once again. If he was allowed the time.

Leopold dipped his cupped hands into the river. The landscape was not so bleak now, not so foreign. The river wound among edifices of rock, headstones the size of buildings. The water flowed red here in the dragon's graveyard. There had been strange splotches of white and mottled gray-black, but those were long gone, carried downstream by the ever-flowing current. Leopold could not see his hands beneath the water. His arms ended at the wrists. The blood of the river was his own lifeblood, flowing out of him and drifting away. For a moment he panicked—his hands, his precious hands, the most perfect artist's tools, as his Muse had shown him.

He withdrew his hands from the blood river and went giddy with relief. His precious fingers were unharmed. Dark water seeped out between them. Leopold lifted his hands to his lips and drank. *She* was here. He could smell and taste her. The dragon's graveyard was her playground. And the teacher said that she would be back. Soon.

None of the joy or honor remained to Jeremiah.
Even in the darkness of the cave, he felt the shadow of
the monstrous sculpture. The eyes of the Gangrel stared,
but they did not see him. The creatures moaned in
agony, but went unanswered by the Prophet.

Anatole's mind had floated somewhere that
Jeremiah could not follow, away from this place of darkness, away from the sculpture of madness and torture.
The Prophet lay unmoving. He did not wander about,
he did not rub his sandals together this way and that.
Jeremiah was alone with the bitter taste of his memories. His bemusement at how Anatole had figuratively
stricken Victoria had been subsumed by horror at the
literal strike against Prince Benison. Anatole had destroyed his clansman after Benison had retrieved for
him the Robe of Nessus, after the prince had seemed,
for a brief instant, to be aware of Jeremiah's presence.

Could he have been? Jeremiah wondered. If that were
indeed the case, the Nosferatu should be thankful that
Anatole, so seldom violent, had struck down the prince,
and by doing so inadvertently preserved the watcher's
charade. But Jeremiah could feel none of that. He felt
remorse, as if the slaying had been his deed, his responsibility, his fault.

Beneath the obscuration of the twisted shadow, he
felt the darkness that he had felt before, in the tunnel,
before the rats, the infernal creatures whose thoughts
had, as if of single mind, called out, *Flesh*. And now
Jeremiah tried not to look upon a giant sculpture of
flesh and stone. He watched Anatole every second.
Although the Prophet had lain apparently comatose
for weeks now, who was to say when he might leap up—
leap up and strike, like he had at Prince Benison.

I have been with the Prophet for months! Jeremiah bemoaned his fate. *But he will not tell me the answers I know he has! What darkness is it that eats away at the heart of the earth? I have felt it. Tell me, damn you! But he will not speak. He will only strike me down.*

But the Prophet did speak. Without warning he opened his eyes and sat upright. "Forty nights and forty days," he said.

And then he looked at Jeremiah. *And saw.*

Jeremiah felt it. He felt the Prophet's gaze. *Dear God. No!* It could not be so. "How…?"

"Begone," Anatole said, no more concerned than if he were brushing a fly from the ceremonial loaf.

Jeremiah staggered backward, away from the Prophet. "Not now! Not now when I know you have the answers! Tell me, I beg you, tell me before I am gone!" the watcher cried.

Anatole simply shook his head, dolefully. "No. I must save all our lives."

And then Jeremiah was fleeing. Away from the Prophet. Away from the sculpture of darkness and the hole into the heart of the earth. Through what he thought was but could not be a graveyard of monoliths and desolation. Through the Valley of the Shadow of Death. His screams from hell on earth echoed into the darkened heavens.

17 October 1999
re: the Prophet of Gehenna

10/16 Jeremiah reports—after weeks of
guiding Anatole, the prophet saw
Jeremiah (for who he was?) and sent him
away; Jeremiah <u>unable to resist.</u>
Anatole left at cave.

Not surprising

Tone of report fairly frantic; does J.
need a (vacation) → *Don't we all, damnit?!*

Anatole follow-up necessary.

→ *Ramona talking about going back to ca—
perhaps Hesha could accompany?*

The tunnels didn't *always* seem to be closing in on her now. Ramona supposed she should be thankful for that. But she wasn't. Not really. *Why the hell can't these guys just rent an apartment building or something?* she wondered. *I mean, they can put on a normal face when they want. Wouldn't nobody know. They could all just have their own building and keep out of sight and be ugly together.*

But Ramona also remembered how she and her friends had hidden in out-of-the-way places and abandoned buildings: the garage uptown, that old elementary school upstate. Hell, she'd slept in the trunk of a car in a junkyard. There was something about the kine that made it hard to blend in so closely—at least for her. And she looked mostly normal. She *looked* like most of the meat, but she knew she didn't belong in that world anymore. It was like sneaking into the boys' bathroom—she could do it, but she'd be waiting to get caught the whole time, and anybody that got a close look… She could imagine how much worse it would be for the Nosferatu, who so obviously didn't belong out there with the kine. It couldn't be that easy for the Nossies to keep up their disguises all the time, so they had a safe place where they didn't have to pretend.

It just so happened that safe place was underground, in tunnels and sewers and crawl spaces. *Don't get too sentimental about it*, Ramona told herself. She sniffed at the air—that seemed to have become a habit down here. "I'll have to get them a nice needlepoint," she mocked herself. "Home is where the shit is."

She made her way along the uncomfortably cramped tunnel. She'd finally learned her way to Hesha's room. Pauline had helped her figure it out. The woman was a bit too much Steppin Fetchit for Ramona's taste, but Hesha's retainer—that's what he called Pauline, his "retainer"—had just enough of a fuck-you attitude that she and Ramona got along okay. The rest of the warren was a loss to Ramona. Down here, she couldn't have found her way to water if her ass was on fire. Then again, she didn't have any inclination to figure out what was where. If it hadn't been for Hesha having been so laid up for so long, she would have made him meet her somewhere upstairs—out on the street. But his recovery from the ass-kickin' that Leopold had given him had been a slow process. Finally, he seemed to be near the end of that road.

His room had a door on it now. Probably the Nosferatu had gotten sick of the stink of his burning flesh. Smoldering turmeric root wasn't exactly Chanel No. Five either. Then again, the Nossies didn't have a whole helluva lot of room to complain. But it was a funny thought.

Ramona knocked. Pauline opened the door. "Ramona, come on in."

Hesha was dressing. He had on crisp gray slacks and was buttoning his starched white shirt. There was some kind of incense burning in the room. Ramona didn't like that smell either, but she guessed it was better than burning skin and Nosferatu stink, if just barely.

"Good evening, Ramona," Hesha said. As he finished buttoning his shirt, Ramona couldn't help but notice how built he was. Expensive clothes covered rippling muscles. Now that he wasn't all festering sores and dribbling pus, he was a good-looking son of a bitch, like a walking advertisement out of *Essence* or *Esquire*. But Ramona wasn't taken in. She knew that just made him more dangerous. She remembered what Liz had said the night Ramona had given her the key to her chains: *Whatever he told you was a lie…. He doesn't care about anyone. He just uses…people, things…. He always gets what he wants…. Don't let him control you.*

Harsh words, and probably true. But Ramona had known the type before—guys who wanted what they wanted, no matter what, whether that was drugs or money or to get down her pants. Just because Hesha might be better at it than those others didn't scare Ramona. She knew what she wanted too. She'd made sure that Liz had gotten away. Hesha hadn't been too happy about that, but tough shit. Now they were going to find the Eye and make sure nobody else got hurt— like her people had, like Hesha had. As long as they were after the same thing, they were on the same team. That was all Ramona worried about.

"Pauline," Hesha said, "See to that list, and that Janet knows to make the necessary arrangements."

"Yes, sir." Pauline headed for the door. "Take it easy," she said to Ramona with a wink, and then was gone.

"You look like you're feelin' better," Ramona said to Hesha after the door closed.

"Yes, I am, thank you. My treatment is almost completed."

His *treatment*. Ramona shuddered. She'd had burning turmeric root stuffed in one hole in her face, and that had been bad enough. All of Hesha's visible scars were healed, but she couldn't help wondering about some of his more…*sensitive* areas. She'd have to remember to ask Pauline about that. Not exactly a turn-on—to burn your man's privates off with damn flaming produce.

"So you want to go with me," Ramona said.

"Yes," Hesha said. "To the cave. Back to the cave."

"Okay." Ramona had been planning to go for some time now, but somehow she hadn't managed to leave the city yet. She *had* to go back. There was no two ways about that. After the horrible battle against the Eye, she had seen her dead, so many of them—Eddie, Jen, and Darnell, Stalker-in-the-Woods, Brant Edmonson, Ratface, and all the others. But not Tanner. Not her sire. She had to find out why. He'd gone into the cave with the first of the Gangrel and never come out. She had to go back to the cave. If Hesha wanted to come too, that would just push her to do what she should have done already. "If we drive most of the way," she said, "we should be able to make it in two nights."

"We'll take a helicopter," Hesha said. "There and back in a night."

"Oh…okay." For a moment, Ramona had the uncomfortable feeling that Hesha was turning her journey into his own. That was fine—to a point. She wasn't about to start letting him boss her around like he did Pauline. But if he happened to have a helicopter handy…that was different. "I forgot that you were Señor Dinero Grande. When you be ready to go?"

"Within a very few nights," he said. "I still have details to catch up on from my convalescence. Even a good staff cannot run itself perpetually."

"Oh, yeah," Ramona said knowingly. "Gotta watch those staffs. Hey," she added, catching sight of red and black gem on a table near Hesha's bed, "maybe you can get your money back for that. Or I bet you could sell it on Fifth Avenue. That and your Rolex would get you a hundred bucks easy. That pay for gas for the chopper?"

Hesha did not grow angry, but neither did he seem amused. He had told Ramona that he could use that gem to find the Eye, to trace its whereabouts, but she had yet to see any results. She mostly believed him when he told her that, for some inexplicable reason, the gem simply was not functioning as it should. *Maybe it needs new batteries*, she'd suggested, and been met with an equally stoic response. She didn't really believe that he'd conned her—she didn't *want* to believe that—but she did enjoy getting a rise out of him by questioning his honor or telling him that he was full of shit.

"You know how to fly a chopper?" she asked.

"Yes, actually," Hesha said, "but I have a pilot."

"Oh, good. My license isn't current. I'll check back tomorrow night."

Thursday, 21 October 1999, 2:17 AM
An isolated burrow
New York City, New York

Calebros bent low to squeeze beneath the low-hanging shelf of rock. It wasn't enough. Muttering curses, he got down onto his knees. Still not enough. He sprawled, not at all gracefully, on his belly and chest and began to slide forward inches at a time. The tight squeeze would have been no problem this way if he'd been able to lie truly flat, but the dramatic kink in his spine jutted upward and grated against the stone. Calebros shifted his weight and wriggled. Only with great difficulty did he make it through.

How many more of these blasted crevices and hairpins must I negotiate? he wondered.

"Stop...right there!" said a nervous voice, not far away.

"Jeremiah," Calebros said soothingly. His grossly dilated eyes could barely make out the other Nosferatu now that his voice had drawn attention.

"Stop!" Jeremiah said again.

"Might I at least stand?" Calebros asked reasonably. "After all, it was you who sent for me." Jeremiah seemed unsure, but he didn't object, so Calebros climbed painfully to his knees. The ceiling was too low to stand upright. Calebros inspected Jeremiah in the darkness. The Kindred who had so confidently and capably shadowed the Prophet of Gehenna was cowering in the farthest, tightest, darkest corner of this dead-end tunnel. He clutched his knees to his chin with one arm. The other was wrapped over the top of his head, as if holding it on.

"The Final Nights are at hand," Jeremiah said.

"I see." Calebros had heard this before from Jeremiah, if not so frantically. It was the same tired prophecy, the same rote words. Yet Calebros had felt the twinge of terror when he'd first read the reports of

Xaviar's claim that he'd battled an Antediluvian. But what the Gangrel justicar had seen was no Antediluvian—just an insane Toreador wielding powers long hidden from the world. *Just!* Calebros chided himself. It had *just* destroyed a small army of Gangrel, and the powers loosed upon the world had been loosed by the Nosferatu, by he and Rolph.

"He knows," Jeremiah insisted, as if someone had contradicted him. "He knows, but he would not tell me! But I saw." He closed his eyes tightly; whatever he saw was too much to bear, and he wished to see it no longer. "I *felt*. He descended into the darkness, yet the darkness did not overcome him. He faced the dragon. I could *feel...*" Jeremiah was wracked by uncontrollable sobs. Bloody tears ran down his cheeks. He squeezed his knees and head more closely to his body.

My God. Calebros watched in horror as one of his most intelligent, if rash, clanmates unraveled before him. *No, the unraveling was already done*, he corrected himself.

"He saw, but he would not tell me," Jeremiah whimpered. "He sent me away." More sobs.

"Come back with me, Jeremiah. To the warren. You'll be safe there."

Jeremiah's eyes sprang open at that. His feet scrabbled against the floor as he tried to push himself farther back into the corner, but he could go no farther. "*Nowhere* is safe!" he screamed, then fell back into the piteous whimpering. "Least of all there, least of all..."

Calebros didn't like the thought of leaving him there. There was safety in numbers; that was why the warren was so vital to their existence. The Nosferatu were masters of the dark places only in comparison to other Kindred. There were still unknown dangers...*Nictuku*, he thought. Jeremiah had once studied under Augustin. *Superstitions!* Calebros told himself, angry that he'd even entertained the thought, angry that Jeremiah had pushed his thoughts in that direction and disrupted the routine of the warren.

"I'll send Pug to check on you," Calebros said, bending down to creep back out of the cubbyhole. "Don't hurt him, do you hear me?" If Jeremiah heard, he gave no indication. But Calebros supposed Pug could take of himself. *I used to think Jeremiah could take of himself.*

Calebros slithered on his chest and belly away from that place. He had seen and heard enough.

Thursday, 28 October 1999, 2:30 AM
Highway 95
Outside Las Vegas, Nevada

"This oughta be far enough," Kragen said. Buttface said nothing.

The cargo area of the van was walled off from the cab and sealed so the cargo couldn't hear what the driver and passenger were talking about. But Kragen didn't really see that it mattered.

"I say instead of just dumping him, we rip his head off and then dump him," Kragen suggested. "And then run over him maybe." Buttface said nothing. "Who's gonna care? Who's gonna *know*?" Kragen asked. "*You* ain't gonna tell nobody, are you?"

Buttface shrugged.

"Hmph. Just what I thought," Kragen said. "You're scared of that uppity little snot from back East. 'Do this…do that.' I'd like to stuff a boat hook up his nose and pull it out his ass." Kragen glanced over at Buttface. "No offense."

The desert and the starry night sky stretched on forever. The tires on pavement sounded a rhythmic hum.

"I mean, he said he was done with him," Kragen said. "'Get rid of him,' he says. 'Take him out in the desert and dump him.' Sure he wants the other Giovanni fucks to hear about what happened, but he didn't say not to rip his fuckin' head off, not specifically. I mean, those fuckin' Giovanni fucks could probably talk to his ghost and find out what happened, right?"

Buttface shrugged.

"Yeah, you're right," Kragen said. "But we could at least run over his leg or something. You know, not his head. It ain't nothing really. Barely feel it, not like a speed bump or nothing."

There was silence for a tenth of a mile. "Okay, okay," Kragen said. "We'll just dump him, like the guy said. Geez."

Kragen slowed the van, then pulled off the side of the road onto the packed desert sand. He and Buttface climbed out of the cab. Before he opened the sliding door in the back, he turned to Buttface and raised a finger to his own lips. "Remember, shhh."

They yanked Benito out of the van. He still had the black plastic bag over his head and tied around his neck, and his hands bound behind him. They threw the Giovanni to the ground. Hard. And then took a few seconds to kick the daylights out of him—just in the ribs; they didn't want to tear the bag and have him see them. *But then we'd have to rip his head off*, Kragen mused, but Buttface was already getting back into the van. Kragen joined his partner, and they tore off down the road.

"…Tell me, oh wise one, which way do I go?"

There was a drawn-out silence, then, "Fuck if I know." Ramona looked at Calebros as if he were crazy. She looked around the murky, cluttered cave-office and said, "Hey, you got another chair around here? You're the one wanted me to wear these stupid boots. Well, you know what? They don't fit right, and they hurt. I don't see *you* wearing no normal clothes, all wrapped up in your rags."

Calebros sighed. "On the rare occasion that I am seen by kine," he explained, "I do not draw attention to myself. If I were up there more often, *as you are*, and I could disguise my nature with a few simple garments, *as you can*, I would do so."

He and Hesha, after repeated attempts, had convinced her to wear boots to hide her permanently clawed feet. It was a problem with some Gangrel. They tended to take on animalistic aspects over time—a sign of how close they were to the Beast, some said; others suggested it was merely proof that the outlanders were little more than wild beasts of the field. Calebros, as Ramona had so pointedly reminded him, had little room to quibble about physical deformities. He did not feel it was excessive, however, to demand that she uphold the Masquerade to the extent readily within her power. He'd noticed her ears too—tapered, like a wolf's. But her hair tended to obscure them, and Calebros felt a need to choose his battles carefully if he was to convince the girl of anything.

Ramona considered his sage counsel. "Yeah, whatever you say." She stared at him for several seconds. "A chair?"

Again Calebros sighed, lifting himself from his chair. He hoped the sound of his vertebrae popping evoked guilt in Ramona, but she showed no sign. He shuffled around his desk, past the candelabra—he'd grown weary of fighting the lamp and smashed it once too often; the base now protruded, upside down, from a bulging trashcan, and Calebros had resorted to more primitive technology—and to the doorway. "Umberto!" The younger Nosferatu arrived in short order. "Umberto, do kindly bring a chair for Ms. Salvador."

Once that matter was resolved and Ramona and Calebros had both taken their seats, Ramona was still obviously displeased with her host. "I never told you my name...my whole name," she said.

"Pilar Ramona Salvador," Calebros intoned. "Formerly of Los Angeles, presumed dead by family and police.... It's my job to know these things. Now, evidently the riddle means nothing to you? Fair enough. There is something else I would like to ask you about."

"Ask away."

"Thank you. First, please listen." He reached for a small tape player on his desk and turned it on. A considerable racket ensued—the noise of a helicopter—then a voice, a female voice straining to be heard, that the cockpit recorder had captured.

"There! There it is!" said Ramona's voice.

"What? Where?" It was Hesha.

"What do you mean? Right there! Look!"

"I don't see—"

"Are you fuckin' blind? Look! Grass, and trees...all burned! And the rocks...like giant tombstones!"

"I don't see!"

"Fuck!"

Calebros clicked off the tape player. "You remember, I'm sure." Ramona nodded. She suddenly appeared very uncomfortable in her chair. "You told us about what you saw...about the horrible experience at the cave, in the meadow with Xaviar. What you were describing on the tape—that was what you were expecting to see, wasn't it?"

Ramona shot up from her seat. "I know what you're gonna say, and I didn't *imagine* nothing," she snarled, jabbing a finger at him. "That Leopold—if that's really his name—him and the Eye, he was raising up these huge fuckin' chunks of rock, and they'd fall over, or *explode*, like a fuckin' volcano or something. I was fuckin' there! I *saw* it. I didn't *imagine* nothing."

"I believe you," Calebros said softly, calmly.

Ramona stood with her mouth open, her rant derailed. "You do?"

"I do. Let me tell you why." Ramona sat, and Calebros continued. "You saw the meadow that way before, when you were with Xaviar, and you saw it that way from the helicopter. But not once you landed, correct?"

"Right."

"When you went into the cave, with Hesha, you saw the sculpture. You both saw it."

"Right." Ramona's teeth were clenched, her fingers becoming claws and digging into the chair.

It enrages her merely to talk about it, to remember, Calebros thought. *Best not go into too much detail.* "This was Hesha's second trip to the cave, as well. The first time, he found Leopold—torpid, Hesha thought. He took the Eye and returned to the city."

"Yeah, and then Leopold came after him and ripped him about five new assholes."

"Um…yes, you could put it that way," Calebros said. "But this is what is important: When Hesha was at the cave that first time, he didn't see a sculpture."

Ramona thought about that, then said, "So? It wasn't built yet."

Calebros reached for a folder on his desk. He brandished the notes that Jeremiah had taken during his observation of Anatole. "I have reports here that describe the statue as of early September."

"But Hesha got his ass whupped…when, in August?" Ramona asked.

"July. July 31."

Ramona reached for a calendar on Calebros's desk, but tossed it back when she realized it was from 1972. "That's still a whole month, and nobody knows where Leopold was that whole time. He could have gone back to the cave."

Smart girl, Calebros thought. He was leading her along the same path of reconstructing events that he had followed. "Possible. The soonest he could have gotten back, if he did, would have been the first or second of August. That would have been approximately a week after your battle with the Eye.

"Now, you know Tanner. You know your other clanmates. Even injured, would they have waited around *an entire week* so that Leopold could come back and incorporate them into that statue? Don't you think that *someone* would have been able to get out, to hunt, at the very least to find blood and bring it to the others?"

Ramona was nodding. "And Hesha didn't find any Gangrel at the cave…."

"Exactly." Calebros knew he had her. He wasn't positive about what he was suggesting, he couldn't be—but it was *possible.*

"So…" Ramona was still a few steps behind; she was putting the pieces together. "The statue was already there…and Hesha didn't see it?" She seemed suddenly unsure. "That's a *big* fuckin' statue."

Calebros nodded. "And it's a big—"

"Meadow." Ramona had seen where he was going as soon as he'd opened his mouth. She was a quick study, a sharp mind.

"Exactly." Calebros was heartened for several reasons. Not only was Ramona following the evolution of his suspicions, but he also felt a burgeoning connection with her. Not an attachment, nothing so maudlin, but an understanding. It would not do for Ruhadze alone to win her trust, and possibly use her against Calebros some night if the opportunity presented itself. Hesha had traveled to Baltimore to pursue the meaning of Anatole's bloody scrawl in the cave, and the Setite's absence pricked at Calebros's paranoia. But that concern was for another time. Ramona was here now, and whatever slight satisfaction Calebros gained from this journey of the mind they had embarked upon, he could not ignore the implications of the destination.

"*Something* masked the statue, the meadow," he said.

"But how?"

Calebros did not know. Theoretically it might be possible, of course, but the magnitude of power that would be required to pull it off…. There was more than the Eye at work here. That was Calebros's belief. That was his fear.

"And why have we seen it sometimes but not others?" Ramona asked, still probing, still questioning.

Better to consider the *how* rather than the *what*, Calebros decided. That route was slightly less disconcerting; less terrifying, truth be told. "You have proved able to follow the Eye. You tracked it to the cathedral," he pointed out. "Hesha tracked it to the cave with the aid of his gem. There seem to be ways of finding it…."

"Except for now," Ramona said. "Not since Leopold—"

"Ripped Hesha five new assholes?" said Calebros.

"*Exactly*," Ramona parroted him in return.

"Wherever Leopold and the Eye have gone," Calebros said, "we are unable to find them. It could be that whatever shielded the cave is masking his whereabouts as well."

Other words from Jeremiah's reports came unbidden to Calebros's mind: *The darkness in the earth, hungering for flesh.*

"Only time will tell," Calebros said. *And it may be that we are out of time.*

Saturday, 30 October 1999, 5:12 AM
Crown Plaza Hotel, Midtown Manhattan
New York City, New York

Nickolai stood before the tall, quicksilver mirror, staring incredulously. The murder he had witnessed was not undesirable—in fact, he had ordered it—but the deed had not unfolded as he had anticipated.

He'd had some time to think about it—the temporal dislocation that accompanied the apportation of another individual was far from an exact science—but had arrived at no firm conclusions. The implications of what he'd seen were problematic at best, potentially lethal at worst. He would make damn sure that the worst did not come to pass. Nickolai did not plan to become a victim of his own creation. He was the last of his line; he owed it to those whose banner he alone carried to survive. Yet the vagaries of undeath had time and again been thrown in his face: from the horrendous slaughter at Mexico City, to the transformed lackey he'd rediscovered and bent to his will.

One thing was certain, however. Benito Giovanni was, once and for all, dead.

Nickolai looked to the mirror. Within the circumference of the ornately rune-carved mahogany frame, quicksilver swirled and twisted. The viscous liquid began to take on a shape, and the glass surface, adhering to that shape, began to bubble and bulge. The shape was that of a man. Or what had once been a man.

Leopold stepped slowly from the mirror. His face, torso, and right leg pressed against the outer layer of glass, bowing it into the room. As the quicksilver gradually assumed his visage, the grotesque Eye was the first recognizable detail. While the rest of Leopold was still but a shadow, a hint of his true form, the Eye became real—wiry vessels, like so many gnarled tree roots in the earth, pulsed with blood along the surface of the white. Leopold followed the orb, pushing through the elastic glass until he stood, covered in blood and ichor, before Nickolai.

"You did well, Leopold. *She* will be very pleased."

The Eye watched impassively. Leopold's other eye was wide and wild. He panted like a feral dog, but slowly, each exhalation several seconds after the last, in perfect synchronicity with the pulsing of one of the Eye's vessels. Nickolai approached him carefully. There seemed to be no antagonism from the boy, but after what the warlock had seen…

Leopold's clothes were foul and tattered. Nickolai had long since ceased trying to replace the neonate's garments after pus had seeped from the Eye and encased much of his body. It was all Nickolai could do each evening to chip away the congealing mess that threatened to crust over Leopold's face and other eye. After destroying two ceremonial daggers at the task, Nickolai had resorted to a sturdier hammer and a screwdriver wielded as chisel. There was the occasional slip, of course, but Leopold seemed hardly to notice.

The ragged tears in Leopold's clothes were more recent, and were part of what alarmed Nickolai. The silk cloth wetted with Benito's lifeblood lay beside the mirror. *I won't need his vitae again*, Nickolai thought. He would feast on the remaining liquid in the vial later. A relatively short while ago, he had wetted the cloth and attuned the mirror. The Nosferatu, it seemed, had learned all they needed to know from dear Benito. *All that he could tell them about me*, Nickolai knew. Rather than disposing of the Giovanni properly, however, the sewer dwellers had dumped him unceremoniously in the desert. So the tidying up had fallen to Nickolai—which was just as well, because the warlock desired to test his control over Leopold. The test had met with mixed results.

Benito was dead enough, but Nickolai had not expected to see the neonate fashion his very bones into a scythe and eviscerate Benito, nor to witness the boy's ribs flay the Giovanni and lay him open to the world. But that was exactly what had happened. And now Leopold was back. Nickolai watched him warily. Those strange, fierce manifestations had not been a direct result of any of the warlock's rituals.

But perhaps an indirect result.

For weeks now, Nickolai had been experimenting with, and on, his guest. Nickolai had grown increasingly convinced that something other than the Eye had been at work months ago in the cave. The Eye, formidable as it was, was not capable of carnage and sick creative brilliance on such a grand scale. Something else *had* to have been at work—during the nights of creation, and on the night that Leopold had reclaimed the Eye.

The Eye had played a part, certainly. Nickolai's experiments had confirmed that. The orb seemed to act as a lightning rod for mystic energies. When Nickolai directed a ritual of any sort at it, the Eye quivered, as if at the touch of a lover. The warlock had three tomes of detailed notes and calculations. He was certain. And tonight had been the test: Destroy Benito while Nickolai pumped energy into the Eye, energy that Leopold no longer possessed on his own. Left to himself, the boy was a babbling cretin, rarely managing a complete sentence or thought these nights. Yet with a bit of supernal aid, he was transformed into an atrocity waiting to happen. The manner in which he had dispatched Benito did not correspond to any of the manifestations of the Eye's powers over the past weeks, yet it had happened. It smacked more of the abattoir of the cave. Perhaps residual traces remained of whatever source had driven Leopold to those heights of depravity, and Nickolai's rituals, though directed at the Eye, had tapped into that source. Perhaps. So many question marks, so many unsubstantiated theories.

In this case, however, the practice carried more import than did theory. For Nickolai's enemies would surely come for him soon. Why else dispose of Benito, if they had not learned all that they needed to know?

But it seemed that they had indeed given Nickolai enough time. He might not comprehend the depths of Leopold's potential, of the Eye's potential, but the warlock now had a potent weapon to wield. And with every additional night allowed him, he learned more.

Turning from Leopold, Nickolai pulled back the cover from a tray of utensils both secular and arcane. He chose a large syringe. *A pint should be enough*, he decided, then turned back to Leopold.

"Hold still, my boy," Nickolai said as he raised the syringe to the Eye. "This will only hurt a bit." *Actually, it won't hurt me at all*, he thought, as he plunged the needle into the Eye.

1 November 1999
re: legacy of Anatole

As usual, nothing straightforward about
Prophet of Gehenna; as many
perspectives as individuals involved.

Ramona claims hillside at cave scarred,
ruined—would seem to fit with Xaviar's
account. But neither Hesha nor Jeremiah
able to confirm. In fact, contradictory
accounts.

Two Malkavians in Baltimore destroyed
after looking at pictures (barely!),
yet others of us unscathed. Clan-
specific response?

↳ Sturbridge might have insight?

Jeremiah still somewhat
troubled after his time with
Anatole.

Saturday, 30 October 1999, 5:37 AM
The underground lake
New York City, New York

"So you're convinced?" Calebros asked.

The distant *plink plink plink* of dripping water sounded almost like thunder amidst the silence of the cavernous chamber. Calebros and Emmett sat by the edge of the lake, the younger of the two recently returned from his sojourn in parts west. Wide, deep-set eyes were accustomed to the dark. Numerous manila folders spread out around them. The slight, pallid illumination given off by the iridescent lichen on the shore rocks and on the walls and ceiling cast the two grotesques in a sickly hue.

"Benito was convinced," Emmett said. "He'd gone to a lot of trouble to find out. So, yeah, I'm convinced. Gary Pennington is, was, Leopold. Anything that Jeremiah said make you think different?"

Calebros shook his head. "According to Anatole, it was the 'young wizard' in Pennington's studio in Chicago, and the 'young wizard' in Leopold's studio in Atlanta."

"*If* you trust Jeremiah."

"I do trust him," Calebros said. "I trust his data. I've studied it closely. The conclusions he suggests…many of them seem warranted."

"He sent you an encyclopedia's worth of *crap*," Emmett grumbled, flipping through one of the closest folders. "I mean, really: 'Anatole begins his sandal rubbing. Four seconds, changes directions. One minute forty-four seconds, changes direction…' What drivel! Jeremiah is off his gourd."

"He was recording the actions of a madman," Calebros insisted. "Why should it seem sane? Regardless, the little we've been able to glean from Anatole seems to confirm what you learned from Benito. Do you disagree?"

"No," Emmett admitted grudgingly. He tossed the folder back down. "I don't disagree. Benito was definitely the man on the ground. He was an accomplice in the murder, but he wasn't the brain. He was used. Just like Pennington, or Leopold or what the hell ever you want to call him, was used. Benito arranged for the sitting, Leopold sculpted—"

"But did Victoria Embrace him before or after he changed his identity and moved to Atlanta? Surely, as prominent as she is, if she'd been involved we would have come across her name before now."

"There's a lot we didn't come across until now," Emmett said.

"Could she have Embraced him after the fact, after he'd fled, and she didn't know?"

"Don't know." Emmett shrugged. "We should check with Rolph again. He should have had an inkling that Leopold was Victoria's childe."

Calebros was about to comment on that, but stopped. He cocked his head.

Emmett heard the telltale sound also. "Was that your freaking back popping or something?"

"No."

The two broodmates eased silently from their seats among the rocks. They zeroed in on the origin of the faint scraping sound—the tunnel, the one down from Calebros's office. They edged closer. The sound was growing louder. Someone was scrabbling down to the lake. Emmett drew his claws back, ready to strike. Calebros picked up a rock that more than filled his hand.

Whoever it was coming down the tunnel was sliding feet first. The shoes appeared first from the darkness—saddle shoes, scuffed, torn, and worn within an inch of their lives, if not beyond. Then the bobby socks, the elastic long since gone slack, fallen down around puffy swollen ankles. The legs were hairy and white, all loose skin and sagging collections of fat. Because of the slide down the tunnel, the poodle skirt and its crinoline had ridden inside out above her waist. Calebros and Emmett profoundly wished that she'd felt the need for undergarments. Hilda scooted the rest of the way from the tunnel and landed on her more than ample posterior with a graceless *flump*.

"Look at you two," she said, flashing them an almost toothless grin. "I thought I might find you down here."

Calebros and Emmett stared at her, both speechless. Emmett lowered his hand, his claws melting back to fingers. Calebros dropped his rock.

Hilda struggled to her feet. "No, no, don't mind me. I can get up by myself," she said as she straightened her torn petticoat and threadbare skirt. "Care for some skinny dipping?" she asked, eyeing the lake.

As Calebros watched her, he had second thoughts about having dropped his rock. This creature had been nothing but grief since she'd arrived bearing the parcel from Rolph. Calebros found his tongue, just barely. "How...?"

"It seemed to me," Hilda said cheerfully, "that there just had to be something behind the bookshelf. Don't know why. Just call it a gift."

"You," Emmett said coldly, "are not welcome here, woman—and I do use that term loosely."

Hilda sidled up to him, raising her eyebrows in a way that made her jowls sway, and firmly grabbed his crotch. "You boys get so grumpy when you've got nobody to wax your beanpole." Emmett pulled away. "Hmm? No like the señorita? That why you two sneak off down here...*together*? Don't know what you're missing." She cupped her hands under her breasts and lifted them above where they sagged at her belt.

Emmett was not amused. "How did you *fit* down that tunnel, you fat heap of—"

"Hilda," Calebros interceded lest events grow too heated. "What Emmett is trying to say—"

"I'm not *trying* to say anything," Emmett said.

"What I *am* saying is—"

"Have you ever heard of London Tommy?" Hilda asked, her flippant manner suddenly turned cold. The raw threat in her voice chilled Calebros. "London Tommy was rude to me too."

"Up yours, you fat fucking whore."

"Emmett!" Calebros gestured for silence. "Hilda!" He did the same to her as she opened her mouth again. The two names, intertwined, echoed through the chamber. "Hilda," he said again more quietly and calmly. "This is a...private place for me. I come here usually for solitude, to be alone with my thoughts; sometimes to speak of important matters with Emmett. Generally, I prefer to—"

"To keep out the fat fucking whores."

"I know where I'm not wanted!"

"Oh? Coulda fooled me! What gave it away?"

Calebros's head was reeling as he felt the situation spinning horribly out of control. He was no good at this. Confrontation with strangers left him feeling weak, although Emmett seemed to make up doubly for the shortcoming. "Both of you, *stop*!"

A tense silence fell over the cavern. "Would you leave us please, Hilda?" Calebros asked.

"That's all you had to say," she sneered at Emmett. "I just wanted to see how you was coming with that ugly thing Rolph had me bring up."

"It's a worthless hunk of shit," Emmett said, smiling, "so thank you very much."

She glared, but Calebros stepped between them to avert further contention and possible bloodshed. "I would prefer," he said pointedly, "that you not mention this chamber or the passages leading to it to members of the warren. The few that know about it know enough to stay away. Can you agree to that, Hilda?" She was still glaring at Emmett over Calebros's shoulder. "Otherwise, I will be forced to see that you return to Atlanta at once."

That got her attention. "I like it well enough here," she said. "I'll not be telling anybody."

"Thank you. And now, if you would…" He gestured toward the way she'd come.

She paused long enough to spit once before crawling sullenly back into the tunnel, a sight from which both Calebros and Emmett averted their eyes.

"It doesn't do any good to provoke her, Emmett."

"Nothing else does any good either."

Calebros couldn't argue with that. Hilda was, in many ways, as repugnant as they came, but she was of the blood, and thus he felt obliged to provide her shelter. Over the years, he had winnowed away the more offensive elements in the warren—the child molesters, the uncontrollable killers and sociopaths, those who were likely to draw unwanted attention to the warren and thereby endanger all who resided there. Hilda might at some point require winnowing herself.

"She did bring this…." Calebros said, pulling from the folds of his cloak a Ziploc bag containing the pieces of a broken clay model and a photograph. "And, contrary to popular belief, it is not 'a worthless hunk of shit'."

Emmett shrugged. "Poetic license. So sue me. Besides, Rolph could have mailed it. He just wanted to get rid of her—for obvious reasons."

"Mail it?" Calebros said. "Would you entrust proof of Petrodon's murder to the U.S. mail?"

Saturday, 13 November 1999, 1:41 AM
The International, Ltd., Water Street
New York City, New York

"I should've gone," Theo Bell said. Injured or not, he wasn't pleased about being left behind while a battle with the Sabbat was going on in the Bronx.

"I need you here," Jan Pieterzoon said. "Pascek could run into trouble on Staten Island. Something could *easily* come out of the woodwork in Brooklyn...."

"Yeah, I hear you," Theo said. It was all true, he guessed, but he refused to be happy about it. "You're the general."

Jan moved closer to the archon, so that his words would not be overheard by the other Kindred and ghouls in the room. "We both know that you could have gone...that you *would* have gone, whether I asked you to or not—if you felt up to it. But something beat the hell out of you, and you need the rest." The words didn't do anything to sooth Theo, but the archon didn't argue. "No one's seen it tonight."

"Nobody that survived," Theo said.

"Perhaps. There've been no reports at least. The Eye thing—are you sure it was the same thing...Xaviar's Antediluvian?"

"It was the same thing Sturbridge brought the picture of, if that's what you mean. We both know it ain't no Antediluvian, but there's gonna be trouble if it shows up again."

"Mr. Pieterzoon?" Hans van Pel called from one of the desks in the office. He held a new report in his hand. Jan went to examine it, leaving Theo to brood in peace.

He needed more blood. Theo knew that much. The little bit he'd had, both last night after the fight and earlier tonight, hadn't seemed to do much good. He felt some of his strength returning, but the burns from the acid, or whatever it was that spewed from that fucking Eye, hadn't healed, hadn't even started to scab over. He just needed more blood. That's what he hoped, but he had a bad feeling about all of this. And that only made him more irritated that he hadn't gone with Federico or that wet-behind-the-ears Mitchell.

Theo almost didn't notice the boy who slipped in the door except that the youth was so obviously looking for someone he couldn't find. He looked to be about fifteen years old, but Theo could tell he was Kindred, so looks didn't really mean much. "Who you need, kid?"

The boy seemed surprised that anyone had bothered to address him. "Archon diPadua," he said. He was holding a folded piece of paper.

"He's gone and not gonna be back anytime soon. I'm Archon Bell. I'll take your message."

The boy hesitated, obviously uncomfortable with the suggestion, but also obviously uncomfortable with refusing an archon. He handed Theo the paper and slipped quickly back out the door. Theo opened the note and skimmed it. "Hey, Jan."

Pieterzoon left was he was doing and took the proffered note. He read it quickly, looked up at Theo, then back to the note and read it a second time, aloud: "Federico: News from Ruhadze. Eye is back. East Village. Little Ukraine." And that was all. "Who brought this?" Jan asked, handing the paper back to Theo.

"Some kid. Kindred, though."

Jan nodded. "He's been in and out with notes for the archon all night."

Theo crumbled the paper. It had blood on it from one of his wounds that wouldn't close. "If I got burned all to shit because of some deal Lucinde made with that Setite…"

Jan looked around nervously and gestured for Theo to keep his voice down. "She's agreed to let Ruhadze have it…if he can *get* it. Apparently he's been after it for a long time. We had no idea it would show up here in New York. *I* had no idea," Jan emphasized.

"Well, it's here," Theo said. He raised the crumpled

wad of paper in his hand. "And if Ruhadze can put it on ice, more power to him. But until he does—"

"There's no one else I can send with you," Jan said. "Federico took our reserves. I sent most of our Manhattan teams with Mitchell. Those that aren't with him are north of Central Park. I'll call them back, and some of the squads from Brooklyn."

"You do that," Theo said, unclasping his shotgun from within his tattered jacket and slipping rounds into the magazine. "They can meet me there."

"I'm here to see Sturbridge," the rasping voice said. The hunched wretch leaned heavily against the great portal. The creature's chest heaved in great broken sobs as if it had grown unaccustomed to the effort of drawing breath for any purpose—much less for something as delicate and ephemeral as speech. Its oversized teeth scissored wetly as it spoke with a sound like knives sharpening.

Talbott's face betrayed no hint of the revulsion his guest had come to expect—to rely upon. In his forty-plus years of serving as the gatekeeper for the Chantry of Five Boroughs, Talbott had witnessed more than his fair share of the disturbing, the inexplicable, the macabre. One more disfigured immortal bloodsucker was not about to put him off his game.

"I will see if the lady of the house is available. Please, make yourself at ease." Talbott gestured the newcomer within. "May I assist you with your parcels?"

The Nosferatu clutched more tightly to the overstuffed bundle of loose-leaf paper, photographs and used envelopes peeking out from beneath one arm. The whole was rather ineffectually bound together in fish paper and bakery twine. A small avalanche of handwritten notes, crude sketches and used carbon paper followed closely on his heels as he dragged himself and his burden across the threshold. "No!" he snapped back and then as an afterthought added, "Thank you. No, thank you, Talbott. Your name's Talbott, right? Thought I saw that here somewhere." He began rummaging among various scraps of paper that stuck out of his bundle at odd angles.

"Talbott it is, and kind of you to remember. Who may I say is calling?"

Emmett looked up from his notes, irritated.

"Emmett. She won't know me, though, so you'll have to tell her it's important. Do that, won't you, Talbott?"

"Have no fear on that account. Can I tell her what this is about, Emmett? Regent Sturbridge might ask *why* this is so important."

Emmett seemed to consider. He rifled through the tangle of papers and extracted a particularly grease-smeared specimen. Wiping it off on his pants leg, he held it out for Talbott to take. He gave the gatekeeper a conspiratorial nod.

To his credit, Talbott accepted the scrap unflinchingly. Glancing down at the paper, he saw it bore a crude, childlike drawing—a single, lidless yellow eye.

"I will return shortly. You may take your ease near the central fountain. There is refreshment to be had there as well. Please feel at home. The shadow of the pyramid is long; there is room enough for one more to shelter beneath it."

Emmett, looking more than slightly exasperated by these polite formalities, grunted, turned, and skulked off in the direction of the fountain.

"You must be Emmett." Aisling Sturbridge took her guest by both hands in welcome. Emmett stood, casting a helpless glance back at his parcel of papers still lying open and exposed on the bench near the fountain. Presiding over the scene, the severe Aztec faces carved into the fountain's step pyramid seemed to regard the clutter with mild distaste.

"You're Sturbridge." Emmett stared at her for an interval far too long to be considered polite. "He said I could trust you. Donatello, I mean. He said you helped him out of a jam, that you said he was…" Emmett broke off in discomfort.

Sturbridge suppressed a smile. "Beautiful, perhaps? Yes, I did tell him that. The first time we met. He is very dear to me, Emmett."

"He's an ugly little bugger," Emmett replied gruffly. "But he's all right. And he said you're all right. And that you'd know if anyone would. Calebros said you were the one at the council in Baltimore. And that you brought the sketch—the one with Leopold in it. And the Eye."

Sturbridge let him talk himself out, but she was no more enlightened than when he had begun. "I'll help you if I can. What is it you're trying to find out?"

A look of frustration flitted across his face. "That's what I've been telling you. Leopold, the Eye, the sculpture. I've got the pictures right here." He pointed back at the parcel.

"All right, then. Let's see what you've got."

Emmett held the packet out proudly at arm's length, as if presenting a trophy. Sturbridge took it carefully. The knotted twine unraveled at her touch. Cautiously, she pulled back the fish paper. The photo staring back at her from the top of the pile showed an unhewn cave wall, smeared in an unintelligible jumble of words, symbols and pictograms—all of them drawn in blood.

The photographer had been very thorough. Along the right-hand side of the picture, a yardstick stood to give the viewer a clear indication of scale. The macabre scrawl covered the wall to the height of about ten feet, as well as much of the ceiling above. Sturbridge whistled low, thumbing through the first dozen or so photos. More of the same. One would hardly believe so much blood was in a body.

"What am I looking at here, Emmett?" Sturbridge spread the photographs out upon the floor, slapping them down one at a time, like playing cards. There was a note of alarm in her voice that was picked up and echoed in the sharp flip of each new photo. Two dozen. Three dozen. She had hardly made a dent in the pile.

"That's the cave. The Gangrel, they are calling it the Cave of Lamentations. It's where… What's wrong?"

Sturbridge cursed, her arm checked abruptly midway through its downward swoop. The photo hung in the air like an accusation. She stared at the picture intently as if unable to let it drop. "That's them. This is where Xaviar's warband was massacred. But this? Christ, look at what he's done to them." She set the photo down tentatively, as if further rough handling might heap some new sufferings upon the unfortunates depicted there.

Emmett did not have to look to know which photo she had come across. "Number forty-three. Leopold's masterpiece. Catalog number, time and coordinates are listed on the reverse. That's not the worst of them, I'm afraid. That one's only the first of the long perspective shots on the sculpture. There's some close-ups of the detail work a little later on."

Sturbridge's tone was distant. "It's so vivid. It's as if they were still…"

"Alive? I don't know that I'd call that living. But some of them did stir. And moan. And some of them turned instinctively to the smell of fresh blood. Like sunflowers. You'll see. It's almost as if they're mugging for the camera."

Sturbridge's mind barely registered his words. She had fallen victim to the steady rhythm of the ghastly parade of images, mesmerized. Slide, flip, slap. Slide, flip, slap. She had no choice but to carry the operation through to its inevitable conclusion.

By the time she had finished, there were hundreds of photographs spread out around her like a protective circle. She crouched at the very center of the diagramma, studying each card before her, its placement, its relationship to its neighbors, as if she were attempting some audaciously elaborate Tarot reading.

She sighed, coming back to herself. "Okay, this monstrosity, it's definitely the remains of the Gangrel warband. Someone, presumably this Leopold, *arranged* them there. Within the sculpture. I don't know what to make of this bloody scrawl. It's all nonsense. No, literally. Linguistics isn't my specialty, but you've got at least six distinct alphabets here. Maybe two dozen different languages all jumbled together. And that's not counting the pictographic, numeric and purely abstract elements. I'd say whatever else this Leopold might be, we are dealing with a sharp intellect that has become dangerously, murderously insane."

Emmett nodded, muttering under his breath, "And he's not the only one. But can you decipher it? Any of it? I was kind of hoping that it might be, well, thaumaturgical. I mean, with all the blood, and the sacrificial victims, and the occult symbols…"

Sturbridge shook her head, her fingertips trailing across the rows of photographs. "That's no blood ritual that I've ever seen before. And I do have more than a passing familiarity with that particular field of study."

Emmett was deflated at having the ground cut out from under his pet theory so swiftly. "Nobody's questioning your credentials, lady. If you say it ain't blood magic, that's good enough for me. It ain't blood magic. Any chance it could be Koldunic?"

She took her time about answering. "No, I don't think so. That's one of the things that's been bothering me, though, the whole time I've been flipping through these pictures. This entire macabre scene feels very 'Tzimisce'. At first I thought it was just that damned sculpture. But it's more than that."

She searched out a particular photograph and handed it to Emmett. "This dragon motif, it's repeated over and over again, as if it were chasing its own tail around the cavern. It is depicted several times in the crude drawings. And the word 'dragon' itself appears in at least five or six languages. And it's one of the three major movements in the arrangement of this scrawl."

"What do you mean, 'movements'?"

"As I see it, there are three distinct movements here, like in a musical composition. The dragon is the second of the three patterns running throughout the scrawl. But these patterns are difficult to pick out, much less to keep your grip upon. Look, here." She indicated a photo at her right hand and then proceeded to trace out the writhings of a great wyrm as it coiled its way through the litter of photographs.

"But what does it mean? And what are these other two movements you mentioned?"

"What does it mean? I certainly would not like to hazard anything so precise as a translation. The linguistic elements are a complete jumble. Offhand, I'd say you would be better off approaching these ramblings by way of the drawings. Although I must admit that there seems little enough of substance to go on there either. Let's see what we can piece together."

Emmett noted that she ignored his latter question. Sturbridge stretched and began to gather examples of the crude, fingerpainted artwork. "You've got all your standard apocalyptic trappings—your dragons, lions, eagles, angels, demons, etc. So I would be surprised if your 'text' did not turn out to contain some prophetic announcement heralding the end of times. But then again, the imagistic content is diluted with rather typical cultist elements—your pentagrams, borrowed Tarot imagery, and band logos. It's hard to tell what, if anything, may be significant. Did you think to bring me a sample of the blood? That might take some of the guesswork out of it. The blood harbors very few secrets from us."

Emmett's hand strayed unconsciously to the pocket of his shabby overcoat, as if to reassure himself that the vial he carried was still secure. But he did not produce it for her inspection. "Would it surprise you to learn," he replied, "that the blood—all of it, so far as we can determine—is from a Malkavian?"

Sturbridge looked skeptical. "You're saying this Leopold is a Malkavian? How does a Malkavian do *that*? It's hard to credit. At the council meeting in Baltimore, Victoria Ash claimed that Leopold was a Toreador of her acquaintance from Atlanta."

Emmett snorted. "How does a *Toreador* do that? So where does that leave us? It looks like we're right back at square one. You've already shot down my best guess—that he was a Tremere. No offense. What about these other two patterns? These movements?"

Again, Sturbridge looked distracted. "None taken," she muttered after a while. "Actually, that was one of the other things that was bothering me."

"How do you mean?"

"I told you this wasn't a thaumaturgical ritual. But just because it's not blood magic does not mean that it has nothing to do with the Tremere. It's those three movements again. The first one is the Eye. That's what started all this. Musically, the Eye is the prelude to the entire composition. It's what empowers Leopold to massacre the Gangrel. The Eye is what pushes Xaviar over the edge and nudges the Gangrel out of the Camarilla. It may well be generations before we see the full consequences of all that the Eye has set in motion."

"Assuming we've got generations," Emmett interjected.

Sturbridge let the pause stretch a bit too long for comfort. "In the Egyptian Book of the Dead, the great god Horus is represented by a single unblinking eye. They say the universe exists only by the grace of Horus gazing upon it. Very soon now, he must surely blink and, when that all-seeing eye closes, all of creation will be snuffed out."

"But you said the Eye was only the first movement, the prelude. The end of the universe is going to be a tough act to follow."

Sturbridge smiled, a gesture without warmth. "The second movement is the dragon. It is a continuation of the initial energy, but a variation upon it, a complication. The Eye is devoured by the dragon, but it is not destroyed. Its influence over Leopold has become usurped, corrupted. Now we see the creation of Leopold's masterwork, his altar of living flesh. It is a perversion of the natural rhythms of both life and death. The music here is the stirring of something deep, something ominous, something forbidden."

Emmett was already making connections of his own, drawing out further meanings Sturbridge could not have intended. "But the serpent can't hold onto the Eye, can he?" he said excitedly. "It nearly kills him. It goes back to Leopold. And then Leopold disappears."

"I'm not sure I follow you."

"That's okay. You just keep on doing what you're doing. Movement the third?"

Sturbridge looked uncomfortable. "That's where the Tremere come in. I don't know how much I can expound upon this. The third movement is the *Malum*. The apple. The forbidden fruit. It's the symbol of our temptation and fall from grace—of the price my people had to pay for their immortality. And, in particular, it is the symbol of the one who laid this double-edged gift before the founders. Goratrix."

"Are you telling me that the final theme of this bizarre composition has something to do with the Tremere renegades, the *antitribu*?"

"Look, Emmett. All I'm saying is that I've been to enclaves where the Fallen Ones had performed their dangerous travesty of the initiation rites. And those places didn't have half the ritual trappings of House Goratrix that these cave paintings of yours have."

"Shit. I thought those bastards were all…gone."

Sturbridge regarded him levelly. "So did I."

Emmett was talking to himself now. "So the worm devours the Eye and the apple devours the worm. Well, what could they do with it? I mean, if House Goratrix got hold of the Eye, or if they got some hold over Leopold, what could they do?"

Sturbridge didn't answer. "We need to find Leopold."

Wednesday, 3 November 1999, 1:30 AM
Morehead Park, Brooklyn
New York City, New York

Hesha found Ramona on the park bench—the same park bench where Pauline had waited for the Gangrel just over two months ago. He noted that she was wearing the boots he and Calebros had insisted upon.

Smart girl.

She was defiant at times—most times—but not so much as to be stupid. She could be reasoned with, and she had proven quite useful thus far. Hesha doubted that he would ever have been likely to wring the *correct* knowledge of how to cure the Eye wounds from her former Ravnos companion. Ramona seemed to have some second sight where the Eye was involved, as well. She'd been reluctant to describe or explain it to him, but she had found the cave. She'd seen it from the helicopter when Hesha hadn't, despite the fact that he'd been there before and they'd been following his own directions, which should have been completely reliable.

"Any luck?" she asked when she saw him.

"With the gem? No. Still no sign."

"What about in Baltimore?"

"My meeting with the Malkavians was…interesting, but they were not able to tell me anything conclusive about the pictures." *My dealings with Lucinde were far more fruitful,* he thought, but there was no need to burden Ramona with such details.

"So we just keep doing nothing," Ramona grumbled. Her index finger, a long and lethal claw, was digging troughs into the park bench.

"We keep waiting," Hesha said. "The last we know of the Eye it was in the city—"

"Man!" Ramona slapped her legs. "If you coulda just held onto the damn thing…"

"Indeed. I would have preferred that myself. It would have saved me a great deal of discomfort."

"No shit."

"As you say. At any rate, here is where I can be reached." He handed her a card. "Since you are less easily contacted on short notice, I suggest you check in with me regularly. A phone call will suffice. And if you do not mind…" he produced a pager from his overcoat pocket and handed the device to her.

Ramona took it. "Probably a good idea." She glanced again at his card. "You not staying down below anymore?"

"I have made other arrangements, though I am in constant contact with Calebros as well," he said. *The creature knows too much to abandon. He, too, is useful.*

Thursday, 4 November 1999, 3:51 AM
A subterranean grotto
New York City, New York

The storm is coming, he tells me, Calebros thought. *Although this city has roiled for years with clashes of Sabbat and Camarilla under cover of darkness, all this has been as nothing compared to the firestorm that approaches.* The remaining power of the East Coast Camarilla, rather than drowning, would fling itself against the rocks. Pieterzoon and Bell would attempt to capture this greatest of cities, which both sects claimed. Generally the Sabbat held sway above ground, except in the heart of Manhattan, home to the Ventrue elite. The streets and most of the city however were Sabbat, if anything. Though the war to the south had drawn much of the riffraff, and the city was safer now than it had long been.

That is how they might win, Calebros's guest had said. *Pieterzoon and Bell might carry the night. It would be a close thing. And soon.* That much Cock Robin knew for certain.

Exactly *how* the Nosferatu justicar knew, Calebros could not say, and it was not his place to ask. But Cock Robin's news was not so different from rumblings Calebros had been receiving from sources both in Baltimore and here. Where his reports had produced merely guesstimates and possibilities, however, Cock Robin spoke of firm dates and times. The justicar brought other news as well.

He leaned close to Calebros and spoke, hardly above a whisper. *"Vitel…gk-girik…destroyed."* Cock Robin's head was stretched and twisted, his pale lips irreversibly puckered and broken by clefts. He uttered words only with self-conscious difficulty, and that he chose to speak to Calebros at all was a badge of honor for the warren chief.

Vitel. Destroyed. Calebros nodded. He knew better than to look the justicar in the eye. Cock Robin was intensely sensitive, even among his own, and prone to violence. Calebros had seen what became of those who angered him, and did not wish to follow in those footsteps.

They had sniffed out the rat, and it was Vitel. Calebros knew many of the details—Colchester had been instrumental in discovering the traitor; Colchester was also a prolific source of information for Calebros—but he had not known that the deed had been done. "Last night?" It had to have been, or he would have known already. Cock Robin nodded. "Who?"

"*Bell. Piet-gk-gk-zoon.*"

Bell and Pieterzoon. Mostly Bell, no doubt. He was a bruiser, but not just a brute. If Colchester had ferreted Vitel out and Pieterzoon set him up, it would have been Bell who'd pulled the trigger.

Despite the wealth of information the justicar brought with him, he was not there as a messenger. It was news of Calebros's that had brought Cock Robin to the city, coincidentally with the Camarilla-Sabbat conflagration that was soon to erupt. "*Pet-gk-gk-don?*"

"Yes," Calebros said. "We have learned of three Kindred that were involved. One has been dealt with. A Giovanni. He will spread word among his clan and serve as a warning. We believe him to have been but a dupe. The second, Leopold, is more complicated. We are watching for him. He should lead us to the third, a Tremere. It seems this Leopold may have been kine still at the time. He was deceived as well, but he cannot be suffered to survive at this point; he's drawn too much attention."

There may have been a fourth, Calebros did not say. He did not have sufficient proof yet, even though Victoria was Leopold's sire, and to mention her to Cock Robin in this context would be tantamount to a sentence of Final Death.

"*Pet-ro-girik-gk-don…revenge.*" The justicar place a hand on Calebros's forearm and squeezed, hardly able to contain his anticipation. The final word, *revenge*, was so clearly spoken and with such intense satisfaction that a chill ran down Calebros's crooked spine. He prayed that the occasion never arose in which he might incite his justicar's displeasure.

Wednesday, 10 November 1999, 8:45 PM
Aqueduct Racetrack, Ozone Park, Queens
New York City, New York

Federico diPadua, the Right Hand of the Camarilla and archon of Clan Nosferatu, sat quietly among his fellow Kindred. Plans were laid, the time for talking had passed—at least for him.

For most of the others as well, but not for Justicar Pascek. The Brujah fancied himself an orator, an inspiring leader of men. *Demagogue* was closer to the truth. Pascek dominated any gathering to which he was a party; such overbearing and boorish behavior validated his innate sense of omnipotence. Not that the man was unable—far from it. Much of his high regard for himself was justified, yet his shortcomings were glaring. Not that anyone would ever say as much. He operated amidst a veil of secrecy, not because deception was at times necessary, but because he enjoyed knowing what others did not, and he enjoyed even more using that advantage to entangle those around him within his vile, paranoid fantasies.

Federico knew the value of secrets; he recognized their utility, but they held no titillation for him. As the evening unfolded and Pascek spoke of what had passed and what was to come, the Nosferatu grew increasingly appalled at the misuse of secrecy. Some had been necessary, of course, but, he wondered, how much?

Michaela, prince of New York, and no darling of the justicars or, Federico gathered, the Inner Circle, obviously had had no previous idea of the scope of the storm descending upon her. Yes, she had agreed to allow the ragtag refugees from the South to flee to her city, and she would use them to press her claim and bolster her title. Unbeknownst to her, this agreement had been but a plan within a plan.

She, along with Pieterzoon and Bell, architects of the northern exodus, had been unaware of the preparations undertaken by Pascek, Lucinde, Cock Robin, and Lady Anne of London, among others. For over a year, detailed information had been gathered concerning hundreds of Sabbat in the New York area, and agents loyal to the Camarilla, Kindred, ghoul, and kine, had been surreptitiously introduced into the city. The Pieterzoon-Bell plan, purely a result of Sabbat aggression, dove-tailed nicely—and in Federico's mind, too coincidentally—with the pre-existing arrangements, and so Pascek and the others had co-opted Archon Bell and the scion of Hardestadt the Elder.

Pieterzoon had not known the full story until quite recently, and later in the evening, when Theo Bell had arrived, he had been fairly disgruntled as well. Although in all fairness, with Bell it was not often possible to discern the source of his disgruntlement; that disposition seemed his natural bent.

As Pascek orated, presenting details and assignments like Prometheus bestowing fire upon humankind, and the extent of the deception became increasingly clear, Pieterzoon's unease grew, as did Bell's irritation. To their credit, each held his peace. A public forum would be *the* absolute worst place to cross Pascek, especially for his own archon.

Lucinde held her peace as well, though she was in on the entirety of the scheme from the start. Pascek's demagoguery was not her style; hers was to appear meek and inoffensive, to allow others to underestimate her. Like Federico, she did her best work away from the spectacle of public attention.

And so Pascek commanded, and Federico watched and waited. He had high expectations—for the battle that was now unfolding, and for the other, more personal drama that was playing out beneath the streets. For it was Federico's own early investigation into the destruction of Petrodon, an investigation handed over to Calebros over a year ago, that was now bearing fruit. The plan within a plan within a plan.

Nickolai could feel them coming for him. Something about the air, even here in the air-conditioned hotel suite, was different. Before the first commercial break of the late local news, his worst fears were confirmed. Gas mains had burst. There was an industrial accident by the East River; bridges and riverside parkways were closed. The Busey Building in the Bronx was scheduled for demolition tonight, so streets were closed. The charges had not been set precisely, and a huge dust cloud had billowed forth, obscuring visibility and creating a public health hazard; citizens within half a mile were ordered to stay inside.

They know, Nickolai thought grimly. *Tonight it will end, or tomorrow night, or the night after. But soon.*

"Is she here?" the voice asked expectantly from the next room.

It was not what Nickolai expected from Leopold these nights. The warlock expected nothing, in fact, other than catatonic stupor. That was what the boy was reduced to. Never much of a conversationalist since the Eye had burrowed into his skull, Leopold had left Nickolai completely to himself—and to his daytime dreams of the Children.

Nickolai poked his head into the bedroom. Leopold was staring at him, eye and Eye. The boy sat at the table, as always, and it, like much of the room, was almost totally encased by the thickening, murky vitriol that oozed constantly from the Eye.

"Is she here?" he asked again. "You said soon."

Nickolai had told him often that *she* would be back soon, the Muse for whom the boy longed. The lie had been required less often recently, as Leopold slipped further and further from reality. But what had roused the boy from his silent vigil tonight?

"She is not…" Nickolai began, but paused. "She is not here with us, but she is in the city."

"Of course." Leopold smiled. Clear ichor dribbled from the Eye down his cheek, a few drops into his mouth. "Soon…"

The time had come, the warlock decided. "I am afraid, Leopold, that there are those who would harm her. If they find her, they will destroy her, and we will see her no more."

The words had instant effect on Leopold. Eye and eye grew wide, a disturbing sight, and a pained expression contorted his features. He tilted his head, as if the Eye were suddenly too heavy to bear upright. "They…they *mustn't*…" he stammered. "They look…I find…"

"I think you are right," Nickolai said. He had long considered this option, but had not been able to bring himself to accept it. Not until this moment. There was so much, he was positive, that he could learn of the Eye, so much he could still do. But his experiments thus far had been productive, and if he did not act, he risked losing that knowledge, never using it. And it was possible, he told himself, that Leopold had exhausted his usefulness. His deterioration was rapidly accelerating. *Best to use what I know for the greater good—for my greater good.*

Leopold stretched and writhed in his chair. Veins both above and beneath the surface of the Eye bulged, and the discharge grew heavier and increasingly frothy, churned by the boy's agitation.

"I think you are right," Nickolai said again. "They crawl beneath the streets, these people that would harm her. You must protect her. Give me just a few minutes so that I can aid you."

Leopold seemed disinclined toward patience, but Nickolai turned away confident that he would be obeyed. Blood listened to blood. The ritual did not take overly long to prepare. Nickolai had sent Leopold before and had also, the warlock hoped, perfected the additional rituals he required. The others would sense him, of course, in time. But that, too, might play into his hands. He had died to the world once, twice really, and that would have been sufficient had he not run afoul of the hideous justicar. Perhaps one more death would suffice.

"Ramona!" Hesha hissed.

She was furious, pulling against him. Her clawed feet dug into the pavement as she tried to push off. She was growling, snarling at him, but she couldn't get her arm free of his iron grip. Finally she turned to strike him. His firm gaze caught hers, *held* hers. He wouldn't let her look away.

"Ramona!" he whispered harshly. "If you do not stop, you will *fail your elders*. Their blood will remain on your hands."

She felt her own hand raised, claws extended, ready to slash into him, to take off his head...but he was calm. He didn't flinch or back away. Gradually, she regained control. She lowered her hand. Hesha let go of her other arm.

"That was him," he said.

"Fuck yes, that was him!"

Hesha had paged her hours ago. She'd gotten on the phone, quickly, and called the number he'd given her. Some woman named Janet had answered. "Mr. Ruhadze requests your presence right away." That was the code they'd agreed on, so they wouldn't have to mention anything over the phone. At first Hesha had told her it would be *demands your presence*, but she'd told him to piss off. So *requests* it had been. Janet had given her the address and directions.

"The Eye?" Ramona had said as soon as she saw him.

"Yes. The gem, it came to life again." Hesha never seemed excited, but he'd been speaking very quickly, walking quickly. "It points us in the right direction, but we still have to find him." He was decked out in black, reinforced leather pants and jacket over a turtleneck, complete with binoculars, hip holster, and whatever else he had in that little backpack of his.

Found Leopold they had—and they'd watched him annihilate two Kindred. Watched and done *nothing*. The setting was completely different this time, but what Ramona saw was eerily familiar. She felt the onset of the ghostsight that Edward Blackfeather had imparted to her what seemed so long ago. She saw Leopold pull the Eye from its socket and hold it aloft. She saw, too, a writhing, serpent-like nerve stretch and grow down from the Eye, until it touched the ground and bore a hole into the pavement. Ramona knew this sight was for her alone—Hesha could not see it, the two Kindred could not see it. Both Eye and nerve pulsed red as blood.

And then the sidewalk fell away beneath the two doomed Kindred. They fell, and there was the sickening hiss of molten rock claiming more victims.

"*Ramona!*" Hesha had hissed in her ear, holding her arm.

She hadn't thought about attacking, she'd just set out to do it. She could do nothing else. She couldn't stand by and watch that thing destroy more of her kind. In the back of her mind, she heard the accusing whispers of her dead. But Hesha had kept her from it.

"You must be patient," he said. "Or you'll end up like…"

"I know, I know." She wanted to feel Leopold's flesh and the meat of the Eye shredded between her claws. "But we just let him go…."

Hesha tried to console her. He was so damned practical and reasonable it made her want to scream. He asked her questions about what she'd seen. She told him. But her mind was playing what *should* have happened: her spilling Leopold's guts on the street, her claws shredding the fucking Eye.

"Come on," Hesha said. She let him lead her away. "We'll find him again. You'll have your chance." Neither one of them spoke for several blocks. Ramona was lost amidst her revenge fantasies, and Hesha was making his plans. "Besides," he said at last, "there's a different way we have to go about it."

Thursday, 11 November 1999, 4:20 AM
Chantry of the Five Boroughs
New York City, New York

There. The blood ran thick and speckled with dark corruption.

Aisling Sturbridge reached out a hand and touched Johanus. He must see, must taste. They all must. For ten nights now they had searched, since the Nosferatu had brought to them the words and the pictures.

Last words spoken by a lunatic, words describing Sturbridge's own dreams: *The last of the light...it fades...high above, far, far away.... The Final Night. Walls too slick...can't climb...surrounded by bulging eyes, blank, bloated faces.*

Words of prophecy, spurred by Malkav's childer, a fortress impregnable until the gates are lowered from within: *The Children down the Well...they point the way.... The Children fear their shadow, but the shadow fades with the last of the light.... The Final Night.*

The lifeblood of the city flowed in the streets and rivers. The veins were laid open to Sturbridge, to her adepts and acolytes. Johanus, her Pillar of Fire, saw and understood. He would not let his regent forge ahead too recklessly. They could ill afford to lose her, not with the chantry depleted through treachery and through duty. The traitors were but ash, but they had weakened the body. Sturbridge had sent away, too, Helena and her jackals to answer the pleas of the Camarilla. But more insidious enemies lurked amidst the blood. Blood of her blood.

Sturbridge had long ago suspected that the city's heart had blackened, yet the lifeblood flowed. For she who knew where to look, the signs were evident, the arteries dripping corruption, hardening, calcifying like so many of the pock-marked edifices of the cityscape. The capering insects feasted upon the blood, scuttled along the arteries, beaten back only to return in force, preyers upon carrion. Sturbridge swatted them away; they did not concern her at the moment.

The corruption amidst the blood—she could see it, taste it. Johanus understood; he would see that the others did. They were so tender of years, as guileless as any of the blood could be. Sturbridge must offer them guidance, while they lent her the vitality of their youth. The blood must boil.

There. The blood ran thick and speckled with dark corruption. She would trace the black trickle and, in time, sever the leprous vein.

Thursday, 11 November 1999, 4:58 AM
The warren
New York City, New York

"Are you sure?" Emmett asked, not in the challenging way of a rival, but rather wanting to ensure that, in haste, mistakes were not made.

There was little time for reflection, for weighing of options. The sounds of frenetic activity permeated the entire warren. Calebros had roused himself from his office to be more readily available to answer those questions that could not wait now that the reconquest of the city as well as the Nosferatu's own hunt were both underway in earnest. He had never seen the warren so crowded and busy. Some hangers-on had arrived with the justicar. Other clanmates had come north with the Kindred from Baltimore; Colchester was about somewhere in the confusion. More Nosferatu, those who had not flown but opted to risk the drive or to follow the tunnels, would straggle in over the next few nights, and the numbers would swell further. On top of that, Calebros was constantly receiving and sending messengers to and from other warrens across the city. The war, the hunt—he found himself at the center of all of it.

Calebros placed a reassuring hand on the shoulder of his broodmate. "You have done your part in this. I need you elsewhere now. Federico was hesitant to hand over the reins as well, but it has been for the best."

"I *know* the city," Emmett protested.

"Precisely. And Federico does not, not so well as you. We must devote enough of our people to the battle. The city cannot be lost because of our…distraction. I must attend to the justicar, to the hunt. You take up position near Federico—he will be with Pieterzoon and the others. They know him, they know his face."

"The face he shows them, at least," Emmett said.

"True enough. Keep in touch with him by messengers—take Pug, and Sneeze. They are quick and surefooted. You speak with my voice, Emmett. There is none other of whom I can say that."

"Will Umberto stay with you?" Emmett asked.

"He will stay *here*," Calebros said. "The justicar is hot for blood, and I must needs stay with him."

Emmett glanced over one shoulder and then the other. "I don't envy you that. I know we're not much to look at, but he…he gives me the creeps."

"He is our justicar, and I will serve him as I'm able. You could take Hilda…"

"Up yours."

"I take it that you decline. Very well. Good luck."

Emmett muttered as he trundled away and became merely one among the constant swirl of bodies, "Fat fucking whore."

A few seconds later, Calebros reached into the swirl and stopped one of the bodies. He grabbed Sneeze by the arm. "Emmett just went that way. Go find him." Sneeze nodded and was gone, back into the swirl.

Mike Tundlight approached from the other direction. "Another message from Ruhadze." He handed Calebros a folded sheet of paper and waited.

Calebros scanned the words. "He's lost him. The gem has gone dead. Nothing to do except try again tomorrow night…but he thinks he'll be able to respond more quickly next time."

"If there is a next time," Mike said. "The damned thing could disappear for months again."

Calebros nodded agreement. "Hesha is not one to act hastily. He has chased the Eye for years—but some of us are on a tighter schedule. Any word from Sturbridge?"

"Cass took your message to the chantry," Mike said, irritation evident on his maggot-white face and in his bloodshot eyes. "Seems the regent is too busy to be bothered. But the warlocks assure us that they are concentrating every possible resource on the problem, and they said this Nickolai is in the city."

Calebros let that soak in; it was the most hopeful news he had received in quite a while. "Good," he said. "How did they know? What did they say?"

"The one I spoke to wouldn't go into much detail—no surprise there. It had something to do with Leopold reappearing tonight. That's how they know Nickolai is near, but they didn't seem to know specifically where."

"Or they're not saying," Calebros speculated.

"But why would they—?"

"He's *antitribu*, but if other clans were after one of our blood, wouldn't we want to get to him first?"

"I see," Mike said thoughtfully, then added, "But I thought, according to our sources, all the Tremere turncoats had...disappeared."

"Vanished, yes," said Calebros. "That's far from a definitive conclusion, and there does seem to be at least one on the loose. If we can manage to—"

"Calebros! Calebros!" cried a small, scratchy voice. Pug wove his way through the milling crowd to tug on Calebros's sleeve. "Calebros. Jeremiah—he's missing. I took him some rats, but he wasn't there. I tried to follow his trail, but I lost it."

"You lost it?" That was not what Calebros expected to hear from Pug. The urchin could find anything.

"He's crazy," Mike said. "Gone in body is as good as gone in mind."

Calebros couldn't argue about the first part of that statement, but still he felt a certain responsibility for Jeremiah. Calebros had been the one to send him away with Anatole. *After he asked for the same thing*, he reminded himself. But there was no time for these distractions. And here was Pug....

"Emmett needs you," Calebros said. "I just sent Sneeze after him, that way. You can find Emmett, can't you?"

Pug seemed embarrassed by the rebuke. "But what about Jeremiah?"

"Are you in the habit of questioning your elders, boy?" Mike asked impatiently. "And in a time of war?" Pug shrank back and turned to go.

"No, wait," Calebros said. "He's right." He sighed heavily. "Emmett will have to make do with Sneeze. Pug, take…" Calebros glanced around the crowded chamber to see who exactly was coming and going. Out of the corner of his eye, he saw someone approaching by whom he especially did not want to be bothered at the moment. "…Take Hilda to help you look. Check back by sunrise. That doesn't give you much time at all. Do you understand?"

Pug nodded and then shot off. Calebros watched surreptitiously as the youngster intercepted Hilda and then, after a brief explanation, led her away.

"Might as well throw him to the wolves," Mike said.

"She's all talk," Calebros reassured Mike, and himself. "And Pug is…well, Pug." He couldn't imagine anyone's libido being kindled by the boy. Although Hilda did seem more fervent than choosy.

"I'd best be going," Mike said, looking over Calebros's shoulder.

Calebros turned and saw Cock Robin making his way across the chamber. Amidst the noise and chaos, a path cleared for the justicar as he marched limpingly along. "Understood," said Calebros.

Cock Robin came very close; he pulled on Calebros's sleeve so that the warren chief would lean down. The justicar whispered unnerving clicking and choking sounds in Calebros's ear.

"Yes," Calebros said, "we will be ready should the opportunity present itself. But I must warn you, the Eye seems to be the only link we have, and it has disappeared before and not reappeared for—"

"*Gk-gk-gk-girik-gk!*" Cock Robin raised a claw to silence Calebros. The justicar wanted nothing of excuses.

"I understand," Calebros said, and he did understand, only too well. It had been his success thus far that had brought the justicar here. There was to be continued success. The justicar expected nothing less. "I understand."

Thursday, 11 November 1999, 8:15 PM
Haubern Estate
Chicago, Illinois

Warm bloodwine. A tad too sweet, but with enough of a bite to be pleasing nonetheless. Victoria sipped leisurely. Unlife was more orderly, less surprising, here in the Midwest. There were all the schemes, of course, the slights remembered for hours or decades, and to be sure, the lupines lurked beyond the city gates—but that was all *out there.* Victoria was in here, safe if not content. For the many weeks now since she'd first arrived, she'd had very little contact with anyone beyond the household; she'd done little but sit and think and brood.

"You'll give yourself wrinkles if you're not careful," Dickie had warned her.

"If I give myself wrinkles tonight," she'd said, "they'll be gone tomorrow night." Dickie had tittered at that. *He's such a fop,* Victoria had thought. *But any port in a storm, and all that...*

Dickie Haubern, of the Chicago Hauberns. Publishing, investing, industry, race horses; more recently insider trading, industrial espionage, counterfeiting, extortion, pornography, prostitution, drugs. He was the black sheep of the family, and it seemed unlikely the family would survive him. He had cornered the market, so to speak, on Hauberns three generations back by disposing of all rival inheritors, and since then had cultivated a single, mildly incestuous branch of the family so that the estate could be passed along legitimately every fifty years or so. All that aside, he was a dear.

He had welcomed her into his household, no questions asked, when she had arrived on his doorstep unannounced. Politics and warfare bored him. Atlanta, Baltimore—he claimed he wouldn't even be able to find them on a map. "Why bother with other Kindred at all, except to keep them at an arm's length, or several arms'?"

he would say. "Clan and sect rivalries be damned. It's the kine we're put here to enjoy, to oversee, to—"

"To dominate, pimp, and live off?" Victoria suggested.

"Don't forget violate. A good violation cannot be overestimated."

His renunciation of Kindred society was, of course, a bold-faced lie. Dickie was a brutal player of the game if his interests were threatened, or if he stood to gain at someone else's expense. But he was sweet and convivial, and he favored Victoria. Always had.

"Victoria," he called to her as she sipped her warm bloodwine. "Victoria, I just received a call from Robert. I'm afraid the old boy is not at all well."

"Robert?"

"Robert Gainesmil," Dickie said, rolling his eyes. "He had to move. Infestation."

"Really? Termites?"

"No. Sabbat. They ate his staff, burned the house down. Poor Langford."

The bloodwine suddenly went cold on Victoria's tongue. "The Sabbat, in Baltimore? In the city?"

"Oh, yes. Hasn't Alyssa brought you today's paper? Honestly, I don't know why I keep her around."

"I think because she's your cousin."

"Cousin. Is that what I told you? Cousin, niece…it all gets so complicated and tiresome after a generation or two." He wandered off in search of the newspaper, leaving Victoria to ponder Gainesmil's fate and that of the Camarilla.

Is it over? she wondered. *Has the Sabbat taken it all?* Or could this be Dickie's idea of humor? He returned shortly with the paper.

"Did you tell Robert I was here?" Victoria asked.

"Of course not, dearest. I never so much as mentioned your name. I gave you my word, and my word is my bond."

"Oh, please don't make me gag, Dickie."

"Well, all right. I might have mentioned your name in passing."

"Dickie…"

"Very well. I told him that you were here…and when you arrived…and that you were terribly unhappy and distracted, and that he should come visit, and we'd all have a fine time." He sighed. "I am such a horrible liar."

"You are a casual and habitual liar, Dickie, which is not at all the same thing. And quite practiced, I might add."

"You say the sweetest things."

He had brought two papers, the *Chicago Tribune* and the *New York Times*. The *Tribune* had a front-page article, below the fold, on an industrial accident in New York City, an explosion and a spill into the East River. The *Times* had a large feature about the accident, as well as a great deal of coverage of other "natural" civic disasters: a subway accident, a botched demolition…. Victoria could imagine the rest. Buried in the paper was also a story on the spate of fires that had swept through various portions of Baltimore, which would be what Gainesmil was talking about.

"Where did Robert call from?" Victoria asked.

"New York," said Dickie. "I hear it's quite the place to be."

"What do you mean?"

"Well, it seems all your friends from Baltimore abandoned ship…. Oh, wait. The ship was already blown up, wasn't it? Along with that brute Garlotte. Anyway, they gave the city up, and while the Sabbat's back was turned, waltzed into New York. Although Robert doesn't make it sound that inviting—lots of fighting, killing, Brujah field day. Robert says none of the important Gangrel are helping, but I say good riddance; they're only half a step up from lupines…."

While Dickie regaled her with his view of current events, Victoria's thoughts wandered. The fighting was taking place hundreds of miles away. It had nothing to do with her anymore. She had faced down the fiends, had returned to the place of her torture; she'd attempted to find out something useful about Leopold—she had to believe that she'd failed at that. She could not believe otherwise.

And yet, word of the fighting tugged at her. *I am not a warrior that I must rend flesh and bone*, she told herself. What good could she, of all Kindred, do anyone in the midst of the carnage? Her hand rose to her jaw, to the tiny self-engulfing dragon. She had done her part. She had survived.

She thought of her moment of decision on the drive from Atlanta, her attempt to cheat the gods, her *need* to deceive them. Yet she had ignored her own test. If she chose chance as her god, so that no other creature could guide her steps, how could she so profane the deity? That was what ate at her soul and kept peace at bay.

"Victoria!" Dickie said peevishly, "you haven't heard a word I've said."

"Of course I have. You were saying that New York is far too cold this time of year."

"I said no such thing."

"Oh, very well," she said, putting her fingers abashedly to her lips. "I am such a horrible liar."

Dickie tittered. "Well, no wonder you ignore me, when I *bore* you with talk of politics. How many times have I said it? Dull, dull, dull, dull, dull." He took the glass from her hand, took a sip of bloodwine, then returned the glass. "But come, let me show you something you will like."

Victoria followed him. The mansion was beautiful. The exquisite Persian rugs, the elaborate chandeliers that shimmered like ice on a chill winter morning, polished woodwork and sparkling tile—some nights

NOSFERATU

walking amidst the finery improved her mood some-what, and she could forget thoughts of her past...and of her future. This was not one of those nights. Dickie chattered on incessantly, but her mind was churning with disturbing visions of gods and elder powers. Chance would have taken her to Baltimore, and then what—to New York? Yet she was here.

Dickie led her to the parlor, where he pushed open the door with a grand flourish. "My latest triumph," he said.

She stepped past him into the octagonal room. The furnishings were all mahogany and crushed red velvet, but what drew Victoria's attention was a sculpted fig-ure resting on a pedestal in the center of the room. She stepped closer.

The figure was a dancer, one arm raised above her head, the opposite leg bent counter-balancing. Details were minimal. The slight hint of breasts and the gentle curve of hips indicated she was female, but the empha-sis of the piece was the strength of form, the suggestion of fluid movement. Victoria had never seen the sculp-ture before, yet she knew it.

"I knew you'd like it," Dickie, pleased with him-self, said from the doorway.

Victoria laid her fingertips lightly against the stone. It was cold. She recognized the hand of the sculptor. "How...?"

"I lucked upon it, really," Dickie said. "And then I almost lost it to some dreadful Ravnos interloper who thinks he's taken over the city, but I persevered. Some local artist, bankrupt or dead or something like that. You know how it goes. They're selling off his effects, and there were a few wonderful pieces. This was my favorite. It reminded me of you...."

Victoria heard his flattering lie for what it was and laughed. She found that once she had begun laughing, small silent spasms that shook her body, she could not stop. She bit her lip as a blood tear traced the curve of her cheek. "What was his name, this artist?"

Dickie paused for a moment. "Pendleton...or Pennington, or something. You've never heard of him, but he had some simply delightful work."

He was right that Victoria did not recognize that name, but she knew the artist well enough. *The gods mock me*, she thought. *They point to where chance would have taken me and then laugh that I am here instead, here where they would have me.* She wiped the tear from her face. She sighed and covered the indistinct face of the dancer with her own hand, leaving a crimson smear across the white stone.

"Um...Victoria...?"

"Call Robert back," she said without turning to face Dickie. "Tell him to meet me at JFK. He should know which hangar." She would do what she must to regain control of her destiny; she would prostrate herself at the altar of chance and beg forgiveness.

Thursday, 11 November 1999, 8:35 PM
Beneath Brooklyn
New York City, New York

Cock Robin did not enjoy riddles, as Calebros had discovered. It had seemed a simple enough thing: Anatole had left them a riddle; shouldn't they all take a crack at it in hopes that someone might solve it? Perhaps it was because the justicar's emaciated frame made it possible to mistake him for a child—if one did not notice his grossly misshapen head. Whatever the cause, when Calebros had recited the riddle, Cock Robin's crumpled lips had begun to quiver and twitch. His eyes had burned, and he'd made queer warbling sounds, like a frustrated cat separated from its prey. Calebros had apologized. Profusely. And excused himself as quickly as possible.

That had been last night, just before they'd retired for the day. Tonight, Cock Robin had not spoken—to anyone as far as Calebros could tell. But the justicar had made it clear that the hunt would continue. If there were no new leads, they would scour the city. They would check any and every location that had the slightest connection to *any* Tremere *antitribu*. Calebros did not relish nosing into those places, what with the certainty of traps and the unpredictability of sorcery. He would have preferred waiting, watching, planning for the eventuality of Nickolai's discovery.

But it was difficult if not impossible, once the inertial surge of events had begun, to slow them again. Not until they had run their course and the momentum was spent. Cock Robin was not one to be swayed or put off. The hunt was on.

They were a silent band of deformed corpses, a macabre parade routed through the sewers. Cock Robin led them. Some of the others had started calling him "the silent one." They never meant to say it within the justicar's hearing, but Calebros recognized the tendency to confuse mute with deaf. The voices were sometimes a bit too loud, or the speaker not aware of his proximity to Cock Robin. Surely the justicar knew. Perhaps that was but kindling for his burning fury. Calebros had come to wish his elder were completely silent. The warren chief dreaded the whispered comments, the strangled, tattered sounds that were Cock Robin's voice.

Let this be done, and he will go his way, Calebros told himself. *If* it was ever done. *If* they survived the hunt. But whether it was this hunt or the next, or the next, Calebros knew that justice would be done. The Nosferatu did not forget.

Friday, 12 November 1999, 2:39 AM
Crown Plaza Hotel, Midtown Manhattan
New York City, New York

Mustn't make it too easy for them, Nickolai thought.
Toward that end, he had not sent Leopold out tonight.
Not until now. He'd left the boy to his catatonia. Was
the Eye literally eating away at the brain? Nickolai idly
wondered. Such a pity that there was not more time for
study.

Leopold was on the street again. The excursion
south had gone admirably last night. Nickolai had decided upon north for tonight. He'd forced himself to
wait this far into the night. *Must pace myself*, he kept
thinking over and over again. Last night had taken a
great deal out of him, and his stores of blood were not
unlimited. Hunting was not an attractive option, not
with the city fairly crawling with Camarilla. *They're
coming for me*, he knew. *Let them come.* But he had to
pace himself, conserve his strength. He must be ready
for them.

Nickolai looked into the tall mirror and saw
Leopold lurking among the darkness between rows of
dilapidated tenements. The Eye glowed faintly, a malevolent red. Blood red. Leopold looked ghastly; he
looked broken and crazed. All true. Nickolai vaguely
supposed that he should feel some sort of regret or loss
at the degradation of his own blood, his only progeny.
But it had been necessity, not sentiment, that had
driven him to Embrace in the first place. Why should
he experience such emotions now, when he had already, almost two years ago, sent away his childe,
devoid of true identity?

It had seemed the prudent thing to do. After that
doubly cursed, self-important justicar had discovered
that Nickolai, unlike all the others of his line, had survived the catastrophe, the slaughter beneath Mexico
City. If they knew he still existed, if *anyone* knew, then

the demon that had slain his kin would find out and would come for him. Nickolai had been sure of it, and he could not stand the idea of facing that again. The very thought nearly made him tremble. So he had sworn to himself that it must not come to pass.

For such a foul creature, the Nosferatu justicar had retained an incredible streak of vanity. It had been so simple to have Benito—dear Benito, who was always happy to extend any favor that he would be able to call due later—arrange for Petrodon's sitting with the mortal sculptor. And what a stroke of genius to provide a picture of the justicar's former self, so that he might be entranced by the evolving marblescape. Had it ever been completed, the beast would have shat itself in ecstasy.

But it never was completed. Instead, Nickolai had struck down Petrodon, and Benito, again proving himself cursedly resourceful, had fled rather than stay and perish like a good little Giovanni. Once the smuggler's guard was up, he was nigh untouchable, nestled away in the bosom of his infernal family. And if there was no convenient killer to be slain at the hand of the valiant, failing justicar, then the sewer dwellers would search and search and search.

In all of this, the young sculptor was not overlooked. Not by Nickolai, and not for long by Benito. When the Giovanni's assassins arrived to erase their own elder's trail, Pennington was already gone. How better to ensure the kine's loyalty than to bring him into the blood, when even death might not put him beyond the clutches of the Giovanni?

The boy had not taken to the change, alas. He'd longed for his old life, the life that would have been taken from him no matter what, and he certainly showed no affinity for the mystical arts, not back then. Still, he'd had his uses. Scourge his mind of the reality he rejected; instill a new identity with foggy memories of an unremarkable past; send him to a new city.

Benito had heard of him, of course. Talent could not be hidden among the claustrophobic little world of the Kindred. But after the first assassin had failed to return, and the second and the third—for Nickolai had watched over his castoff childe—Benito had understood that the mysterious patron was out there somewhere, and that each move the Giovanni made threatened to uncover the trail that led to him. Better to bide his time.

There matters had stood until Benito had been foolish enough to accept the invitation to Atlanta. He should have known better. Nickolai never should have had to warn him away. But the keepers of secrets had been onto poor Benito by that point anyway, Nickolai supposed. They'd followed the spoor that led from Petrodon to him, and now they'd discovered the trail from him to Nickolai.

Let them come, Nickolai thought. He watched Leopold in the mirror and pulled the brazier closer. The warlock placed a kiln-hardened earthen bowl on the warm metal rim and dipped a golden knife into the bowl. When he removed the knife, a trail of the juices he'd removed from the Eye stretched along behind the blade. He crossed the coals, north to south, east to west, dripping. The coals sputtered and red smoke billowed up, partially obscuring the mirror before him.

Nickolai held the sanctified blade above the smoking coals until he felt the heat coursing through the leather handle, and the skin of his palm beginning to crisp. He raised the knife to his own eye, watching unflinchingly the shapes in the mirror through the billowing smoke. When the first drop of blood struck the coals, the image in the mirror rippled, as if the vitae had landed in the midst of a calm lake of quicksilver. Ripple after ripple after ripple flowed clear and true. And the Eye glowed more fiercely red.

Saturday, 13 November 1999, 1:30 AM
Pine Street, the Financial District, Manhattan
New York City, New York

Emmett listened to what Umberto had to say, then clicked off the phone and tucked it back into his pocket. He was comfortably situated on a second-story limestone ledge of the skyscraper that towered above him. Sneeze sat nearby expectantly. The boy had done well so far—that meaning that he hadn't gotten lost running messages back and forth between Emmett and Archon diPadua several blocks away at the Camarilla temporary headquarters.

Federico had sent his last note just over an hour ago. Seemed Polonia had been spotted in the Bronx, and the Nosferatu archon was running over to Throgs Neck to pull Prince Michaela's bacon out of the fire. That wasn't exactly how Federico had stated it, but Emmett was used to reading between the lines.

At the moment, he was considering what Umberto had just told him: that Hesha had checked in with the news that the Eye was on the prowl again tonight, third night in a row. The only reason Umberto has passed that tidbit along to Emmett was that Calebros was out hunting with Cock Robin, everybody's favorite justicar.

Emmett was well aware of Calebros's deal with Hesha to find the Eye and then turn it over to the Setite, but in Emmett's opinion, Ruhadze could do with a little more backbone. While the snake was stalking Leopold and the damn Eye, the thing was taking out Kindred left and right. It had appeared on the Lower East Side two nights ago and wiped out at least a couple of sorry-ass Brujah. No great loss there. But then last night the thing had gone underground and waxed two Nosferatu and a few more Brujah to boot, including kicking Theo Bell's ass. Pug had come blabbering back to the warren half hysterical.

Emmett had heard enough. He was going to see that something was done about this Leopold freak, and if Hesha didn't like it, that was his tough luck.

In the East Village, Umberto had said. *Little Ukraine*. Emmett scribbled a brief note, folded it, and handed it to Sneeze.

"Take this to Federico," Emmett said. "I *know* he's not there. Don't interrupt me. Go like you're supposed to give it to him, then give it to Pieterzoon. Or better yet, to Bell." Federico's last note had said that the Brujah archon had returned in bad shape from his run-in with the Eye. *I bet he's pissed as all get-out*, Emmett thought. *Good.*

"You want me to *what?*" Ramona asked incredulously, barely remembering to keep her voice down. "Are you out of your fuckin' mind?"

Hesha did not seem surprised by her reaction. He was decked out in what Ramona thought of as his city safari suit: black turtleneck, reinforced leather pants and jacket, holster. He was holding his backpack open between them.

"I know it sounds odd," he said in a perfectly calm and reasonable tone.

"No," she said raising a finger at him. "Living in the sewers, that's *odd*. This…this is just fuckin' stupid. *You* want *me* to attack that Eye with a *leaf*. Have I got it straight?"

"Not the Eye, the nerve. It will work," he insisted.

Ramona peered down into the backpack. "What—you got the demon-possessed-fucking-eyeball instruction book in there?"

"My research—"

"I got a better idea, Mr. Research. How 'bout *you* attack that thing with a palm leaf? How's that sound?"

"I can't *see* the nerve. You can. I'll be diverting its attention. I'll be in more danger than you."

"Who's gonna be closer?" Ramona asked.

"I'll be close—"

"Who's gonna be close-*er?*" They stood silently. Ramona peeked back around the corner. She could see a shambling figure about two blocks away. She recognized his irregular gait. She turned to Hesha. "I don't believe this. You say we'll get the Eye. I go along with it. I help you out. And now you want me to wave broccoli at it. You know, you need me a lot more than I need you."

"It is a palm leaf," Hesha said curtly, his patience thinning. "And we need *each other*, unless of course you'd like to go out there on your own and end up like your clanmates."

Ramona glared at him. Hesha's gaze was just as cold. She held out her hand, not quite believing that she was really doing it. "Give me the leaf." She paused before she slipped around the corner. "If this doesn't work, I'm gonna stuff the biggest chunk of flaming turmeric root you ever seen right up your ass."

"If this doesn't work," Hesha growled, "that will be the least of my worries."

"Hey," Ramona said, pausing at the corner again and peering around, "Leopold must be a popular guy. Looks like we got company."

Saturday, 13 November 1999, 2:12 AM
The International, Ltd., Water Street
New York City, New York

The fog of war. Jan found it maddening. He had marshaled his forces, dispatched them where he thought they were most needed, and now there was only waiting. Battle was raging in the Bronx. House-to-house fighting. It was impossible to keep the police away completely. Even if the Camarilla carried the night, the Masquerade would be at best frayed. And there was no guarantee that they would triumph. As word trickled back, it was becoming evident that Cardinal Polonia was fighting as a Kindred possessed.

Justicar Pascek was engaged to the south as well. There was no way to shift reinforcements from Staten Island. Also, unless Theo Bell could accomplish what had proved beyond an army of Gangrel, the Brujah archon could be fighting his last battle. Jan had hoped, but never expected, to get them this far, but Hardestadt would care little for preliminary successes if tonight turned against them.

"Jan," said a familiar but out-of-place voice, intruding upon his dark thoughts.

He turned to see Victoria Ash for the first time in over two months, since she had left for Atlanta and disappeared. Robert Gainesmil stood behind her. As usual, Jan's first thoughts upon seeing her were of her perfect beauty; but his second thoughts were his suspicions of her time among the Sabbat.

She must have read his face or guessed his thoughts. "Jan, I know you don't trust me, and I don't care," she said sharply. "You can have your Camarilla and your damned war. But Leopold is here, in the city."

Jan nodded. He was unaccustomed to her directness. "In the East Village," he said. "Theo has gone after him."

That was all Victoria wanted to know. She turned on her heels to leave the office, then stopped and turned back to Gainesmil. "Give me the keys."

He did so, somewhat befuddled. "I can drive you," he said.

"I know how to drive," she said. "And what good would you be anyway?" She strode from the office, leaving Gainesmil and Jan in her wake.

Saturday, 13 November 1999, 2:15 AM
East 4th Street, the East Village, Little Ukraine
New York City, New York

Theo walked down the center of the street. He didn't see much point in playing coy, nor did he want to be in an enclosed area with the thing he was after. This was not a lively section of town after dark, even less so after the chaos of the past few nights. Sure, some kine were going to see whatever happened, but what were they going to do—call the cops and say they saw some big, black vampire fighting with some ugly, near-sighted motherfucker?

The street was dark despite the streetlamps. Theo made a note to watch out for the damn lightposts. He wiped a leather sleeve across his face. The burns still hurt. A lot. That was one thing that this Leopold had to answer for. Frankie was another. Lydia and Christoph too. Christoph's head, arm and shoulder were torn up pretty good. Lydia was in worse shape, though. Her face and chest and hands were burned all to hell, and none of the blood Theo had given her had done any good, just like with his own burns.

He felt stronger walking down the street than he had hiding out in that office with Jan. It was the anger, the fire in his belly, that kept the Brujah going. If that wasn't enough, he figured, he was fucked.

As he continued on, he thought about the note that the kid had brought for diPadua. Somebody had been keeping track of Leopold and keeping the Nosferatu informed. Was the note from Hesha himself? Didn't seem quite like his style, Theo thought. Did Lucinde have more to do with this? Jan had said that she'd agreed to let Ruhadze have the Eye. *He's welcome to pick up the pieces*, Theo thought.

When Theo saw the other solitary figure a few blocks ahead, he knew it was Leopold. The way that the bastard carried himself was familiar even at that distance. Theo's burns began to sting and itch more than they had, or maybe he just noticed them more. He quickened his pace and strode purposefully toward his prey. Leopold didn't seem to notice him. Eye or no Eye, Theo would be damned if he was going to sneak up on a fucking *Toreador*. Last night the bastard had caught him off guard. Tonight it was going to be straight up. When Theo got within a block and the figure was still lumbering the other way, the Brujah stuck two fingers in his mouth and whistled.

The creature stopped, and slowly Leopold turned around. His bulging left Eye seemed to cast a faint light on the street.

"Hey, motherfucker," Theo said, cocking his shotgun. "Remember me?" He kept walking closer. Leopold's right hand was a bloody stump, wrapped in rags but not healed.

Apparently Leopold did remember, and remembered what had worked so well last night. Theo heard the moan of metal twisting. He ducked as a streetlight swung just over him. He dropped and rolled and was back on his feet in seconds—just soon enough to leap over the metal post as it swatted at him on the backswing.

"Will—not—harm—her!" Leopold growled

"What the hell are you talking—" but Theo was dodging again from the metal post aimed at his head. He dove closer to the center of the street, out of the reach of streetlights from either side, if they didn't uproot themselves and come charging after him. They were all swinging now, on both sides of the block, like the legs of some giant, overturned beetle.

Theo rolled to his feet again, but before he could get off a shot, the ground was falling away beneath his feet. He leapt at the last second, his feet pushing off pavement that was crumbling to nothing, and landed hard. He squeezed off a quick round from his SPAS 12—

and a flash of white phosphorous exploded against a parked car behind Leopold.

Shit! Theo was diving again, dodging, always moving. More fissures opened, in his path, under his feet. It was everything he could do to avoid being trapped by the earth itself. His lunges kept taking him back into the reach of the flailing streetlights. Every dodge ended in another and another after that. His speed was an advantage, but he could feel his strength draining away. Sure, he needed to avoid Leopold's attacks, but fighting to stay alive wasn't the same as making ground.

He was *not* going to his Final Death fighting a Toreador. He needed to get closer. Close enough to get his hands around that scrawny neck and snap it in two. And he knew, as one of the metal posts struck a glancing blow off his shoulder, that he needed to do it soon.

Ramona had been expecting this Theo Bell guy to get his head handed to him, although Hesha had made it sound like the Brujah was a real hardass. Maybe so. He hadn't even tried to sneak up on Leopold. Just walked up, *intentionally* got Leopold's attention, and then started fighting for his life. He was hanging in there so far, barely getting out of the way of whatever Leopold threw at him, keeping a step ahead, but Ramona could see him starting to slow down, starting to wear out. That wasn't all she could see.

She would have known that he was Kindred even if Hesha hadn't told her, even if the ghostsight hadn't shown her. Bell was too fast to be kine, his movements a blur. He jumped and landed and rolled and got up and jumped again, all so quickly that Ramona had trouble keeping up with him. He got off a second shot that missed. That first shot had almost hit Ramona, who decided to keep behind cover for the moment.

From her hiding place, Ramona saw what no one else could. As she looked on and Theo raced around the street trying to get closer, Leopold plucked the horrid Eye from its socket. He held the orb aloft, not in his hand this time, but atop the bloody stump where his right hand once was. The Eye twitched and throbbed like a living thing. It shone like a blood-red moon. Fizzling ichor welled up upon its surface and dripped hissing to the ground.

Ramona could not tell where her normal sight ended and the ghostsight began. They were seamless. She couldn't distinguish between what was real and what wasn't. But she knew from Hesha that others did not see the orb held high; they saw it still part of Leopold's face. She knew, too, that others didn't see the writhing, snake-like nerve that, even now, was stretching from the back of the Eye, reaching toward the ground and burrowing, pulsating, drawing strength from the earth. She had seen the fibrous nerve in the meadow before the cave as well, when the Eye had destroyed her kinsmen. But now there was no army of Gangrel. There was only her, cowering, and one foolhardy man trying to survive against the Eye. Ramona knew she must strike soon. She had come this far and felt she could force her body no farther. But she must! The man standing against the Eye didn't have much longer. That, too, she could see.

Slowly, painfully, Bell was working his way closer to Leopold, but for every two feet he advanced, he ended up giving back one through his evasions. Every so often, one of the malevolent streetlights caught him, just glancing blows, nothing solid, not yet. But they were starting to hit him more often, and the craters opening in the street were beginning to spread and connect one to another. Footing was rocky and treacherous.

Where's Hesha? Ramona wondered. It didn't matter. She had to strike without him. She had to take advantage of Theo's battle, for soon he would fall.

It happened the moment she thought it. A sheet of pavement rose above Bell like a tidal wave. It blocked the sickly light of the Eye and drowned him in shadow.

The black wave rushed toward him. He fired his shotgun and the flowing wall of asphalt exploded, fragments flying everywhere. He dove, but not quickly enough this time. The remnants of the wave slammed into his legs and sent him spinning. He landed hard, and before he could dodge again, the closest lamp post pummeled him from behind. He slumped to the ground, and the post, instead of rearing back for another blow, wrapped around him, a constrictor engulfing a hard-won meal.

Ramona started to rise from her crouch. She looked at her weapon, the *palm leaf* in her hand, and was again gripped by misgiving and terror. *This is crazy!* she thought. But she could wait no longer, or Theo, like her clansmen, would be lost. She had hesitated on that field of battle, and they had died.

"Leopold!" came the cry, but it was not Ramona's voice. Her head whipped up and she saw Hesha, pistol in hand, out in the street. He fired, and the bullet struck Leopold square in the chest. The bearer of the Eye staggered a step but did not fall. The Eye cast its blood-red gaze upon Hesha.

When the corruption revealed itself this, the third night running, Aisling Sturbridge knew that she would discover the fortress of her enemy. Discovering the fortress and breaching the walls, however, were very different tasks.

She followed the lifeblood of the city flowing through the streets; she tasted the corruption of her own blood and, recognizing it as her own, she could not lose her way. To the heart of the city she led her adepts and acolytes, loyal Johanus ever a step away. Only a little way from their own sanctuary did they travel. South beyond the lupine refuge, not so far as the tallest and thickest of the bones and headstones of the dragon's graveyard. The river of blood twisted through avenue and artery until it reached the fortress, and there it formed a fiery moat.

Johanus stepped forward to the edge of the infernal abyss and tested fire against fire. The acolytes joined him, gave their strength to him, as Sturbridge probed the walls of the fortress itself.

They were erected with no little skill, towers and abutments, wards placed much as she might have placed them. And therein lay the weakness. Though the hand of the builder was foreign, the architect was the same, and what Sturbridge comprehended she could destroy. Thus was the power of death over life and the secret of the Children.

She called her flock back from the chasm. There was no need after all to quench the flame. Instead, she called upon it, and it responded. The beast of blood and fire rose and spread its glorious wings. For a lingering moment it stood towering above the children, above the city, above the boneyard…and then it fell upon the walls.

Fire and blood engulfed the fortress, swept against the walls and drove the defenders from the battlements. The fortifications were strong, and it appeared that they would stand firm for quite some while.

But suddenly, unexpectedly, cracks formed along the walls. A giddy cheer arose behind Sturbridge, and the beast, smelling blood, roared at the prospect of triumph. Tongues of flame licked at the faults. Harmless clefts became gaping fissures. Once the first tower collapsed, the end was quick to come. Walls collapsed inward. The beast scourged the earth within, and the blood of the moat was purified by fire.

Saturday, 13 November 1999, 2:40 AM
Crown Plaza Hotel, Midtown Manhattan
New York City, New York

The initial explosion gutted the twenty-fifth, twenty-sixth, and twenty-seventh floors of the hotel. Glass and fragments of granite were flung outward with such force that they would be found in buildings across the street the next morning. The blast shattered windows as far as two and a half blocks away.

The fire swept through floors down to the twenty-third and up to the thirtieth before emergency teams could arrive at the scene.

Ramona, frozen where she stood, palm leaf in hand, marveled at Hesha. He might not have possessed the same blinding speed as did the larger Theo Bell, but just the same he avoided Leopold's attacks with a mesmerizing grace and fluidity. Ramona wasn't sure if the scales that seemed to cover his exposed skin were real or of her ghostsight. And his body appeared to move in ways it should not, stretching farther than possible when he leapt for a signpost, twisting as if not constrained by joints as he dodged fragments of pavement hurled at him by bucking waves of street.

After the first few seconds, her watching became almost detached, for to care about the outcome, about Hesha or Theo, was to open herself again to fear. She was discovering that her thirst for vengeance might not be so strong as that fear.

Maybe Hesha could beat Leopold. Maybe he didn't need her to destroy the Eye after all. As she watched his desperate dodges and attacks—rolling, firing, twisting, firing, many of his shots tearing ragged holes in Leopold—she knew her false hope for what it was. Hesha, like the other man before him, was holding his own, but making little headway. He survived, but barely.

Theo, she noticed, seemed to have recovered his wits. He was still wrapped tight by the coiled lamp post, but, taking advantage of the respite Hesha's attacks created, the larger man was now struggling. He was straining against the metal, but the coil grew tighter as he pressed against it.

But then, suddenly, before Ramona's eyes, the coiled metal went stiff. At the same instant, the sound of a distant explosion reached them, and Leopold staggered. Not in response to Hesha's bullets, and no one was close enough to have attacked, but still Leopold's legs seemed to fail him. To Ramona's ghostsight, he seemed paler and less substantial, diminished somehow beneath the Eye, which along with its umbilical nerve was throbbing more fiercely, desperately.

It's hungry, Ramona realized. *It's not as strong as it was.* She took a step, sneaking closer. *It's not as strong as it was a few moments ago, and even then it wasn't as strong as the night at the cave.*

Before her, Hesha was advancing on Leopold, and Bell was still straining against the now-rigid, curled lamp post—except now he was *bending* it. Not a tremendous amount, but enough that he was able to slip free of it. He staggered to his feet, picked up his shotgun, and fired a blast that caught Leopold square in the chest. It knocked him back and left a large patch of smoldering flesh. He did not fall, but he was *hurt.*

Ramona saw images from that other night: wave upon wave of Gangrel charging to their deaths, erupting monoliths, and pools of molten rock. Something was different tonight. Something that allowed two battered Kindred to hold their own against Leopold, against the Eye. Why hadn't she seen it before? Maybe her terror had blinded her, but it was true. They were advancing on him now, Hesha's face inscrutable, Theo's gaze red as blood.

Leopold seemed hesitant, unsure. No new pits opened before his assailants. No wave of pavement rose to break their bodies. Ramona saw her chance and charged. She was behind Leopold. If Hesha's bizarre plan didn't work, then she would rip the nerve and the Eye apart with her claws and her fangs—but she would not be a prisoner to her fear, to her past.

As she rushed forward, headlights appeared up the street. High beams, a car approaching at high speed from beyond Leopold, beyond Hesha and Theo. Ramona felt as if a spotlight were cast on her alone. She hesitated...and as she paused, her ears caught a strange sound, a sound she'd heard before—the wet split of flesh torn asunder. To her shock, she saw sharp bones slice through Leopold's clothes—*his own bones*, piercing his skin and protruding from his emaciated corpse. The ghostsight—that must be why she saw that. It *couldn't* be real. His bones couldn't actually be stretching out beyond his body.

The car was roaring closer. Two blocks away. One block. Ramona shot forward, blood in her heart and the names of her dead on her lips. She was mere yards from Leopold, from the phantom nerve she must sever, when the bones, Leopold's ribs, lashed out and struck her like a collection of scorpions' tails.

The impact stopped her in her tracks. The bone lances pierced her arm, her chest, her stomach, her legs. She was joined to Leopold, attached to him by his own impossibly long bones. Shock gave way to raging pain and to the sick, churning realization of failure. She was leaning forward but could not move. He didn't even bother to look at her. The pulsing nerve was feet away, but the palm leaf slipped from her hand as her fingers went numb, her own nerves severed rather than that of the Eye.

In her despair, she looked to Hesha and Theo. Only then did she see that they were impaled as well. Leopold had lashed out with his body, or the Eye had resorted to using him as a weapon. Either way, Hesha's chest was pierced by one large bone spear that had run him through. Theo was pinned more like Ramona. Ribs had punctured his knee and belly, his shoulders, and one ran through his upper lip and out the side of his face.

Ramona hung limp. She was surrounded by bent and broken streetlights, craters, asphalt and concrete rubble. She and Hesha and Theo were flies entangled in a web of bone. All the while, the car was barreling toward them, bounding over broken pavement. Finally it plowed into a hole far deeper than those preceding it. The nose of the car bottomed out and the vehicle came crashing to a halt.

Once the engine died amid the echoes of crunching steel, a strange quiet fell over the street. Ramona looked helplessly at Leopold, so close. He was sagging where he stood, pale and shriveled, the three Kindred he was joined to holding him upright as much as his deadly bones held them. The only sounds in that instant were the fizzing discharge of the Eye, Hesha's moans of pain and frustration as he writhed on his spear, and the hiss of steam escaping the car's ruptured radiator.

Then one of the car's doors opened, and an incredibly beautiful woman climbed from the wreckage.

Victoria could not believe the devastation she stepped into. Wreckage as if the street had been bombed, strange rolling hills of pavement. And Leopold, weak, palsied, his own bones somehow splayed out a freakish distance impaling three Kindred: Theo Bell, bleeding and stunned, closest to her; some dirty child the farthest away; and to the side she recognized Hesha Ruhadze, whose man Vegel she'd spoken to what seemed now like so many years ago. And in the center of it all stood Leopold, dwarfed by the malevolent Eye that she'd seen in the sketch Sturbridge had brought to Baltimore.

"Leopold," Victoria said gently. She set her gaze upon his face—not the Eye, but his face, his other eye. She looked for signs of the artist that had been so desperate to win her good graces back in Atlanta. She looked for any sign of *herself*.

The young wizard's sire is within the clay.

"Leopold," she said again, stepping forward past Theo, past Hesha. They watched her, Hesha struggling, Theo beginning to take stock of his situation and pull against the bone. She continued walking slowly and calmly toward Leopold. She slipped off her heels so as to make her way more easily across the rubble.

He watched her approach, warily, longingly. She came very close to him, close enough to scent the vitriol as it dripped from the Eye and sizzled on the broken pavement.

"I never knew, Leopold," she said. "You have to believe me. I never knew. Everything would have been different." She couldn't tell if he heard her, if he understood, if he *believed*. All she could see was that he was completely drained. He was a hollow shell, a pedestal of flesh upon which the Eye perched. Slowly, she reached out a gentle hand to him. "I never knew. I am your sire."

Leopold was trapped, entangled by the barbs of an unbreakable thorn tree. Before him the red river flowed through the streets of the dragon's graveyard. The teacher was gone. His wisdom and power lost. But *she* was rising from the crimson water. Leopold could not remember if this was precisely as he remembered her. Her visits had always been so fleeting, her beauty real to his Sight, but ephemeral nonetheless.

She was reaching out to him with her delicate hand. *Be careful of the thorns*, he wanted to say, but words failed him. She had been part of every creation he'd given life, and her mere presence brought back to him the rapture of his masterpiece. How long he had struggled, despite her help. She had teased and abused and cajoled him, but she was here with him now, ready to embrace him.

She spoke, and her words dripped blood and honey. "I am your sire." She claimed him as her own. It was not her blood but the teacher's that ran in his veins, he knew in that instant. She was not his sire but his Muse. None of that mattered, though. She claimed him as her own. They were of one spirit for eternity. And Leopold knew peace.

Ramona could hardly see the woman walking slowly toward Leopold. The Gangrel was lost amidst her own private agony, of body and of spirit. She was run through in five places. She had failed her dead again. It was small comfort that this time she would join them, this time she felt their pain in her own body. She hadn't run away.

But she had hesitated. With her strength fading, she was still capable of accusing herself. She had stood frozen in fear, she had waited for the perfect moment—a moment that would never come. She had failed her dead, but at least she would join them. She owed them that.

She looked up again, to Hesha. He still struggled, though the bone that entered his chest and exited his back was curled upward behind him. There was no way he could pull himself from the spear, yet he fought on.

Theo, too, she saw, was fighting still. She could see the anger, the hatred in his eyes. One of the ribs had skewered his face. Grimacing against the pain, he pulled his head back. Slowly at first, and then with a rush, his skin slid over the intruding bone. That one rib, at least, did not extend far beyond him. Unable to maneuver the rest of his body, he craned his neck to the side. Inch by inch, he pulled his face back over the bone. His eyes were squeezed shut. Broken fragments of teeth fell from his mouth—and then he was free. Of that bone. Four others held him firmly in place.

Ramona, through the haze of pain, was amazed by Hesha's determination, and by Theo's will. They had no chance of freeing themselves, not in time to help. Ramona remembered the woman. She was as close to Leopold in front as Ramona was behind, as close as Ramona was to the nerve. But Leopold hadn't struck down the woman. Ramona's pained thoughts drifted from wondering if the woman needed help to resenting that she hadn't been attacked. He hadn't flung metal posts or waves of pavement at her. *What about the acid?* Ramona thought. *She's close enough to spray with the fucking acid!*

And now the woman was talking to Leopold. *Talking!* Ramona couldn't make out what the woman was saying. Her own ears were ringing, complaining of the damage done her body. *Don't fucking talk to him!* Ramona raged. *Tear his fucking heart out! The Eye! Slash the Eye!* But the woman stood close and spoke kindly to him— to the monster that had destroyed Ramona's people. The woman reached a hand out to him….

That was more than Ramona could take. She strained against the rods of bone that pierced her body. Pain flashed through her like fire from every point of intrusion. Her right arm was numb, skewered at the shoulder. But she leaned hard with her left. She was already leaning forward, propped up by Leopold's bones. The palm leaf—part of Hesha's plan, Hesha's stupid, insane plan—lay upon rubble just below her. She felt her skin tearing, the wounds stretching. Her taut fingers were razor claws, pincers closing on the large leaf. She had it! But now what?

She looked down at the bones impaling her, the five ivory spears. Despite the pain, or maybe because of it, she laughed grimly to herself. *Guess he ripped me five new assholes.*

And then she drew on her rage. Theo was fighting, but he couldn't have as much reason to hate as she did. To hate and to *fear.* Ramona began telling over the names of her dead: *Eddie. Jen. Darnell.* And with each name she thrust herself forward on Leopold's bones. They protruded too far behind her for her to free herself, so she'd be his lunch and make sure he fucking choked on it.

Ronja. Peera Giftgiver. Ramona forced her body, inches at a time. *Crenshaw. Bernard Fleetfoot. Mutabo.* A stake through her heart, sun burning away her flesh, acid eating at her face—all of it was happening at once. *Lisa Strongback. Aileen Brock-childe. Brant Edmonson. Tanner.* Blood was running from her wounds, pooling on the ground beside the sickening, pulsing nerve that drew strength from the earth. Ramona's blood, blood she had stolen...

Zhavon.

With the last of her strength, Ramona's hand fell forward. She clutched the palm leaf as surely as pain and death and fear. It passed *through* the nerve, not cutting into the fibrous sinew. Ramona could feel no resistance to the leaf. She must have missed. She had to strike again. But the leaf was a leaden weight in her hand, her arm dead. Her fingers failed her, and the leaf slipped from her grasp. She screamed in outrage.

Or was it the other woman who screamed? Ramona wasn't sure. Her strength was gone. She was falling....

Falling? But the bones?

Ramona slammed into the rough ground face first. She looked up and saw the bones, like a path to Leopold's heart, from outward in, turning to ash. And from the three paths of ash, jagged bursts of lightning shot into the sky, streaks of gold, red, and green. For an instant the streaks met above Leopold, and there standing above him was a towering, monstrous apparition, its dark face a demonic snarl, its sole eye bulging with malevolent glee. Then, as Ramona watched in pain and horrified wonder, the figure was gone, and Leopold's frail body crumbled to dust.

Theo fell to his knees and then forward, face first onto the rubble. Every part of his body was in agony. He was exhausted. But he couldn't spare any time. Not yet. He tried to direct what blood he could to his knee. The gut shot was painful, but there was nothing much he needed in there. And his fingers all seemed to work, so the shoulder wounds could wait. His face felt like it was ripped off. *Never was much of a looker*, he thought.

Slowly and not very steadily, he climbed back up to his knees. He spat teeth onto the rubble. If he'd been kine, his face would've been gushing, and he'd have been choking on blood. He made it to his feet. Hesha was already staggering toward Victoria. The other chick was lying on her face behind...behind where Leopold had been. Now there was just a pile of dust—no, not *just* a pile of dust. There was something resting in the dust.

Theo saw his shotgun lying on the ground nearby and had to make a concerted effort to bend down and pick it up. The walk to Victoria felt longer and harder than it should have been. Every gouge in the street seemed a deep trench, and every pile of rubble a mountain. Theo wanted to hurry—they should get away from here before cops started to show, or kine in the neighborhood grew overly curious now that all was quiet—but it was all he could do to keep moving.

"You're back," he said to Victoria when he reached her side, and before he realized quite how much talking was going to hurt. He clamped a hand over the left side of his jaw.

She didn't speak to him. The Toreador just stood and watched as Hesha, kneeling by the Eye and the dust that had been Leopold, took a Kevlar case from his backpack. The Eye, perched atop Leopold's remains, was bluish purple. It no longer throbbed or moved at all, and a lid-like membrane had closed around most of the orb. Victoria seemed disinterested in what was going on. She was still a beauty, in that uptown kind of way, but she seemed empty, lifeless—even for a Kindred. "Fate plays its cruel tricks," she said to no one in particular.

Theo gave her a sideways glance. "Uh, yeah...right." After a moment, she turned and, without so much as looking at Theo or acknowledging Hesha, walked away. She seemed consumed by a tired, cold anger, or maybe it was just regret. Theo didn't understand either way, and didn't care. He was too exhausted at the moment to worry about a Toreador's hurt feelings. He wasn't sure why she'd shown up, or how the hell she'd managed to face down Leopold. It seemed to have been the scrawny kid that had finished him off, but Victoria had gotten his attention all right.

She said something to that Leopold freak, Theo mused. He shrugged. *Whatever works.* Watching the Setite stooped over his bag, Theo was still partially stunned himself. *Get my ass whupped by one Toreador and saved by another, all in one night.* He shook his head.

Hesha had unzipped the Kevlar case and laid it open. It was full of thick mud or clay. Intent on what he was doing, he smoothed the substance with his hands.

Theo cocked his shotgun and tried to speak without moving his mouth any more than necessary. "You're not planning on takin' that, are you?"

Hesha didn't look up from his task. "Archon Bell," he said politely, as if he didn't have a gaping hole in his chest, "perhaps you were not informed. If you check with Mr. Pieterzoon, you will find that Lucinde has granted me this."

"I look like Lucinde?" Theo asked.

That gave Hesha pause. He stopped and looked up at Theo. "I believe Justicar Pascek signed off on the agreement as well."

"*Shoot it*," said the bloody, half-crippled Kindred who was crawling toward them. One arm hung useless, dragging along. She'd shown up at some point in the fight. Theo couldn't remember exactly when, but she, like Victoria, seemed to have come in handy.

"Ramona," Hesha said, unperturbed, "you did well."

"Fuck you," she snarled, then looked at Theo. "Shoot it. Shoot *him* if you have to. Shoot it." She was angry, but there was desperation in her voice too. "Don't believe anything he says. We were gonna destroy it."

"Ramona," Hesha said, "I never lied to you. We agreed that I would see that the Eye caused no more harm. I doubt I could have accomplished this without you, and I don't want us to part on unpleasant terms. But I will have the Eye."

Beneath the Setite's calm words, Theo sensed desperation of a different sort—fanaticism. He instinctively tried to gauge the extent of Hesha's injuries, what the chances were if it came to violence. Theo didn't like it one bit—the back-room deals, the sly promises, and to a *Setite*, for Christ's sake. *You may not have lied to her*, he thought, *but I bet you sure as hell didn't tell her the truth*.

Hesha went back to his work. He gingerly lifted the Eye and placed it into the clay, settling it firmly into place. "Archon, you might wish to take up the matter with Lucinde or Jaroslav, but in the meantime, I must see this to a safe place." He carefully closed the case and resealed the zipper. "If it makes it any difference, I promise you, both of you, that you will never have to face this again. And, Archon, a portion of turmeric root, still smoldering and pressed firmly against those burns, will allow the blood to do its work. They will not heal otherwise."

"Hmph," Theo snorted. *Right. Flaming whatever-you-said*. He wanted to blow the fuck out of the thing that Hesha was packing away, like Ramona had pleaded. But decisions, the archon had come to learn, were not always his to make. "Go on. Get out of here."

Ramona, too weak to fight anymore, sagged to the ground. Hesha slipped the quiescently bulging case into his backpack and was on his way.

Saturday, 13 November 1999, 3:52 AM
A subterranean grotto
New York City, New York

Calebros sat in the flickering light of the candelabra. He stretched and popped his back; he allowed himself to rest. Elsewhere in the city, in the Bronx, the war still raged. But the hunt was over.

Umberto had passed word along to him and Cock Robin as they had scoured the city: The Eye was captured; Leopold destroyed; and more importantly, as confirmed by the Tremere, Nickolai was no more. Sturbridge had tracked him somehow—Nickolai, betrayer of his blood, murderer of Justicar Alonso Cristo Petrodon de Seville. The Tremere messenger, flushed with victory, had been unusually forthcoming. Not intentionally, perhaps. But he had mentioned the explosion in Midtown and linked it to the final, mystical blow.

So much that had weighed on Calebros's mind was resolved. Even Cock Robin seemed to take his own sort of grim pleasure from the news, though he would have preferred to have done the deed himself, Calebros was sure.

The Sabbat was still struggling, Cardinal Polonia personally laying waste to Kindred. Calebros, upon his return, had sent Emmett with most of the hunting parties to Throgs Neck. If they could break Polonia's power, the city would still not be won, but the Camarilla would be so much closer to that goal.

Calebros himself was taking a few minutes to savor the successful labor of several years and countless of his clanmates. Soon he and Cock Robin would follow Emmett and see what further aid they could give. There was no time for him to retreat to the lake, but Calebros was tired and hungry. He rose from his desk and followed a different, seldom-traveled tunnel.

They heard him coming, as they always did, and the howling began, guttural cries of pleasure at his approach. The smell of the long, narrow chamber was very strong, and very familiar to Calebros. Sweat, body odor and wastes. The inhabitants wrapped their thin fingers around the bars of their makeshift cells and cages and rattled them. Many scampered back and forth in the few cramped feet allowed them. Calebros could never avoid a wash of nostalgia for the hard realities of the kennels.

Most of the children in the cages had long since forgotten all but the faintest traces of their former lives. It was best that way, Calebros believed, as Augustin had believed before him. For the few, the strongest, who would be brought into the blood eventually, it was better not to have a past to pine for, better for it to be washed away over the years. That way the Embrace was truly a gift, and one's place within the clan was one's only place. Even so, Calebros recognized in himself the occasional hints of regret, the rare longing for those distant, pale memories, for what might have been.

Ah, but how much harder it would have been, taken directly from the mortal world and thrust down here, away from the sun forever.

He walked along the row of cells, some wrought-iron bars sunk deep into stone, others small steel cages tucked into cubbyholes or tied to the back wall. Everywhere, expectant eyes watched him pass, each occupant hoping to be chosen—to be nourished, or to provide nourishment.

Calebros stopped before one of the cages, and the boy—it seemed to be a boy—thrust his hand through the bars. Calebros grasped the arm tightly just below the elbow. The boy knew to make a fist, to squeeze. Calebros waited, waited, as long as he could. As the veins in the skinny wrist and forearm rose, so did his own desire, his hunger. The boy tried to hold still, though one of his feet was bouncing against the back of the cage. He grunted and moaned in anticipation. And when Calebros could hold himself back no longer, he tore into the arm.

The world was a chaotic din, the children and youths pounding on the walls, wailing, and rattling metal against metal. Blood spurted into Calebros's mouth. A strong pulse sounded at his temples and attempted to drown out the external sounds. He felt whole in this place, one with these demi-humans, some who would be lucky enough to join him in time. He remembered his own blood drawn forth by Augustin's fangs; he remembered, later, standing with his sire as Emmett was chosen. The blood coursed into him, through him. Which one of these human larvae might one night prove him- or herself worthy to join the clan, so that the circle might continue…?

Calebros stopped drinking suddenly. Blood pulsed onto his face, ran down his chin. Absently, he licked the boy's wound, healed the flesh, and rushed from the kennels. The howling followed him through the tunnel, but already it was forgotten.

The circle…the circle!

He rushed back to his desk and began rummaging for the particular folder he needed—Jeremiah's reports from his time with Anatole. And all the while, the words were running a circle through Calebros's mind: *One in a minute, and one in an hour.*

There, the folder. A *circle, you fool, a circle!* Calebros berated himself. *On the face of a clock—the second hand makes one each minute, and the minute hand makes one each hour.* He flipped pages furiously until he found the early notation he was looking for: "*Anatole places his hands inside his sandals and then rubs the soles together.*" That was part of what he wanted, but not all. Calebros skimmed farther down the page, on to the next page, and found it: "*…constantly rubs his sandals in circles, first one way and then the other.*"

The Prophet was leading him somewhere. *Walk a*

mile in but seconds to deliver my letter. Literally? Unlikely. Nothing so straightforward with the Prophet. Perhaps a progression. *Walk a mile…in the shoes of your enemy? Sandals, in this case?* But Calebros had already connected the sandals. Had he skipped ahead somehow? And what did seconds have to do with it? Reference to the clock again?

…*Seconds to deliver my letter.* A message? The riddle was a message of sorts, or there was a message in the riddle?

Calebros impatiently flipped more pages. Where was Anatole taking him? Where had the Prophet taken poor Jeremiah? Had Jeremiah recorded the right details? He *must* have. Anatole would have seen to it somehow. The Prophet had known all this would come to pass. He'd known about Jeremiah even before Calebros had sent him. Anatole had planted seeds with Donatello in the cathedral that would grow and bear fruit with Jeremiah much later.

Seconds…letter…

Calebros scanned ahead through the reports. "*Anatole begins his sandal rubbing. Four seconds, changes directions. One minute forty-four seconds, changes direction…*"

"Seconds!" Calebros said aloud. Anatole knew that Jeremiah was timing him—knew that he *would* time him. Calebros had to abandon chronology; he had to acknowledge that causal and temporal relationships did not necessarily exist with the Prophet. Planting the seeds for the fruit he knew would be needed….

It had to fit. Jeremiah had timed the sandal rubbings, timed them in *seconds.* But how did that deliver messages? A message, rather. No, not a message, a *letter.* The answer had to be here. Seconds. What did seconds have to do with a letter? And what did Anatole's sandal rubbing have to do with anything?

Four seconds, changes directions. One minute forty-four seconds, changes direction. Calebros slid his finger down the page to the notes from another night: *Four seconds, changes directions. One minute forty-four seconds, changes direction.* These were the first recorded times for the given nights. They were followed by various times, all between four and one-forty-four. It must mean something that they were the same. But then Calebros cursed when he saw the next night: *One second, changes directions. Twenty-six seconds, changes directions.*

What, Calebros tried to discern, was the pattern? Most of the recordings were four seconds followed by a minute and forty-four seconds. But every so often, seemingly at random, there was the one and twenty-six substitution, and on those nights the subsequent times all fell within *that* range: 1-26-1-14-1-14-7-5-12...

A combination? he wondered. *Or a mathematical relation? One and twenty-six, four and one-forty-four.* He started scribbling down the math. One-forty-four was divisible by four...thirty-six times. Was there a significance there? Thirty-six months? Three years? Was something going to happen in three years? The numbers all started to run together in his mind, then...*not one-forty-four. Seconds! One minute forty-four seconds is one hundred four seconds, not one hundred forty-four.* And one hundred four divided by four was *twenty-six.*

Calebros slammed his pen down in triumph. Even when the initial numbers were different, the *ratio* was one to twenty-six. *And how is twenty-six related to a letter? Each letter is one of twenty-six!* Calebros hastily began making a chart along the margin of the report: 1=A, 2=B, 3=C.... The four nights were merely multiples!

And the last line of the riddle, *Which way do I go?* Which *direction.* Jeremiah had already recorded the changes in direction. They signified the end of one letter's time and the beginning of the next.

Quickly, he began flipping *back* through the report, gathering all the times that Jeremiah had listed. *What if he missed something? Something vital? Ah, but the Prophet would have seen that that didn't happen. Best to see what's here, though....*

It did not take long before Calebros saw the numbers transformed into letters into words into sentences. It did not take much longer than that for him to realize that he should find Cock Robin—*right away*. There was not a moment to spare.

part three:
beginning of
the end

Saturday, 13 November 1999, 4:41 AM
Beneath Manhattan
New York City, New York

Their restless, bloodthirsty gazes followed his every movement. Especially the stare of the silent one. Pug could feel them watching him. Knowing that their hatred was not directed at him did not calm his nerves. He'd already brought them farther than anyone else could have, but if he failed now, if he lost the trail, their denied vengeance might be directed toward other outlets—like him.

Calebros had led him into the still-burning hotel. How desperate did the chief have to be to do *that*? It was because of the silent one, Pug knew. The silent one wouldn't rest until this was over. After two nights of the relentless hunt, Pug thought he might rather have just kept helping that strange Hilda woman search for Jeremiah. In the hotel, Pug and Calebros had stayed away from the fire crews. They were everywhere, as was the smoke and the water. It had turned out that the floors Calebros wanted to check were too far gone. There wasn't much of them left, really. Nothing that Pug could have picked up a scent from. They'd left, defeated, and there it would have ended.

Except Pug found the trail. He'd found it where none of them had expected, where they had congregated beneath the hotel. While Calebros and the silent one had decided what to do next, Pug had noticed the familiar scent, the scent from the photograph. It had been touch and go through the tunnels since. It was touch and go still.

He moved forward slowly, cautiously, approaching another storm grate. Untold scents from the chaotic upperworld flooded into the tunnel through the metal cross-hatching. The wave of competing stimuli engulfed Pug—litter blowing overhead, food wrappers, stale urine, motor oil, the ever-present, all-permeating exhaust fumes. He hesitated, doubted, faltered. The strand he followed was so faint!

"Concentrate, Pug," said Calebros from behind, understanding but anxious, impatient.

The silent one watched, glowering. He clicked his jagged fingernails together. The sound, like spiders clattering up Pug's spine, made the hair on his neck stand on end. He hoped that the others didn't smell his fear. But he knew the silent one did.

Concentrate, Pug! he echoed to himself Calebros's words. The extraneous smells, the clicking spiders in his mind—*Concentrate!* Set them aside. Then he heard the nervous shuffling. Behind Calebros, the others, too, were unnerved by the silent one, the monster among monsters. They wanted desperately to prove themselves to him, to play a part in his vengeance, but none could match his brooding ferocity.

Pug caught the trail again, moved forward, felt the beginning of the collective sigh behind him, instantly lost the scent. The tunnel split ahead, just beyond the storm grates—their quarry must have known that, must have risked rising this close to the surface for just that reason. The downdraft whipped the maddeningly churning scents into a cavorting frenzy.

The silent one let out a deep, throaty warble, a peculiarly disturbing sound.

"Which way, Pug?" Calebros urged.

"I…I don't know."

"You must know," Calebros said quietly. "Take your time. Here." He reached into his pocket, took out a folded Ziploc bag, and handed it to Pug.

Pug opened the bag carefully, sniffed at the picture inside—a handsome kine, the former justicar before his change, before his first death or Final. The picture was not their quarry, but their quarry had handled the picture, had touched it and left his scent upon it. That was long ago, much too long for any normal bloodhound to pick up a scent, long enough that Pug was having trouble even without the distracting wind and smells from above. He handed back the bag, then closed his eyes and covered his ears, trying to ignore the mocking breeze that smacked at his face, and to concentrate instead on the plethora of scents the air carried. He tried, as best as he could, not to hear and feel the agitated trilling of the silent one awaiting results....

There. The left tunnel. As they continued, Pug moved more quickly, felt more sure of himself. The tunnel split again, but he barely paused before taking the left fork. The urgency of his clanmates drove him forward. His increasing confidence was exceeded only by his sense of relief that he had not failed those who depended on him. Not yet, he hadn't.

There were still competing scents, distracting odors that threatened to overpower the true path, but Pug was up to the challenge. He had the trail. He had the scent of the Kindred they pursued and didn't think he'd lose it again. It seemed normal again, natural. Not like before at the storm grate. Something there had been...*not right*. Even with the wind-borne smells from the upperworld, he shouldn't have had so much trouble. He never should have come that close to losing the trail and not finding it. He shouldn't have needed the picture again. Maybe it was the Tremere they were following. Maybe he'd stopped and tried to conceal his passing—and almost succeeded.

What mattered, Pug reminded himself, was that he'd found the trail. Now, after the fact, he was halfway miffed with himself for having been so nervous. It wasn't like they would have tossed him back into the kennels had he failed...at least he didn't think so. But it wasn't over yet. They were still right there behind him, after all. The silent one, Calebros, all of the others. Still depending on him....

Concentrate, Pug reminded himself, not wanting to subject himself needlessly to the overwhelming pressure of those other thoughts, of that slippery slope.

He led them deeper into the storm sewers, away from the upperworld. He followed the trail as easily now as if their prey had unrolled a ball of twine as he went and left it to lead them along. The Kindred hadn't attempted any of the usual tricks to obscure his passing. He hadn't waded through the shallower sections of the sewer if there was an alternate dry route. He hadn't tried to disguise his scent with garbage or overflow from the waste sewers. It was as if he thought he'd be home free by this point. He'd counted on his gambit at the storm grate. But he hadn't counted on Pug.

Concentrate, Pug told himself. Whatever trick the Kindred had used at the grate had almost worked, and he could certainly try it again. Magic, Pug decided. To have given him that much trouble, the trick must have been magic. *Concentrate*.

Just a few minutes later, Pug, with his nose almost to the ground, was concentrating so intently in fact that he didn't notice the feet that stepped toward him from the darkness. He did notice, at the last second, the lead pipe that smashed down across his skull. Everything was very suddenly confused.

He looked up just as the blow fell. The pipe struck above his right eye and along that cheek. The darkness of the tunnel was instantly replaced by bright flashes of light. Then Pug was weightless.

Shouting. There was shouting in the distance, muffled, incoherent. He tasted blood—his own blood, or what passed as his own blood. But that taste was quickly diluted by another, rank liquid. He opened his eyes—tried to, wasn't sure if he was successful. Darkness rushing.

Hands grasped at him. Pug struggled to get away, to shield himself from more blows. But he was merely fumbling. They grabbed him, held tightly against his weak thrashing, pulled him roughly but met resistance. Water. They were pulling him through the water.

Slowly, he was able to orient himself again. He'd

fallen into the flow channel of the storm drain. *That was clumsy*, he thought vacantly. No, not a clumsy fall, he remembered. The pipe.

A struggle was still going on, not far away, on the walkway where his three clanmates were now towing him. Pug caught a glimpse of Calebros's wide face, all jagged fangs as he tore a savage bite from one assailant's shoulder. The silent one, too, was a blur of violent motion, claws slicing and rending. The other Nosferatu attacked ferociously, giving no quarter. Bodies already littered the tunnel.

Pug and his rescuers ducked as a projectile flew past—an *arm*, the hand still clutching a lead pipe. The arm landed in the foulness of the water, and the pipe pulled the limb under.

The enemies were not faring well. That Pug could discern as his senses cleared. The attackers, though immersed in battle, moved lethargically. Their pipes and scraps of wood rarely connected with a target, as the Nosferatu darted in and out among them, striking blow after blow. Pug had never seen Calebros move so quickly and was shocked too by the force of his attacks. The elder's every blow was a scythe of destruction. Bodies were piling up.

And then it was over as suddenly as it began, even before Mike and Paulie were able to hoist the still slightly dazed Pug back onto the walkway. Some of Pug's clanmates were rifling through the pockets of the few bodies that remained relatively intact.

"What were they doing here?" Pug, wringing out his clothes, asked no one in particular.

"They were dead. Already dead," said a quiet voice. Calebros. He sniffed at one of his own talons, stuck out a gray, pimpled tongue, and tasted a bit of the meat that wedged beneath. He nodded, confirming his assertion.

Pug looked around at the bodies—body parts, mostly—scattered about. It was difficult reconstructing exactly how many assailants there had been. At least seven or eight, perhaps as many as a dozen? But despite the degree of dismemberment, there was little blood. "Kindred?" he asked.

"No," Calebros said. "Little more than corpses."

The other Nosferatu had finished ransacking the bodies and taken anything remotely of value: shoes, clothes, spare change, fillings. An ominous, throaty warble signaled the silent one's impatience to continue. The creature's deformed head, with its distended, vaguely avian chin, reminded Pug of a vulture. But Pug could also see—it was clear in the pale, icy eyes—that the silent one was not content merely to find carrion. He wished to create it.

"You'd best lead us onward," said Calebros.

Pug nodded, turned back to recover the trail, and was relieved to have something other than the silent one to concentrate upon.

She could see how it got its name: "the Shaft." The
tunnel was roughly two car-lengths wide where it
started, just below street-level Brooklyn. It was steep
right off the bat, but almost immediately it turned
sharply downward and continued from that point nearly
vertically. There were ladders and ledges and carved
steps and handholds all along the way—and more tunnels, hundreds of tunnels stretching out in every
direction from the central shaft. Hilda had fallen in love
with the place the minute she laid eyes on it. Pug had
brought her here in their search for Jeremiah. That had
been two nights ago. They'd come back last night, and
still they had barely scratched the surface. A Kindred
could spend lifetimes down here and never explore all
the tunnels. If Jeremiah was lost near the Shaft, chances
were he was going to stay lost.

Pug had said as much last night, and Hilda couldn't
argue. But tonight, when the odd little fellow had been
called away to help with the hunt, Hilda had sneaked
away and come back. She couldn't care less about the
hunt or the Sabbat. Petrodon had been a bastard, and
nobody in the Sabbat had ever treated her worse than
folks in the Camarilla. So here she was.

The last thing she had expected was to run into
someone else.

She'd been in the shaft for hours when she heard
him, following along, coming from the same direction
she'd just come. Coincidence? Down here with hundreds of tunnels and passages turning and twisting back
on themselves? Hardly.

She briefly considered hiding. Instead, picking up
a large rock from the tunnel rubble, she bashed him in
the head the instant he turned the corner. He was plenty
big, and it must be true what they say about big fellows,

because he fell plenty hard. She had considered the possibility that he was a friend, but he still had no business following her.

He lay stunned for a moment. He wore an old suit, but he was obviously very hairy, mangy patches of brown and gray. He didn't move, except for his large black eyes, no whites whatsoever, blinking rapidly. He had a nasal cavity instead of a nose, and the longest of his jagged teeth protruded through half of his lip. After a few minutes of quiet groaning, he managed to sit upright. "You would be Hilda?" he said somewhat groggily.

"Guilty as charged, glamour boy."

He rubbed his head and gave her a lusty stare. "I like a girl who can help me get my rocks off."

"I'll get your head off your shoulders if you don't watch it. What are you doing here? Just in the neighborhood?"

"Marston Colchester. Thanks for asking."

"I know who you are. Up with the Baltimore crowd. I seen you around the warren."

"And you still bash me in the head?"

"I said I seen you. I didn't say I liked you."

"Help me up?" Colchester asked. She offered a hand and pulled him to his feet. She noticed the way his clammy fingers lingered on her own. "I wasn't following you, by the way. Jeremiah and I go way back. Pug said he might be around here somewhere. I just saw that somebody had come this way and thought I'd check it out." Then he grabbed her ass. He grinned, waiting for a reaction—

And seemed surprised when she latched on to his crotch. "Hmm," she pondered. "Must be siesta time south of the border."

Colchester jumped back from her. "Well...*ahem*...about Jeremiah..."

Hilda moved closer. "What's wrong, sweetie? You wouldn't get a girl all flustered and then run away, would you?"

He started backpedaling. "Like I said, he and I go way back."

"I had a Rambler once. The seats went back *all* the way."

"Uh…Pug said that he thought maybe—"

She bashed him in the head with the rock again. He landed like a load of bricks, and she was on him in a second, tearing away the old suit. She rubbed herself up and down his abdomen and ripped away the buttons that had barely managed to hold her too-small blouse together. Her bountiful flesh fell in rolls across his face.

"Dear God, I've died and gone to heaven," he muttered beneath her.

Hilda reached down between his legs and took firm hold of a surprisingly turgid appendage. "Siesta must be over, eh, flyboy?" But when she looked, she saw that the appendage did not belong to him. Instead, it was a fleshy tendril that had somehow entwined itself around his leg and up to his waist. "What in the—?"

Suddenly the tendrils were everywhere, lashing the two Nosferatu like bloody, rubber hoses. Hilda jumped to her feet, but her own legs were quickly entangled, as were her arms, her neck. The tendrils pulled her back down. They pulled her along the tunnel floor toward the central chasm. Colchester was struggling, but she couldn't see him. He was a mummy wrapped in flesh instead of cloth.

Hilda pulled and kicked and bit, but to no avail. Finally all that was left to her was to scream. The sound, like Hilda herself, disappeared down the Shaft.

Saturday, 13 November 1999, 5:50 AM
Beneath Manhattan
New York City, New York

Although it was Pug who followed the scent, Calebros and company were close on his heels, leaning low as if they too could discern the trail. Mike Tundlight and Paulie and the others seemed to have, for the moment, forgotten their fear of Cock Robin. All kept close. Each time Pug picked up his pace, the entire pack of Kindred, nine in all, surged forward to keep up. They were driven by a thirst for vengeance.

Calebros was pleased that they were so sure of him. Or perhaps it was the words of the Prophet in which the Nosferatu placed their confidence. *The wizard does not burn, but seeks peace among the dead.* One of several messages Anatole had left—prophecies as much as messages, for he had set the messengers in motion long before the events themselves came to pass. He had loaded the messengers down and then pointed them toward Calebros. And was it merely luck or happenstance that the warren chief had deciphered the messages tonight, when another night or two might have been too late? Calebros had never been a strong believer in coincidence, and after being caught in the wake of the Prophet was even less so. He believed that the discovery of the hidden messages had to have come so closely on the heels of the note from Sturbridge for a *reason.* She'd informed him that Nickolai was destroyed in a great conflagration, but the regent had provided no proof. And then the revealed prophecy: *The wizard does not burn....* Calebros found it easier to accept the cryptic ravings of a madman than the bland assurances of a Tremere.

Even so, he had not been sure, not completely. Not when he alerted the justicar and gathered what clanmates had not been sent to Throgs Neck. Not even when Pug had found the scent beneath the burning hotel. Too many possibilities for error, too many potential avenues of failure.

But when the corpses had attacked, *then* he was positive. Not Kindred, but walking corpses. Thaumaturgy. Blood magic.

The others seemed to have sensed the final throes of his doubt. Cock Robin had pressed Pug more relentlessly, and the boy, to his credit, had forged ahead. They all had moved as quickly as possible behind their guide, who now brought them to a familiar place, a place Calebros was not completely surprised to see.

Pug came to a halt, and all the hunting party with him. Ahead, the tunnel ended at a stout wooden door, and before the door stood a Nosferatu familiar to Calebros. The warren chief turned and signaled to Mike, who promptly took two of their number, Thurston and Diesel, and retreated back the way they had come.

By the door, Abe Morgenstern scraped his toes in the muck and bowed placatingly. "Good morning to you all," he said nervously, "and welcome to my abode." His head was small, too much so, as if headhunters had gotten to him but not finished the job. Morgenstern was *antitribu*, but among the sewer dwellers that did not mean death on sight. Much could be learned by speaking to one's enemies and, on occasion, trading information with them.

But Calebros and his hunters were in no mood to trade anything tonight. "We will have him," Calebros said, eschewing pretense and civility.

Abe flustered easily. His entire head, little more than a skull with skin pulled very tightly over it, turned scarlet. "He's not…I'm sure I don't know what…"

Cock Robin stepped past Calebros, and in the blink of an eye had laid open Abe from neck to groin with the single swipe of a razor claw. Surprise more than pain registered on Morgenstern's red face as the justicar shoved him to the side. At the same time, Calebros noticed a strange sound in the background—like a chorus of fingernails tapping on stone, faint but not far away.

There was no time to ponder, however. As Morgenstern fell to his knees and tried to stuff his withered intestines back into his belly, shouting and the sounds of struggle rose from behind the door. With one fierce blow of Cock Robin's fist, the wood splintered, and the band of Nosferatu rushed forward.

They crashed through the first room, barely a widening of the tunnel filled with boxes and garbage, and into the second. Thurston was on the floor, writhing and jerking spasmodically. Blood flowed from his nose and ears—and the blood boiled. Mike and Diesel were struggling with another Kindred, a middle-aged man. He was not as physically imposing as they, but there was sorcery in the air, as Thurston's simmering blood attested.

Nickolai, Calebros thought, *the murderer I've sought for so long.* "Yield, Tremere!" Calebros called. There were many questions he would ask, secrets he would pry loose. Mike and the others had circled around and blocked the warlock's escape, but he was not yet subdued.

The Kindred answered Calebros with a sneer and latched a hand onto Diesel's chest. The Nosferatu reared back his head, mouth wide to scream in pain, but only a thick gurgling emerged. And then his blood. Boiling and foaming, it poured from his mouth and ran down his body. As he fell away, Mike still wrestled with their prey. As the other Nosferatu piled into the room, Nickolai grabbed Mike's arm and an ethereal emerald light spread over it. Within seconds, the arm withered and shriveled. Mike screamed.

With an alacrity that surprised even himself, Calebros clambered over the boxes and crates that filled the room to block the far exit himself. Mike, clutching his crippled arm to his body, staggered away from Nickolai. Cock Robin and the four Nosferatu behind him stepped forward threateningly.

"Yield!" Calebros commanded again. He spoke

quickly, before another blow could fall. "Your clansmen think you destroyed, as you wanted." *The wizard does not burn, but seeks peace among the dead.* "They won't be looking for you. I know you fled the hotel; you fled them." Calebros had sought vengeance for so long, but now that the moment was at hand, he discovered he desired *answers* far more. How exactly had the murder played out? How had Benito and Leopold been drawn into the web?

"Yield? So I can answer your petty questions, you wretched beast?" Nickolai sneered. He was pale and drawn. "I think not. The world is better off rid of your pathetic Petrodon, and it will be better off rid of you." He reached a hand for Calebros, but the Nosferatu proved too quick, jerking out of the way.

But that left the door unobstructed, and Nickolai lurched toward it. Calebros could not both stay out of the warlock's deadly reach and prevent his escape, so he fell upon the Tremere. Pug and Paulie were there with him too, piling on. Nickolai roared with anger and slapped a hand at Calebros's face. The warlock's fingers found purchase against a deep-set eye and a gaping nostril—

And nothing happened. Calebros waited a moment for his face to wither or his blood to boil away, but nothing happened. Nickolai screeched his rage and squeezed, as if he meant to crush the Nosferatu's skull with his bare hand, but no mystical surge of energies tore Calebros asunder.

The wizard, his strength spent, crumpled to his knees beneath the blows that Pug and Paulie rained down upon him. "I yield," he said, defeated, hardly trying to fend off the abuse heaped upon his shoulders.

"Enough," said Calebros, halting Pug and Paulie. "He has done his worst."

That was when Calebros heard the strange sound again—like fingernails drumming on stone, the fingernails of hundreds and thousands of fingers. As Calebros stood over the kneeling Tremere and Pug and Paulie backed away, the sound swelled, grew louder, almost deafening. Nickolai seemed confused by the noise as well, and the Nosferatu were craning their necks and looking about.

All except Cock Robin. He stood squarely in the doorway that divided the two rooms of Abe Morgenstern's pitiful haven. The justicar's fists were planted firmly on his narrow, twisted hips, his gaze, full of hatred immeasurable, did not shift from Nickolai.

He cares nothing for the answers we could find, Calebros realized looking at the justicar in that instant. *Nothing for what we could learn of the Tremere and their sorcery.* Cock Robin did not wish to exploit Nickolai; he wished him destroyed.

The roaches began streaming into the small room by the hundreds and then by the thousands. They covered the floor and climbed over each other, and when they became too deep on the floor they scurried across the walls. Even the Nosferatu were unnerved by the onslaught. They stood rigidly still and looked anxiously at one another as the flood of insects reached their ankles, and then their knees. If any of them had spoken, his voice would have been drowned out by the clatter and chitter of millions of insects.

Only Cock Robin remained unconcerned. Only he watched, unflinching, as the roaches began tearing away the undead flesh that was Nickolai. His screams were muffled by the rattle and buzz of the scavengers. But then he was beneath the flood, and at some point, his screams stopped.

Friday, 19 November 1999, 11:00 PM
Office 7210-A, Empire State Building
New York City, New York

Lucinde's Ventrue ghoul below had pressed the button for the elevator and then gestured for Calebros to enter when the doors opened. *As if I didn't know how the blasted thing worked*, the Nosferatu thought. That alone might have perturbed him had he not been of a foul temper already. He was not in an all-fired hurry to pay his respects to Prince Victoria Ash of New York City.

She sat across the table from him, all splendor and makeup and pearls. It was not official yet. She was not actually prince, not yet. But Calebros had heard the rumblings; he'd received word of the maneuverings and machinations, the unsavory deals. This Council of Twelve, as Lucinde so grandiosely referred to it, was but a perfunctory show for the masses. The fix was on. Otherwise, Pascek would have stayed in town.

The six clans were each represented around the table. That's what they were calling the Camarilla already, *the six clans*. Never mind that no one seemed to know for sure if Xaviar had followed through with his threat, if Clan Gangrel was truly no longer part of the sect. Certain individuals would remain loyal, no doubt. The outlanders had never been a model of top-down leadership. But for the time being, Lucinde and her ilk had sufficient cause to exclude the Gangrel from decision-making. One less wildcard with which the Ventrue and Brujah intelligentsia would be forced to deal.

Calebros himself would have skipped this charade had not Cock Robin insisted that they attend. That alone had been worth the trip—seeing the reaction of the others in the room, most of whom had not even known that the Nosferatu justicar was in the city. Lucinde, who jointly with Pascek had called the meeting and remained to act as chairperson, represented

Clan Ventrue along with Jan Pieterzoon, who had served so well over the past months. With Pascek's absence, Theo Bell, seemingly fully recovered from his exploits, and Lladislas accounted for the Brujah, the latter looking decidedly disgruntled. Victoria had Gainesmil beside her for the Toreador. Regent Sturbridge had brought a Tremere underling along, and two brothers, Eric and Jonathan Chen represented the Malkavians. They appeared disturbingly normal.

"Greetings and welcome," Lucinde addressed them once the gathering was complete. She seemed deceivingly young and vulnerable among the hoary old Kindred at the table. "The city is ours," she announced. "Fate has smiled upon us."

Calebros thought he noticed Victoria flinch at the words. No doubt she, too, felt the assumption of victory to be premature. It was true that the Sabbat's organized resistance had been broken at what was becoming known as the Battle of Throgs Neck, and Cardinal Polonia forced to retreat from the city, across the Hudson into New Jersey. A humiliating defeat for the newly ascendant cardinal, but that only made him more dangerous. Sabbat packs still roamed portions of the city, and many attempted to return home each night, now that the war to the south was over and the grand alliance forged by the late Cardinal Monçada was defunct.

The Camarilla organization had largely collapsed as well, now that the majority of Sabbat had been scourged from the city. Polonia might have lost his battle, but he had struck down Prince Michaela and her last known childe. The lack of mourning among the survivors was fairly conspicuous. Once the generals and justicars moved on, a proxy would be left as prince, and the struggle for the soul of New York would begin in earnest. Every night would be a war, and Calebros had little optimism for Victoria's skill to lead in that capacity. She would attend the festivities, the balls and the galas and exhibits, much as Michaela had frequented Wall Street and Broadway, but the street was as much a player in New York as were the boardrooms and theatres. So few of them realized that. Bell did, and maybe Pieterzoon after the past weeks.

"We pay tribute tonight," Lucinde was saying, "to our heroes both standing and fallen. To Archon diPadua, the Right Hand of the Camarilla, and the Hero of Throgs Neck." She nodded solemnly toward the representatives of Clan Nosferatu.

Oh, please. Calebros fought his urge to gag audibly. Yes, Federico had taken a saber to the head and slipped into torpor for God knew how long, but did anyone in this room actually *believe* that Lucinde felt bad about that?

"To Archon Bell, the Scourge of Harlem; to Jan Pieterzoon, our able field commander…" The bestowal of honors and sobriquets seemed to take hours. Calebros shifted in his seat periodically, setting off chains of popping vertebrae that everyone else at the table did their best to ignore.

"But we must also look to the future," Lucinde said at last. "The routines of the night have been disrupted, and already there is strife among our own." Calebros wondered when there *hadn't* been strife among their own. "Hunting grounds must be established in the territories we've gained, or re-established where Kindred have fallen. New Kindred enter the city in great numbers, some having fought by our sides, others seeking their destinies. Justice must be administered. Boundaries must be secured—"

"What you're saying," Theo Bell broke in at last, "is that the city needs a prince. Right?"

"I am," Lucinde said, slightly flummoxed. "But—"

"Pascek left a letter for the council about that." Bell produced a folded paper from his new leather jacket, waited long enough that everyone could see Pascek's personal wax seal, and then opened the letter. "The justicar *instructed* me to read the whole thing…" his eyes ran down the page, "but Lucinde here seems to have hit the hot spots already. Important part's at the end." He slid the letter across the table to the Ventrue justicar.

Lucinde retrieved it and her eyes took in Pascek's words a bit more carefully than Theo's had. When she came to the bottom of the page, she folded it and placed it back on the table. "To fulfill the duties of prince of New York, Justicar Pascek nominates Victoria Ash."

Nods and murmurs betrayed the lack of surprise. Calebros, like Cock Robin beside him, responded not at all. The city could not function without the Nosferatu. It mattered little who was prince. Calebros would advise the new prince as faithfully as he had the old. *But what would the others think if they knew Victoria was the sire of that thing that wreaked such havoc? Would they be in such a hurry to make her prince? What would Bell say? Dear God—what would Xaviar do if he found out?* Calebros darted a glance at the seat beside him. *What would Cock Robin do?*

"And I," Lucinde added, "am honored to second the justicar's nomination. Let the clans speak."

One after another they gave their blessings: Sturbridge, then Eric, elder of the Chens. When Theo mumbled his assent, Lladislas, formerly prince of Buffalo, cursed, slammed his pen to the table. He stood and stormed from the room. "He agrees too," Theo said.

As junior member of his delegation, Calebros had no vote—but he could stop the proceeding in an instant, merely by revealing Victoria's secret. Those who'd already spoken would reconsider. So tempting…yet what purpose would it serve? Victoria would be spited— no small accomplishment that, and satisfying. But the city would wallow in chaos, and the Sabbat would be that much more likely to reverse its losses. Cock Robin's bloodlust would be stoked by the revelation. Calebros knew that. Then Victoria might not only be passed over for prince, but might suffer some horrible "accident" as well, and then Calebros might never find the answers to the questions he still had about Nickolai, about Benito, answers he thought Victoria must have. Cock Robin would care only for the blood.

And so in the end, Calebros remained silent. *She's in my debt, and she doesn't even know it*, he thought. *Not yet she doesn't.*

Cock Robin nodded his approval, and it was done. Victoria had been the perfect compromise candidate. Neither Lucinde or Pascek would allow a member of the other's clan to gain the position, especially after the mess Michaela had made of things. Nor would the Ventrue or Brujah have considered a Tremere, not after the warlocks had guarded their precious citadels rather than supporting the string of Camarilla princes that had fallen from Atlanta to Washington. The Nosferatu were seen as but servants to the "worthier" clans, the Gangrel were gone, and no one was going to consider a Malkavian except as a last resort.

But someone had to rule. Otherwise the elders and neonates flooding into the city would tear themselves apart fighting for territory and influence. *They might do that anyway*, Calebros thought.

So it was that Lucinde, justicar of Clan Ventrue, conveying the decree of the Council of Twelve, turned to Victoria Ash. "The mantle is passed to you, Victoria. Do you accept it?"

Victoria had met no one's gaze since the beginning of the proceedings. She had sat uncharacteristically quiet while Lucinde and Theo had spoken; she had not seemed to notice as Lladislas left, or as the votes were tallied. Now, she looked around the table, from one of them to another. She removed her hands from her lap and placed them flat on the table before her.

She wanted Atlanta and gets New York instead, Calebros thought. *Not a bad deal.*

•

"The mantle is passed to you, Victoria. Do you accept it?"

She had known this moment was coming, but still she felt blood welling deep in her throat. She feared she might vomit right there on the table. Her great ambition was within reach, was being placed into her hand—and she did not know if she could take it.

Of course she desired to be prince. Atlanta would have been sufficient, but this...*this!*

Yet she did not know. She could feel the itching of the mark on her jaw. The gods of Fate were cruel and capricious, but she had pledged herself to them. She had vowed never to defy them again. Once she had denied them and followed the road to Chicago. As her penance, she had watched her newfound childe destroyed before her eyes, her hand offered to him.... What vengeance would they unleash, what pestilence would they inflict, were she to ignore them now?

No, Fate must needs be consulted, and Victoria, though her desire in the matter held her heart in its crushing grasp, must abide by the decision. Pascek had set forth her name; his words would tell the tale. There was no time, and too many people watching her, to count his every word.... The paragraphs, then. If their number was odd, like the five boroughs of the city, then she would assume her rightful place. If otherwise...no, she would not think of it. Fate could not continue to abuse her so.

"May I see the letter?" Victoria asked, a slight tremor in her voice.

Lucinde stared at her for a moment, uncomprehending. "Pardon?"

"Justicar Pascek's letter. May I see it?"

Profoundly confused, Lucinde looked at the letter as if it were lethal poison, and then back at Victoria. "I assure you, the seal is authentic, and Archon Bell is—"

"I doubt neither you, nor Archon Bell, nor the letter," Victoria said icily. "But I would see it."

Lucinde passed her the letter, and Victoria opened it as if it might crumble to dust in her fingers. She took a long time reading it. Watching her eyes, Calebros saw her start over twice. The silence around the table deepened unbearably. Finally, Victoria was done with the letter. She set it down and placed her hands again flat on the table.

"No," she said quietly, jaw clenched. She stared daggers at her own hands. Calebros could see the tension there, skin taut over thin bones, knuckles white even for her pale complexion. "No," she said, speaking more quickly and forcefully this time. "I do not accept the mantle."

"Ah…Victoria," said Gainesmil beside her, "if you need time to—"

But she had already pushed back her chair, and without explanation she stalked out the room much as Lladislas had minutes before. Ten shocked, gawking creatures of the night watched the door swing closed behind her.

It was Lucinde who eventually broke the silence. "It's not often that…really I don't think I've ever…" She reached for Pascek's letter and read it silently again, as if the answers she sought might be found within. But the letter provided no satisfaction and she dropped it back on the table. "We must delay this meeting…this decision until—"

The pounding on the table startled them all. All except Cock Robin. He smashed his fist against the table just twice. And when he had their attention, he took Lladislas's pen, and on the back of Pascek's note the Nosferatu justicar began to scratch large, childlike block letters.

It all seemed so odd. To hide from the dark *in* the dark. Jeremiah couldn't decide if it made sense or not. Either way, he couldn't bring himself to use a light of any sort. He'd broken his flashlight—stomped the bulb and thrown the batteries away—lest he turn to it in a moment of weakness. So like it or not, sensible or not, he would wait in the dark. He resolved not even to think of the light again....

The worst part was that he knew that the light wouldn't really have made a difference. Not to the things out there. *Nictuku.* He said it quietly to himself, feeling the different ways that his tongue pressed against the roof of his mouth. "Nic-*tu*-ku. *Nic*-tu-ku. Nic-tu-*ku*. Nictuk-*u*." They didn't need the light any more than he did. They would smell him. They would smell the *blood.*

There was worse out there too, of course.

Poor Colchester. Marston might have understood. *I could rescue him,* Jeremiah thought. But it would mean going...*down there.* He wasn't sure what was down there, not exactly. Anatole wouldn't tell him. *Damn the Prophet!* Jeremiah lunged at the ground, seized two rocks, and smashed them together in an explosion of shrapnel and dust.

"Damn the Prophet," he said, defeated, despairing.

"Not much use hiding if you're going to smash rocks together," said a voice.

Jeremiah spun to face the intruder. He could make out a vague outline but no details in the gloom. The shape seemed familiar. "Calebros?"

"No," said the shape. "Not Calebros. Tell me, Jeremiah, why are you hiding?"

"Why?" he said, laughing sarcastically. "Because the eldest of our clan are prowling the night, hunting. Except you say they are an old wives' tale."

"Calebros says that," the shape said. "I know better. But why else are you hiding?"

Jeremiah's eyes narrowed. He moved closer to the shape, peered back in the direction of the shaft, and then whispered, "Down there...in the darkest places. It's there."

The shape moved closer also, and spoke in a quiet voice. "How do you know this?"

Jeremiah rubbed his thumb and fingers together before his face. "Can't you feel it...in the air? I can almost smell it too. It's dark and cold and angry."

"Everyone *should* feel it, Jeremiah. But the kine, they don't. And most of the Kindred ignore it. But you...you know."

"You never believed me before," Jeremiah said, pleased by this turn of events.

"I told you, I'm not Calebros. But he is of my blood. *You* still haven't told me how you know, how you learned the smell. You spoke with the Prophet, didn't you?"

"I did," said Jeremiah. He thought for a moment that he was angry at Anatole, but he wasn't sure why that would be.

"Come with me, friend," said the shape. "You must tell me about your time with the Prophet."

Jeremiah was pleased to have a friend again. He'd been alone in the dark, *fearing* the dark, for so long now. He gathered up his few belongings in his canvas sack and left that place.

Tuesday, 30 November 1999, 11:07 PM
The underground lake
New York City, New York

Calebros did not crawl full into the water. Instead he sat naked on his haunches, waist-deep, on the shelf of rock near the shoreline. If previously he had been haggard and at a loss for time, now it was worse, a hundredfold. And the whispering earth would tell him nothing he needed to know at the moment. It would not tell him which middling heroes of the Sabbat war deserved which tunnels and neighborhoods to claim as their hunting grounds. It would not tell him which disputes to settle in whose favor. It would not tell him how to be *prince* of such a sprawling and chaotic city.

He glanced over at the shore, at the crown that Emmett had fashioned him from a mangled hubcap, begemmed with cigarette butts and some kind of unidentifiable, molded fruit. "King of the Sewers," Emmett had called him during those first heady minutes back at the warren, before the reality had settled in. The hubcap was not heavy, yet the crown had weighed heavily on Calebros when he'd tried it on to humor his broodmate.

Cock Robin was gone. He'd drunk his fill of vengeance and then, though perhaps the least political of justicars, had managed to install his protégé as ruler of the city. After Victoria had walked out, Calebros had been as shocked as anyone to see his own name rendered in Cock Robin's awkward scrawl. Theo Bell had seemed to like the idea that his justicar's motion had failed, and was the first to voice support for the Nosferatu. Sturbridge had taken her time before agreeing, and then the Malkavians threw their support behind him. Lucinde and Gainesmil had acquiesced once the vote was carried—for the good of the city, so there would be no doubt of the new prince's legitimacy. Unanimous selection.

The nights since had been pure toil, and prospects for the future were not much brighter. Yet the feeling of dread within Calebros had nothing to do with territorial disputes or Sabbat raiders. He could not shake sense that something far more ominous hung over him and the city, *his* city.

He tossed a single pebble toward the center of the lake and watched the ripples spread. Then he threw a handful of stones and tried to count the points of intersection among the concentric circles. But there were too many. Far too many. He looked down into the briny water and saw his own reflection, distorted and wavering. He looked into his own eyes.

It was an eye that had begun so much of what had transpired, and now Hesha was gone with that Eye. Strange how circumstances had brought them together. *Circumstances. Coincidence.* Calebros thought of the Prophet and knew that those other words held no meaning, no truth. There was a *reason* for all that had happened. But what reason? And whose?

His mind was reeling. Thoughts mundane and abstract converged, collided, became hopelessly enmeshed. Calebros rose from the water. He gathered his clothes that were lying on the shore and climbed the tunnel back to his desk. If anything could help him make sense of his tangled thoughts, it would be his Smith Corona.

30 November 1999

FILE COPY

Personal

I find myself too involved in events to observe objectively. So many questions—seemingly unconnected. But the task is not to find *if* the pieces fit the puzzle, but *where* they fit it. Seeing only the tip of the proverbial iceberg atop the water, we must somehow map the underlying, unseen dangers. Who (or what) has lost and gained from the results of this past year's extraordinary events? The Camarilla lost much in the way of territory, but the Sabbat has (practically) lost New York and finds itself as fractious as ever, or more so. We Nosferatu have gained our revenge for Petrodon's murder, yet I have more questions about what led to the foul deed. The answers may have gone to the grave with Nickolai. Or does Victoria know? And what insanity prompted her to reject her greatest achievement? Her Leopold is gone. The Eye, too, is out of sight. May Hesha use it wisely. But the question remains: What is the thread that binds these questions together? What is the cause of so many intrigues—the Eye, Petrodon, Nickolai, the war—resolving at the same time and upon the same stage? I can sense it, but not perceive it. Perhaps the answers are in the addled messages of the Prophet. For instance: "An angel must enter the hell of the dragon's belly before this age passes, lest all ages come to pass." If so, I fear I lack the insight to decipher them. He left his coded words and his bloody scrawl upon the Cave of Lamentations. I shall seek what it was he found, and pray that I have time enough.

Prince Calebros

Tuesday, 30 November 1999, 11:31 PM
The underground lake
New York City, New York

Once each of the ripples had run its course and the face of the lake was as smooth and slick as glass, a single, fleshy tendril broke the surface. It stretched toward the shore, where it twined around a discarded, bent hub-cap and pulled it back to the depths.

About the Author

Gherbod Fleming lives in a subterranean grotto. He is the author of **Clan Novel: Gangrel**, **Clan Novel: Ventrue**, **Clan Novel: Assamite**, and **Clan Novel: Brujah**, as well as the **Vampire: The Masquerade** Trilogy of the Blood Curse—**The Devil's Advocate**, **The Winnowing**, and **Dark Prophecy**. Fleming is currently writing part of White Wolf's Predator & Prey fiction series.